SOUL CLAP ITS HANDS AND SING

SOUL CLAP

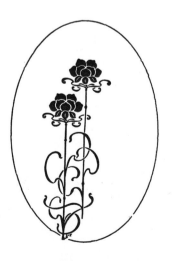

ITS HANDS AND SING

stories by Natalie L.M. Petesch

South End Press Boston

First printing
Library of Congress Number: 81-51386
ISBN: 0-89608-119-2

Typeset in Garamond
Produced by the South End Press collective
Printed in the U.S.A.

SOUTH END PRESS/BOX 68 ASTOR STA/BOSTON MA 02123

for Marge Petesch

ACKNOWLEDGEMENTS

The author wishes to express her thanks to the editors of literary journals for their permission to reprint the stories in this collection. "Be Not Forgetful of Strangers" and "Main Street Morning" originally appeared in *New Letters*; "A Journal for the New Year (Resolutions, Memos and Whimsies)" in *The Georgia Review*; "The Assassins" in *Kansas Quarterly*; "Doing It Like Velasquez" in *The Remington Review*; "In America Begin Responsibilities" in *The Dekalb Literary Arts Journal,* originally under the title, "Jacob K."; "The Man With the Pinto Bean Hair" in *Slow Loris Reader*; "Ericka" originally appeared in *Different Drummers* (Random House); and "The University Interviews Felix Mateo" in the *The Akros Review*.

This collection of short stories was completed with the assistance of a Literature Fellowship from The Pennsylvania Council on the Arts.

Contents

Be Not Forgetful of Strangers
1

A Journal For the New Year
(Resolutions, Memos, Whimsies)
17

The University Interviews Felix Mateo
28

Main Street Morning
41

Lunching With Tenney
57

Shopping
69

A Love Letter to Peter Dalosso
83

Why My Father's Birthday is St. Valentine's Day
91

By The Sweat of Your Brow
104

The Man With the Pinto Bean Hair
114

The Emperors of Ice Cream
123

Ericka
136

The Assassins
151

The Exile
164

In America Begin Responsibilities
178

Doing It Like Velásquez
192

An aged man is but a paltry thing,
A tattered coat upon a stick, unless
Soul clap its hands and sing, and louder sing
For every tatter in its mortal dress,
Nor is there singing school but studying
Monuments of its own magnificence;
And therefore I have sailed the seas and come
To the holy city of Byzantium.

From *Sailing to Byzantium*
W. B. Yeats

Be Not Forgetful of Strangers

Corte Delta, Texas
Early Morning
Greyhound Bus Station

Dear Martha,

Well, we started. Waited so long for the bus to leave, I almost changed my mind. At first it seemed like I was the only elderly lady there, then, as the line got longer outside Gate 6, I noticed another woman waiting who looked to be about my age. We sort of exchanged glances, like we were embarrassed to be going someplace alone unless it was to visit our children or take care of a sick grandchild, maybe. This woman had a sort of sling over her shoulder, what they call a baby-Snuglie, only instead of toting a baby she was carrying a tennis racket and a pair of those running shoes with stripes on them, you don't need that kind of shoe for an errand-of-mercy: she was getting ready to have a good time, I saw that. It made me feel sort of jealous seeing how she seemed to know exactly where she was going, whereas I, though I'd chosen travel instead of the rocking chair, I still had a lot to learn, for instance: do *not* leave your luggage unattended, do *not* sit right behind somebody who smokes, do *not* sit opposite the toilet at the rear of the coach, do *not* sit right near some worn-out mother travelling to California with two crying children, etc.

Later

But at last we were on our way. The lady with the Snuglie took a seat toward the middle of the bus, by the window. I did the same, figuring she knew better about these things than I did. I didn't try to start any conversation, but just picked a seat and looked out the window. I was no forlorn widow begging for company, I said to myself, I've got my own thoughts in my head. And as soon as the bus got started, I started this letter. Here it is.

Love,
Louisa

I've been studying the timetable. We'll get to St. Louis about suppertime. I'll decide then whether I want to stay overnight, though the thought unsettles me. I can hardly believe it myself, Martha, but you know I've never slept by myself in a hotel room in my whole life? Now, how could that have been a fact of my life and I hadn't even *noticed* it? But you know how it was, Martha, first we went to the local high school, then twenty whole miles away by ourselves to that nice junior college in Arlington. Then married the next year, though *you* at least stayed long enough to get a degree and learn to play the flute. Then five kids like contrary-Mary's marigolds all in a row. I remember how one day I woke up to the thought that I hadn't been out of Corte Delta since Shirleann was born. Then the Depression hitting us like the smallpox, and feeling lucky not to be on welfare like so many we knew, because at least Arnie and Mel together knew how to get what few construction jobs there were and they *were* good at fishing and hunting rabbit, weren't they? But I don't want you to be thinking about those hard times, you don't need *me* to remind you. The point I'm making is, how could we have gone anywhere while the kids were growing up, when Mel and I hardly had time for a conversation, much less for this kind of vacation where you step up to the desk and you register and you go out to dinner and you order something you've never had before and you leave a nice tip for the waitress whose face you don't even have to remember because she's so far away from your home, you know you'll likely never see her again? No, we never did that, Mel and I.

More later. It's getting dark. I can hardly see to write by these little egg-shaped lights they have above your head: they look a little like the cigarette lighter on your dashboard. Give you about the same amount of light too.

You wouldn't *believe* what I just paid for a doughnut and a cup of coffee. Why, I can remember Mel working a whole day for a dollar once...

Dear Martha,

A sinking spell...Not the kind you're thinking, though, not fear of the unknown, just the opposite. Hold on a minute, you're going to be surprised.

Just let me backtrack a minute, see can I explain.

We'd driven all night and there was this twenty-minute rest stop, just before sunup. Those of us that were awake, we got off the bus to see the view. We just stood there watching the purple sky get softer and lighter till the whole world seemed one big ball of light. Somebody said it was probably the moisture being drawn up to the light that made it look like thousands of tiny bits of mica. Then suddenly I was crying. Without looking at anybody, I climbed back into the bus like I didn't even want to look at the sun. But when the bus started up again I followed the colors as long as I could. It was like riding some magic carpet and as long as I could see it, the carpet would stay in the air. Then the lady-with-Snuglie offered me some hot coffee from her thermos and I just sat there feeling mean and ornery. Because I'd never seen anything quite so beautiful as that sunrise before and *that's* what suddenly spoiled everything for me, Martha, like the sky had been filled with poison instead of all that light...Like right in the heart of the excitement of seeing all these things there was this question I've asked myself many times this trip: what were we thinking of, Martha, burying ourselves in Corte Delta when everywhere around us, if we had time to look, there were these *events*?

Much later, Same day.

And now I'm thinking about you in your house this time of day, and I see you blowing a bit of dust from the needle of the record player, holding up the arm with your good hand while you press the coffee cup close to your body with the other, and suddenly I can hear your favorite piece, as plain as if you were playing it in the bus, over and over, Brahm's *Tragic Overture*.

How come I waited so long?

Nearly 5:00 p.m.

And now here it is going to be near dark in St. Louis when we get there and I'm either going to have to go straight on to Chicago, riding all night, which wouldn't be *too* bad, some do it and seem to bear up under it, or get out and do what I set out to do after all—see a piece of this world before I quit it.

Well, I got out and took a cab to a hotel. The cab driver who recommended the hotel was real nice and we talked a little about the price of gas and the high cost of auto insurance these days. And he told me about how they've about rebuilt the whole downtown area, and how interesting it'd be for me to go down on the levee or to take a walk through some of that West End neighborhood, they have these pretty old porches and bay windows there. And the ride to the hotel *was* pretty, with the evening light having just a tinge of ivory in it like our August moon. And the cab driver said I really should take a tour tomorrow around the city. He was very polite, and I thought at first, well this is all for a tip, but even after I'd tipped him he stood by the cab talking to me and he was just as polite as he could be and he carried my bag into the lobby. Anyway I tipped him a dollar. It probably *was* too much, and it does seem strange to just be giving away money after all these years. But being free with money is a pleasure I've not had much of *either.*

Of course there was another tip for the boy who carried my bag up in the elevator, but I didn't feel the need this time to be all that generous, since he had hardly any distance to go, and I could just as easy have carried my bag up in the elevator myself. He switched the airconditioning on for me, then he was gone too and I was alone in my room.

Well, I lay down on the bed for awhile, like a guest in my own home. I was not really tired, and everything was perfectly still except for the air conditioner which was a bit too loud and had a sort of buzz in it (Mel would have known how to fix it, I thought).

Now listen to me, Martha, because you're hardly going to believe what I'm about to say. Here I was in this lovely room, clean and comfortable, everything done for me, not a thing to do but watch television or go to sleep, when suddenly this odd feeling came over me. The walls seemed to get whiter than white, and the paintings (of bull fights and of señoritas looking out at you from over their fans)—all this suddenly seemed to me something that maybe I was not really living at all, but maybe was only imagining I was living. And a wonder came over me that everything that I knew to be real and believed to be happening could have this strangeness about it as if it could disappear any minute and I would wake up from it—or even worse yet, that it could disappear any minute and I might *not* wake up from it, but somehow just be kept a prisoner in my own mind, hanging in the middle of Nothing forever...It was like a horror movie on the late late show that you know can't be true, but scares you just the same, so you turn it off.

Well, I was feeling upset and so I did what probably millions of alcoholics and bums and prostitutes and travelling men and divorcées and lost people waiting for money, for doctors, for drugs or pills or lovers or maybe even for death, have done before me, I pulled open a drawer, looking for something, and there was a Bible there. Now, you know, I don't put much stock in heavenly messages by *that* route, I don't much like the idea of treating my religion as though I were playing bingo and just waiting for the right number to show up under my fingers. But there I was, with nobody to talk to, and the only good thing on television was something I'd seen already, and besides, those programs aren't so funny when you're all alone. So I picked up the Bible, feeling sort of timid about it, as though it might hurt me as well as heal me, and what should I open to but, *Be not forgetful to entertain strangers,* which *did* seem inappropriate, considering the circumstances. So I just shut it again, and took one of my pills for motion-sickness and fell asleep right away.

Slight delay, waiting to start for Chicago.

Well, I *did* sleep—long past breakfast and would probably not even have woken up for lunch if the maid hadn't come in to make up the bed. But I have had to give up my chance of seeing some of old St. Louis—at least going this way, maybe coming back home I'll have better luck—because with one thing and another, I missed everything, including the early bus, and now we're starting for Chicago just at the evening hour, a sad time to go anywhere. Folks should start out for places in the morning, like they were hoping to arrive home by sundown. People getting on the bus at this time of evening look sort of dazed, like they've all come to a party where they don't know anybody and they have to figure out where to locate themselves so they will look like they belong *some*-where. Some of the young kids, though, look like they've left home and they don't care, they'll never go back. As soon as they get on the bus, they shove their bags far back onto the upper rack, punching them angrily the way I've seen winos kick their dogs. Then they turn to look at the road and in twenty minutes they're asleep, you don't hear a peep out of them.

Now that is a long way around to tell you about what happened. Mostly I guess I was comparing these youngsters with Mr. Peterson. This Mr. Peterson, he didn't exactly pick me out from all the others on the bus, I won't be so vain and foolish as to say *that*. I'll just say that he noticed a seat that was empty and it happened to be right across the aisle from mine. The first thing I noticed about this man, besides his being about my own age, I mean, was that he was so at ease with himself. He looked like he'd just walked into the kitchen to get something from the refrigerator and was coming back to join the rest of us watching TV in the living room. He is a small man, which makes him look to be younger than he is (sixty-eight), and he was wearing those frameless glasses you don't see much any more. He seemed not to have a care in the world. He just nodded and smiled and asked me where I was going, and I said Chicago, and he said, "Me too." And then he asked me if I were visiting folks in Chicago, and I said "No"—rather sharply, I guess. He was quiet for awhile after that, then he opened up a package of mints and offered me one. He said he'd been on the bus for three weeks and he had travelled all the way across the United States and had been in twenty-three states and was now returning to Harrisburg, Pennsylvania. He asked if I had ever been to Chicago. I said no. Again there was silence.

Of course I knew what was happening, but at my age, you think you've put all that sort of thing behind you, back when you were first told not to talk to strangers because they might get the wrong idea about you. But here was this man I'd never seen before in my life telling me all about his daughters and his grandchildren and how he had decided to go on this trip after his wife died last year because he was going crazy anyway and he thought it would be better to see a few things than to go crazy all alone in the house by himself. At first, each of his daughters (he has two) came to stay with him awhile, then he went to stay with *them* awhile. But after a bit he got tired of visiting back and forth. Then he told me how his wife had died, "with the thing finally reaching her tongue so she couldn't speak to me anymore—and that was the worst thing of all, her not being able to speak to me anymore—" he said.

Then he put the photographs away.

So I just naturally told him about my own kids, though early on I'd decided not to be carrying around a lot of pictures to be pulling out every time anybody asked me how many kids I had, so I had only the one of Mel and me and everybody in it together. But Mel didn't show up too clear in that picture and for some reason that seemed all right because there's not a photograph in this world or the next that could show Mel as he really was, his jokes and his charm. After all, the only place he needs to be clear is in my own head, nobody else could get an idea of all those years together from some old photograph.

We'd been riding about two hours (time does go so fast when you're talking to people) when he asked me what I'd sort of known right from the beginning he *would* ask me: where did I plan to stay in Chicago? Of course this was the point at which I ought to have turned my head to look out the window as if I hadn't heard him but then I remembered what the Bible had said, and now here was a stranger who looked to be in his right mind—polite, and not likely, you know, to take advantage of every situation.

So I came right out and admitted I hadn't the least idea, that the place I'd stayed at last night had been recommended to me by the cab driver and it hadn't turned out too badly except that the airconditioner had a buzz in it and—I stopped myself just in time: in another minute I'd have been telling him straight out that I'd been scared to death to sleep alone in my hotel room. Mr. Peterson must have seen some confusion in me because he said, looking away, "Well, there are a lot of good places in Chicago. It's merely a matter of personal taste and money."

Well, putting it on that *level* and not like he was trying to impose his opinions just because he had done all that travelling already and had so much experience, made me say, "I can't afford just everything. I do have to...make it last." I wasn't sure myself what I meant by this, whether I meant that I wanted my money to be enough to last me the rest of my life, or whether I was simply letting him know that I had a budget for this trip which I did *not* intend to spend more than. No matter what. No matter who. Though of course he was no gigolo, he had his own pension and his social security, as he'd told me right off, like a man who wants to let you know he's worked all his life and doesn't need to ask anybody for anything anymore.

He dug into the pocket of his shirt and took out a little brochure about a hotel near Lake Shore Drive which he said he'd been to once before and which was very reasonable, "everything considering. I mean," he explained, "considering that it's close to everything."

I thanked him and looked out the window so as not to seem to show too much interest.

After a moment's silence he bent across the aisle. "I *personally* recommend that hotel," he said.

I merely nodded as though it were a matter of some interest but of no real importance, and folded the brochure into my pocketbook. He nodded approvingly. Then he began to tell me about his trip, the things he'd seen and the places he'd been, and he was wishing it could go on forever, because he had got used to being in a different place every day, and talking to different people, and that was what he found most interesting: that people came from all walks of life and had done so many different and interesting things and wanted to talk about them. He paused and looked at me inquiringly.

I was about to say that if anybody thought raising five kids was not doing a lot of different and interesting things, well, let him try it. But suddenly I felt embarrassed or ashamed of something, as if I had to protect Mel from something he hadn't done properly. So I said, "We never had much time to travel." It would have seemed too much like whining to have added as I might have, "Nor much money either," and besides, it was more than I wanted to say, to sound as if I were complaining about Mel's not having made more money than he did when the man worked hard every day of his life for his family and it was not his fault. No one knew better than I that it was not his fault. No, I was not going to sell Mel short the first time he left me alone in order to impress this stranger. So I repeated, and I sounded to myself as if I were annoyed, though I wasn't really, "My husband and I were just too busy, we had plenty to do with the kids growing up and all."

Then he *did* seem to get snappish, like I'd accused him of something he was not guilty of. "Well, they're grown up now, aren't they? It's time to think of yourself." Then—maybe feeling that that was a little too forward for a stranger, it really *was*—he opened up a little notebook he was carrying with him and started studying it, like there might be some interesting remark in it which he could use on me. Not to let on that I was feeling upset myself, I brought out the magazine I'd bought in the hotel lobby. So for a long while we ignored each other, and I dozed off. When I woke, it was pitch dark and Mr. Peterson was gently patting my shoulder. "Rest stop," he said, "and it'll be the last one before Chicago, so you'd better get up and move your legs a bit." He helped me out of my seat and I was grateful for the help, I must say. There's no lonelier feeling than a rest stop in the middle of the night.

When I came out of the ladies' room, there he was waiting for me, to make sure I got back on the bus safely. Somehow after that there didn't seem much point in making a fuss about our getting off the bus together in Chicago or about his hailing a cab for the two of us together. When the cab driver asked, "Where to?" I just took the brochure out of my pocketbook and handed it to the driver without looking at Mr. Peterson. From the corner of my eye, though, I could see a line of satisfaction around Mr. Peterson's mouth and when he pointed suddenly, saying, "See there? That's the Sears Tower, the tallest building in Chicago. Gives you a wonderful view of the city!" he sounded happy and excited.

Next Day.

Martha, you're not going to believe this! When we got to the hotel, the cab driver thanked Mr. Peterson for the tip and said, "Well, I hope that you and your wife have a nice vacation." "Thank you," said Mr. Peterson and he didn't even look at me.

Then the minute we were in the hotel lobby, somebody came and took *my* bag from Mr. Peterson and walked to the front desk with it. The desk clerk handed him a card and a pen to register with. There followed what felt to be a long silence, and Mr. Peterson looked at me. "Well?..." he asked.

For an answer all I could think of was to hand him some money and walk away, for all the world as if we really *were* man and wife.

WAIT! Before you begin praying for me, don't jump to any conclusions. What he had done, that kind thoughtful man, he had just signed us in for a suite with adjoining rooms.

Still, all the way up in the elevator, it *was* quiet. I was burning with shame. Even if Mr. Peterson *did* seem to be the gentlest of souls, what would he think of me for having allowed matters to turn out this way? These questions were rushing around in my head so that I could barely speak for shame when suddenly we were at the door of the suite and he handed me my key, let me into the suite and showed me how to lock the door from my side...I tell you, I *was* ashamed of my suspicious mind.

Waiting for departure time.

Martha, what a day this has been. In one day I've seen more different things than in the ten years before, and I feel so strange, like somebody's been embezzling from my bank account all along and I've just found out about it and I can't track down the robber, never, because he's like some faraway robber in a fancy opera cloak and shining patent leather shoes who makes long trips to Europe and Hawaii and the Caribbean and only comes back to Corte Delta now and then to gobble up my life with a long spoon.

Let me tell you all the things Mr. Peterson and I did today! First thing this morning he said, "I have this list of *Things to See and Do in Chicago*. It's really a question of timing. Would you rather go see a matinee and then go to a nice place for dinner, or would you rather skip the matinee and see something of Chicago first? After all, you can always attend a matinee in Houston."

Well, you can be sure I didn't correct him and explain how far Houston is from Corte Delta! In fact, I was so pleased I didn't dare speak at all. Instead, I took out a handkerchief and polished my glasses for about five whole minutes, not even looking at him. Then we just naturally started out walking on Lake Shore Drive, with Mr. Peterson talking in that nice quiet way he has, pointing out everything like he'd lived in Chicago all his life. You'll hardly believe me when I tell you I walked at least five miles, and my feet were so tired I could hardly walk downstairs later to dinner, but we did go *every*where.

The first place we went to we took a taxi, but only because Mr. Peterson is a gentleman of the old school, and he seemed to feel that that was the way to do. But I soon persuaded him that, after all, we both knew how hard it was to save money and wasn't that why we were both on the bus instead of driving our own Cadillacs? And he saw the sense of that, so after that we just rode the buses. Like a pair of school kids, we were, running to catch the bus, Martha, I'd never dreamed that a year after Mel's death I'd be running after buses, a thousand miles from home with a strange man.

Anyway, first we saw the Art Institute and then we walked around the Loop and under the elevated—I do wonder how folks get used to all that noise—and had lunch at the Blackhawk where I had the most wonderful salad and then again a nice little stroll (I didn't want to complain, but I was already dead tired). Then after awhile, Mr. Peterson consulted his map and said, "Would you like to get a view of the city from the Tower?" So of course I said "yes" (one thing I've learned on this trip is that if anybody offers to show you something, say *yes* right away, because how do you know what it is you've been missing all along till you've seen it?).

So Mr. Peterson bought tickets (I do try to insist on paying my share, but it is hard because Mr. Peterson is so old-fashioned) and we went up to the Sears Tower. It is 100 stories high, 1350 feet in the air! Well, we got off at the skydeck and I'd hardly looked out at the city which was like some kind of mirage, with the sunlight striking the office windows and the cars below like little yellow blue red and black cough drops, when suddenly I had this awful dizzy spell and if Mr. Peterson hadn't held me up I might have fainted right there in front of everybody which would have been too embarrassing for words, I would have been so ashamed to have caused all that commotion. And I thought, too, how am I ever going to be able to explain to Mr. Peterson what happened?

But anyway I didn't need to explain to him because he was the one explained it.

Coming back down to the street he held my hand and said he was sorry, truly sorry, that he wouldn't have exposed me to that for anything in the world, that he hadn't known I was afraid of heights. And I just laughed kind of shakily and said I hadn't known it either. Mr. Peterson said maybe we ought to go right back to the hotel so I could rest awhile, that maybe he'd tried to pack too much into one day, maybe he was taxing my stength. But I just laughed again and said it was nothing, that the weakness wasn't in my legs, it was in my head. Then he laughed too, but we did go back to the hotel and I went straight to my room and took a shower.

Mr. Peterson rang me up on the phone after awhile to ask how I was (though he could easily have heard me moving around in the clothes closet and switching the TV channels). I said I was just fine and that I was ready to go out and see the museum he'd wanted to see, the one with the coal mine, and within five minutes we were on our way again like nothing had happened.

Well we went out there but it was all so clean and safe I couldn't believe any miner could ever have worked in such a nice place. Without ever having been in a real mine, I felt they had to have been a lot dirtier than *that*: no miner ever went on strike to get improved working conditions at a mine like the Chicago Museum of Technology and Science and I said as much to Mr. Peterson. He shook his head slowly and then he told me all about how he had worked for a steel mill for thirty-two years. And I declare, Martha, it does break your heart to think of a man working in noise and danger all day long, every day of his life, for over thirty years.

So we stood there in the middle of the sidewalk, and I guess he must have seen how sorry I felt for him, because while he stood there, the sun shining on him, a kind of trembling went through him, and his thin white hair seemed suddenly thinner and whiter and he moved his lips as though he were going to say something but he didn't. And all the way to the hotel we sat on the bus holding hands.

Now this is the part where I know you're going to start praying for me. I can tell you, though, before you go into anything about Sin, that there was no sin to it, not what *you* mean by sin. It was just that we'd both lived long enough to know that there's more than enough grief in this world to go around, and all this kindness we felt toward each other was something we couldn't afford to waste anymore. So I guess that's what it was then, that we just wanted to be *kind* to one another, we didn't want one little speck of hurt to come down on us ever again.

So please don't lecture me about my morals, Martha, unless you can prove to me that I can expect a whole lot of times like this, when a kindly-intentioned man from my generation will want me to lie down beside him to stroke the white hairs on his chest and to comfort and solace him for all his loss and loneliness, if you can prove that to me, well then I'll admit I was wrong and will repent of it.

But just let me tell you about it. That evening when we'd got back from the museum, I heard Mr. Peterson lying in his bed in that other room he was locked into. I heard him coughing and keeping his TV real low so as not to disturb me, and Martha, it was I who got up and rang his room and said, wouldn't he prefer to watch TV in my room, since mine was a color and his was black and white? He gave a great sigh and said that surely would be nice and he came in his neat little bathrobe. He sat down for a moment in front of the television set. Then presently he said, "Louisa, don't you think this is a bit silly? What harm can we do one another?" Knowing exactly what he meant, I just nodded and climbed into bed. He turned off the stupid television program that was on and he climbed into bed too.

What I was not prepared for, was his sobbing. When I asked him *What is it?* he turned to me and, laying his head on my bosom, he said he was crying with relief, his terrible ordeal was over, he wouldn't ever have to go back to his home alone.

I sat up in consternation then, "Wait a minute, William," I said. "You know you're an awful nice person and I like your company, but what are you saying? I can't go home with you, I got my own home and my own kids..." And I almost said, "my own life."

Well, he calmed down and became his own reasonable self again. And he began to explain to me how much better off we'd be together—we'd have a lovely home, we'd make trips back and forth to Florida and California, we'd share our families, our friends, we'd never be lonely again. For a minute I almost forgot how many long years it had been since a man had talked to me like that. So when I got up to get us each a drink of water and I caught a glimpse of myself in the mirror, I was surprised to see this stranger in the mirror, her body rather drooped and pouchy, her hands wrinkled, her face resembling my own face but full of hardships and wrinkles.

Well, Martha, I managed to be gracious and as I brought him the water I said to myself, maybe this is what comes of being immoral, immediately you get problems. Then I laughed and said, "William, you better go back to sleep." Well, he just grinned at me and leaned back and went to sleep like a baby.

The next morning we tried to be as calm and natural toward one another as if nothing had ever happened. We dressed and packed our things and had breakfast and we arrived at the station nearly an hour ahead of time. Then we stood there, both of us sad and silent and hanging onto our luggage as though they were our lives. My bus was the first to come in and as I walked through the departure gate I started to cry, it just didn't seem right to let that poor man go home to Harrisburg all by himself, with none but his daughters to look after him during this, the loneliest time of his life.

Yet now that I have had some time to think about it all, about Mel, and how I took care of him all through his long last sickness, I have to ask myself, would I be willing to go through that kind of suffering again? And what if it should be me who took sick and not Mr. Peterson, and he had to care for me after knowing me but a few short years and not for nearly my whole life the way I did Mel: how could I expect anybody to look after me the way I did Mel? how could anybody expect that?

And yet at the same time, maybe if I hadn't met Mr. Peterson right off like that, at the very beginning of my travelling, I wouldn't be thinking like this, weighing everything pro and con like a money changer in the temple. Maybe if I'd done all my travelling, I might be ready to settle down in Harrisburg or Corte Delta and try it all over from the beginning again. But the way it happened, Martha, it's caught me off guard, and I don't know what to think. Maybe when I get home I'll have time to write to Mr. Peterson and he to me and we'll get to know each other, and then if I did get married and settled down again in Harrisburg or Corte Delta, it wouldn't be like I'd married a stranger.

A Journal For The New Year Resolutions, Memos, Whimsies)

Why I Should Want to Live:

Because a pair of birds, a sparrow and a bluejay, are struggling with each other for bread outside my window, on Mrs. Thalmann's rooftop. One is winning. The sparrow. He seizes his prize, he flutters upward like a sigh of God. Mr. Bluejay starts to pursue, but for some reason can't seem to muster up enough aggressive will power. (*Think*, Mr. Bluejay, can't you recall your territorial imperative?) Suddenly he has capitulated.

Moral: even the common sparrow may win over these thieves of bluejays.

MORE OF THE ABOVE: 10:00 a.m.

Because twice a week, shortly after sunrise, the milkman comes up to my front porch and says, "Good morning, Mrs. Hallison. Beautiful day comin' up, I think." He's always right too. Unlike that 6:00 o'clock forecaster who peddles the weather like campaign promises, purveying and perjuring the very sunlight.

Because the mailman, a nice young man, smiles at me as he hands me my social security check, looking me in the eye like an honest jailer who is assuring me of my safety for another month. He always *hands* me my check.

Because my son needs to feel that he has not "deserted" me: he merely took a job 2000 miles away.

And my daughter-in-law needs to feel that she has "done everything possible."

And my ex-husband, living well in Mexico on the devalued peso, needs to feel that he no longer owes me anything: his conscience is clear. The divorce settlement "gave" me the house, the children, and (at the time) twenty more years to contemplate the workings of Justice.

And my daughter needs to feel that her visits console me for that cruel invention, Old Age (brought to us by the same friendly used-car dealer who sold us Death). Actually, this is the best reason of all.

Still December 31
4:30 p.m. and growing dark

A Different Sort of Memo: Why I Might Want to Die:

Because there is nothing to look forward to anymore.

Because there is everything to look forward to, but I can't afford it.

Because I am bored unto death with the care and feeding of Mrs. Robert Hallison (address mail to Ms. Sandra Hallison, please).

January 1
7:00 a.m.

SOME RESOLUTIONS FORMED WHILE WATCHING THE NEW YEAR'S EVE PROGRAMS:

Will take only two tabs daily, and these with meals only. That will dissipate the effect, perhaps. Three tabs make me feel sleepy or euphoric; the first condition prevents me from living what there is left to live; the second condition (is it preferable?) prevents me from dealing with so-called reality. But two should keep the pain at a tolerable level: the rest is up to me. Maybe they'll soon have a sugar cube to deal with this—since even the president's mother suffers from it. In her case, though, not crippling. Whereas I sit here trying to hold the pen straight, clumsy as a child with chopsticks. When I was young I was called a curly-haired beauty. Now, curly-handed.

Will write at least three letters every day. When I'm up to it, that is. No: even when I'm not up to it. How do you know whether you're up or down to something till you've done it? Would anyone, for instance, become a mother who waited till she was up to it? No way to know these things. "Lord, we know who we are but we know not what we may be." Saw Laurence Olivier in a re-run of that play on TV the other night: *he* doesn't look like that anymore either. And to think we *both* look a lot better than we will, ha ha.

> January 1, 9:00 a.m.
> The Morning News Giveth Rise
> To a Few (Negative) Ideas

LIST OF THINGS I WILL NEVER BECOME RECONCILED TO:
  War
  Orphans crying
  People starving in Bangladesh, in Pakistan, in Africa, in Indochina, in Latin America, in...
  Veterans' Hospitals
  People wanting to learn things and being denied access
  Shame
  Scorn
  Nursing Homes
      (Not necessarily in that order)

January 1, 4:00 p.m.
(A nice cup of tea, I had)

MORE RESOLUTIONS: DO'S AND DON'TS:

(a) Will *not* feel sorry for myself.

(b) Will *not* live in the Past (but the Past is my lifetime annuity...)

(c) *Will* have the clock radio fixed. At least to know what time it is when one wakes up in the middle of the night...waiting for the cock to crow.

(d) *Will* have the furnace checked. Last time I was upstairs (winter before last) it was 53 up there. It's either the furnace or the thermostat. Used to be too hot upstairs when Robert was with us. He'd come down complaining about the thermostat: too hot for Cynthie and Timothy, or even for the dog, Schlepper, who always slept with one of them. Robert used to say he *had* to keep the bedrooms the right temp. because they were always having something (why do they speak of "having" the flu, the chickenpox, the mumps, as though they were something we could use and enjoy?)

Though, thank God, no polio. Used to have nightmares about one of them catching it those hot summers, then everybody getting it—a houseful of paralytics. But we've been lucky. Even Mother died "in the best of health." Like me: in perfect condition except I couldn't even stand up straight enough to fall properly into my own grave.

Somebody should educate us for these Last Days. Attention Curriculum Designers: an undergraduate course in Arthritis, Then Advanced Spinal Arthritis, and finally, a Graduate Course... (I *did* take a "home study course" in How to Get On and Off the John & In and Out of Bed.)

ANYWAY, fix the clock radio for sure.

MEMO: CALL EVERYBODY TOMORROW TO SAY— WHATEVER I CAN THINK OF TO SAY.

The fact is, with postage so costly, it's now cheaper to call up than to send greeting cards. Also, gives me a reason to phone people I wouldn't think of bothering with my aches and pains during the year. So, tomorrow, will start a phone-in, beginning with Martha, Etienne, Murphree and Sherry (so named for Ann Sheridan, whom she used to resemble. Must remember she doesn't like to be called Sherry anymore, but simply Carol.) All of them widows, of course. The Black Plague of achievement killed off their husbands. Now they sometimes wonder aloud: *was it real?* And I too wonder: can anything seem real after Death has wiped it all out, like a declaration of bankruptcy? All their planning for the future, for their retirement together, becomes the history, as it were, of somebody else. Etienne, Martha, Murphree, now left with new identities, totally severed from the past as by continental drift. No one remembering what their young lives were except Themselves.

January 2, a beautiful, sunny morning. Even the sparrows have forgotten their eternal hunger.

True to my RESOLUTION, called all of the above. None was in except Murphree—a percentage rating which evoked glooms-and-dooms of self-pity. How easy it was for them to escape their loneliness, simply by walking out of the house. I once read an account of a man who, after many years of imprisonment had finally been released: he said the thing that took him the longest to get used to was that the doors were not locked. Likewise my friends can still rise in the morning, *open a door*, and congregate somewhere—in a restaurant, a shop, a park bench. In melancholy chorus, they can share the disillusions of a lifetime. Whereas I...STOP!!!! NOTE RESOLU-TIONS ABOVE: *Will-not-feel-sorry-for-myself* hereinafter referred to as Resolution (a).

O.K., Mrs. Hallison. *Write.* Point pen downward, jab at the paper the way you would knitting needles. Form letters loosely the way the Sisters taught you in school, when they still taught Penmanship: so many thousands of circles shaped into CAPITAL LETTERS, thus OOOOOOOOOOOOOOOOOOO like designing your own mantra.

Murphree was strange, rather remote. Guess she hasn't forgiven me for the way I acted before Christmas. You'd think an old friend wouldn't hold it against you. Can I help being bitter? (That's a rhetorical question, Mrs. H., you don't need to answer.) I had called her around the first week of December to come help me decorate the tree. The way one always says it: "*Come help me decorate the tree*"; i.e., it's the tree that's important, not the help. It's meant to be a joyous communion, not an S.O.S. I didn't think I needed to change the language after all these years. She came over, all her Christmas spirit transformed into fussy charity. Doing-good. She came with a basket of food, like I was going hungry. She humbled me, she did. That made me angry. I didn't want to be angry, I wanted to decorate the tree. But of course, from my wheelchair, I couldn't reach any but the lower branches. I would try to stand up a bit, resting my weight on the arms, as I do on occasion. She'd say, "Now, Sandra, you be still. You know you'll fall and break a hip or something." I didn't "know" any such thing. I wanted to try to reach as far as I could. She'd practically grab the tinsel from my hand, like I was blind as well as crippled. Finally I just wheeled my chair out of the room and went into the kitchen. I was close to bawling, that was the thing. And when she showed me all the cooked food she had brought in her basket, I just growled, "Murphree, why did you do this? I'm not going hungry."

The fact that she knew that sometimes I do go hungry, not for lack of food, but because sometimes it's just too much trouble to fix it (I still have a few problems with that stove—the oven's too high), the fact that she *knew* this was what spoiled my Christmas. And since that day she's not come by.

So. I called her just now. A new year, isn't it? It's implicit at the new year that we forgive our friends, and if not exactly love our enemies, at least not hate them so hard.

Murphree's been a friend to me many years now. So why

can't I forgive her being charitable to me? But I hated it. I hate being on the other end, the receiving end. When Robert met me, I was a pink and white candy-striper at the hospital. How I used to love to bustle around the complaining, alienated *powerless* folks—reminding them there was still sunlight and energy in the world. I didn't know my enthusiasm must have seemed to mock their helplessness.

ANOTHER RESOLUTION. Try to be grateful. Like when the Meals on Wheels lady comes by. Usually I'm so sullen (when I'm not downright mean), you'd think she was coming to cart me to the knacker's right off. But I do so resent the publicity, the proclamation to the whole neighborhood that this grand Rescue Action has been set in motion viz., the lady is about to receive a *hot lunch!!!!* You'd think I was receiving extreme unction.

But, *yes.* I do resolve to cultivate Gratitude (you can cultivate a taste for anything). And to prove my good will, I will try to knit a sweater for the Meals on Wheels lady. If I can handle this pen, I ought to be able to maneuver the knitting needles. It would take about four or five skeins of yearn. That's a slip. Of course I meant to write *yarn.*

Later

I should, of course, be grateful if *any*one comes to see me. Such a bore one can be, even to oneself. "How are your pains today, Mrs. Hallison?" Mrs. Hallison replies: "Not bad, not bad. I've seen better pains, but these are good enough, thank you for asking, ha ha." But they don't like that kind of joke. I do believe sometimes they'd rather you whimpered, then they could console you: "Things are not so bad as you say, Mrs. Hallison. Like *my* mother had this and that and she did thus and so, and she's walking around again good as new. Etc."

I found myself guilty of precisely this kind of brainwash while "conversing" with Mrs. Thalmann. I had wheeled myself onto the back porch, and there she was, out taking her "walk" with her walker, looking like your average, every day stroke victim, exercising her constitutional rights: i..e., to take a step, to falter, to tremble, to take another. Send a message to the sodden brain. There! Very good! And now return...(Reminded me of Cynthie when she was a year old, falling proudly into Robert's arms after discovering she could stay on her feet to the count of ten.)

Mrs. Thalmann is confined to her apartment. There's no elevator in her building; even in good weather she can't get down to the sidewalk unless someone assists her down the stairs, then waits for her to return. Expensive custodial care...But adjacent to her building is a small garage on whose rooftop Mrs. T. takes her walk. In this space, approximately 10 by 15, but perfectly flat, so that she can maneuver her walker, on this rooftop where a few days ago bluejay and sparrow struggled for their bread, Mrs. Thalmann also struggles. Twice daily she comes out to exercise. No one speaks to her. Passersby who see her walking on the roof gripping her metal walker like an altar railing, pretend that this is the usual thing: every little old lady walks the rooftops in our city; it's as if they had finally convinced themselves that Mrs. Thalmann had been born with this end in mind—to walk her walker round the rooftops.

So, it being the New Year, and myself plumb full of resolutions to be *friendly, articulate, conciliatory,* and *grateful* (see above), I say to Mrs. Thalmann, "How are you today?" Dumb question: I'm instantly ashamed. Is there no other way to say hello? How are you today, how's your shroud, how's your terminal cancer, how's your pending operation, how's the cold damp hole you live in, eating baby food and dog biscuits? But what's *really* dumb about my question is that I know she can barely speak. A speech therapist comes regularly. They're trying to teach her how to talk again...The whole left side of the brain (or is it the right?) is involved in this process, and as I speak to her I seem to see her brain scanning the iambic syllables, the way we are taught in h.s., the rhythmic sounds leaping in the air: *how-are-you-today?* I seem to hear the agitated effort of the brain cells to catch fire, like the engine in a stalled automobile. *Cough, cough,* will she make it? *You don't have to answer my dumb question,* I feel like screaming. *It's not important! It's not worth the effort!*

But it is important to her. She wants to prove that she can do it: it's not for me that she's going through the colossal effort of controlling the unmuscled seizure of the jaw, the wandering eyelid—but for herself: to prove that she's improved, that the speech therapist will triumph over darkness.

So I wait in my chair. (Where am I going anyway? There's no hurry.) I wheel myself closer to the railing so that if she manages one single comprehensible word, I won't have to look blank because I didn't quite *hear* it.

She purses her lips now in a succession of movements resembling those by which the pure Mother of us all, the vermiculate worm, winds its way through the millions of meters of darkness into the light. She bursts out at last: "BETTER! GETTING BETTER!" But while I am still smiling and nodding my pleasure to hear this, a groan of complaint seizes her. She shakes her head angrily. Something else remains to be said. I move up, right against the porch railing, listening intently.

"But...so...much...money! So...much...money!" Again and again she says it. She has learned how to say it and will now never cease saying it: "So...much...money. I...have...no...money. My...son...my...sister."

No need to amplify. I understand all too well. It is I who am speechless now, and I sit over in my chair as though whiplashed by this repetition. I pull my neck in like a bird, ready to depart. It's a subject too dismal to pursue. Then suddenly Mrs. Thalmann manages to say: "You...have...money." Her voice has no inflection, so there is no way of knowing whether she is merely stating it as a fact or...as an accusation. But I understand her very well: I understand that my social security checks seem to her like *true* money, not because it is much or even because it is mine, but because I can still decide for myself how to use it. Whereas she, whether it is her own money or not, has very little to say anymore about what people spend it on. Compared to her, I'm a princess in disguise. As all this dawns on me, my attempt to exchange jolly season's greetings falters. I'm not willing to fake any more enthusiasm over her improvement. I nod again—neutral, ambiguous— and wheel myself back into the house. After such an exchange one might well confine oneself forever to watching bluejays and sparrows. I think of Whitman's line about living with the animals, who are so peaceful.

January 4

I am not doing so well with Resolutions. Cynthie arrived, just back from her business trip, bringing youth and high comedy as well as strawberry preserves from a Mennonite farm she passed on the way. What mother would not smile on her deathbed to have such a daughter? But the conversation with Mrs. Thalmann has sobered me. The sight of that walker is a threat I cannot cope with. *Mens sana in corpore sano.* O.K. So the health of the body has flown: in a kind of reversal of time the body has become stone before it has become dust: and now what of the *mens sana?* I am plunged into anticipatory guilt at the suffering I will inflict on her: how will she deal with a mammering imbecile mother who will perhaps accuse her of a million crimes of which she will be utterly innocent, who will wail and wet like some changeling put on her Christmas tree instead of the true doll she always wanted? A sick old doll who, instead of lisping adorably Ma-ma, Ma-ma, may be an angry madwoman muttering Cynthie, Cynthie, where are you, where are you cruel, cruel child to have let me die?

The suffering I feel at the suffering I may (unknowingly) inflict makes me look at her with a sadness which she senses: "Don't be sad, Mother, " she says. "There are worse things... though I know it's hard to imagine..." She looks away guardedly, hoping she hasn't said too much.

Alas, not hard to imagine at all: it hovers on the brink of one's imagination like the void which awaits Mrs. Thalmann if she should try to fly off her roof.

So we eat lunch together, Cynthie and I. My daughter's visit is the best thing that has happened since Christmas. I am endlessly astonished at her wit, her vigor, her—suddenly the words *her mortality* fly into my head. The thought assails me: could *she* die? This idea is enough to make me accelerate my own end, to spare myself *that* horror, at least.

She has another business trip to make and will be out of town ten days. Will I be all right? I try not to be too hearty in my response to this: she knows perfectly well I will never again be *all* right, so what's the use of lying? The one thing she is concerned about is that I live on a busy street with easy access for any burglar. We don't dwell on this. What I am supposed to do if someone comes to rob me of my "wealth" is an unsolvable mystery we both prefer not to discuss.

Cynthie kisses me goodbye. I watch her as far as the eye can follow: I will watch her thus from eternity, I guess. I turn on every light in the house; I wheel my chair into the bedroom; then I take three tabs and fall asleep.

The University Interviews Felix Mateo

What they never talk about is that at sixty-five you're *ready* to retire. Who wants to go on till he's eighty, riding the freeways, eating lunch in twenty minutes, sharpening pencils, making squidges in the old accounts? Listen to me, when you get to be my age there's only one thing you want and it's not sex, money or politics—it's *fun*. And you don't want anybody rushing you about it either, you've been through all that: at last you've got time to put together a decent shirt and tie before going to the movies; there's no more pressure, the struggle to survive is over: you've survived.

All these I had: time, money and maybe ten, twenty more years of the loafing life to look forward to. I'd worked like a horse for forty-odd years and now was preparing to roll in the grass. *So why did I let them put me back into harness?* Well, let me tell you it was for me myself alone, and not for the color of anybody's eyes. And because it was free. After earning every nickel yourself that you've spent, how could I turn down such an offer?

So this was the way it was: one day my youngest grandson, Rinaldo, he calls me up and says: "Matt, I'm going to put you through college."

I laughed. "Ho, ho ho." What a kid. "You got yourself a bigger lemonade stand now, have you?"

Then he says, "No kidding, Matt. This one's on me: my treat. They've got this new program where if *I* buy a college education, then one swinging grandparent gets his free. That's you: Matt, the Swinger."

"Ho, ho, ho. Swinging by what? My tail?" Still, I was flattered. Imagine that kid thinking about me at a time like that, when *he* was about to get his Big Chance. I mean, he was about to get rid of all of us authority-types at once, if you know what I mean.

I guess Rinaldo remembered that I'd always wanted to go to college—though of course back in the Thirties when the bottom had dropped out of the world, a married man with a family could hardly get a job, much less go to college. It's true that at the time I was young and strong and I thought of my future as still being all ahead of me, so it hadn't seemed so bad, waiting for an education, it had seemed something you *could* wait for: everybody was waiting for something back then: most of all we were waiting for the Depression to be over. See, I'd met my wife Lottie, in my last year at Jackson High, and she was pretty as a picture, and we got married, and by the time the Crash came we had two kids with a third on the way, and for the next ten years it was the fastest race in the West just to keep food on the table and coal coming down the chute. Very soon after Luke was born (they were named Matthew, Mark and Luke: God must have caught on to our game because He stopped things and we never *did* make it to John) it'd become clear to me that I had to get myself a car so I could move the family out of Jackson to a bigger city where maybe I could get a job that would keep us all together. Which I did. I did for a fact get me a car, a Ford it was, and we moved to Detroit. Of course at the time it seemed like ten million people just like us were headed for the same place looking for work, and for a couple of years things were so bad we were about ready to give up and live on the dole. Then finally the hard years were over and there *was* work, in fact more work than you could handle and

longer hours than ever you thought a man in his right mind
would or could work—building ships and planes and quonset
houses and all those things they needed for the War Effort.
You'd better believe it, we hung onto our jobs with our teeth in
those days because if you didn't put in your time, no matter
how many hours, they'd find somebody else to do it for you all
right, but then later they might decide you weren't essential to
the War Effort after all, and they could send you right off to
fight in the war. But fortunately my job really *was* essential,
and I stayed home and tried to bring up my boys to be good
citizens. I sent them to the parochial school, which you know
costs *some*thing, it's reasonable but it's not free, of course it's
worth every cent, what kids learn there they don't teach you
anyplace anymore, and I always felt it was the least I could do
because Lottie was religious and it meant a lot to her. Besides I
was bringing home a bigger pay check than in all the ten years
previous, though it was surprising how it didn't go very far,
our kids were big and ate like giants almost from the day they
were born.

But back to how my education got to be delayed. Suddenly
Matthew, Mark and Luke were big enough to be breadwinners
themselves, same as their old man. But naturally Lottie and I
figured they'd need more education than we ever had, we
didn't want them to have to wait for a war to get a decent
job—so we sat down and calculated a bit, balancing War Bonds
versus second mortgages and figured out a way for them to go
ahead and be an engineer or whatever they wanted so they
wouldn't have to work as hard as their father did, besides my
being worried all the time about how long my job would last.
And in fact when the war was over, the place I was working at
started making small electronics stuff and I was too big and
clumsy and high-powered for that—they found women were a
lot better at that sort of thing—anyway, I left of my own
accord before they, later, laid all the men off.

The way I got this little store, I started out keeping books
for Luigi, he was the previous owner, Luigi couldn't write
anything except his name on a check, though he was as smart

as a whip I'll tell you *that*. Well, after Luigi died, I bought the place and I've kept it nearly thirty-five years (I've only been sick twice, once I had pneumonia and then once I got a little infection in my thumb here, I don't even know where it came from, I had to have a little minor surgery on it). Anyway, I did all right, I can't complain, and my boys did go to college, every one of them, but by that time I was pretty near a grown man myself and Going to School was not something I was thinking about anymore. Besides, as I say, I married Lottie and then almost right away the Depression came, so I hadn't quite finished high school, something I didn't like to go around bragging about. It didn't seem quite right that a man with college-educated sons, one an engineer, one a teacher, and one a medic (he drives one of those emergency ambulances, like you see?) should have been a high school dropout.

Well, to go on with what I'm telling you. One morning at seven-thirty Rinaldo came by to pick me up, and we both went down and commenced our college education.

Naturally you're going to ask me how I'm enjoying it, and to tell the truth, the first week or so I didn't like it at all. There was too much noise, there were too many kids racing around, changing courses, tracking the professors down to see if they could get in their classes, and those who weren't running around in a frenzy seemed to have nothing else to do but lie on the grass with their girl or boy friends. I didn't have anybody to lie around on the grass with, so it made me feel old and lonely, just looking at them.

For instance, this is how bad things were, if you'll believe it; the first few days I just walked up and down the halls looking into classrooms to see if there were any guys my own age, and I didn't see any...it was like I was the last passenger pigeon. I must say, though, the kids were nice to me, they were friendly and encouraging. Still, they had their own lives to live and I couldn't even *begin* to tell them about mine: it wasn't even what they call the Generation Gap: it was the whole damned U.S. History Since 1914.

So I walked around from building to building, checking

out the campus—the Library Building, the Public Health and Environmental Science Building, the Law School and the Medical School and the Dental School and the Nursing School, trying to look like I was the janitor or something. And during that first week I also sat around the cafeteria a lot, just thinking and puffing my pipe. In the cafeteria you could be inconspicuous (nobody pays much attention to an old man smoking his pipe and reading a newspaper) so from where I sat I could hear conversations on both sides of me, without even moving my head...Now, this being invisible wasn't without its bad side. In fact, my worst day here was ticked off by my sitting around the cafeteria, just listening to conversations that way. Like one day during the second week I was just sitting there in a booth, smoking and having a cup of coffee and beginning to feel kind of confident about myself, you know, feeling I was doing all right here, I'd been up since early morning, I'd attended two classes already that day, and now I was waiting to get to a third one that afternoon called Social Change (I'd sacrificed my usual afternoon nap to get this class squeezed in, you understand, but I'd been in a regular go-for-broke mood when I registered).

Well, as you might imagine I was pretty tired but I was also feeling quite smug about it all, thinking, "Felix Mateo, you're going to beat this game yet and Rinaldo will be bragging about how his Grandpa Mateo graduated from college. Well, while I was thinking this and puffing away at my pipe, along come a couple of girls who sit down in the booth next to me, and my attention is naturally drawn to one of them—a tall, blonde girl who sits directly facing me. She and her girlfriend both have apparently come straight from the swimming pool: her hair is still in wet ringlets around her face and she is wearing a tee shirt which says *College is for Lovers*. She sits right there in front of me without seeming to see me at all and her friend asks her how did she do today, and she says: "Well, I did fifty laps. It was a little much, but I wanted a nice round figure. Usually I do about twenty laps. But if I want, I can get a second wind and do it again: that's a great feeling when you get your second breath, you feel so *strong*."

So I sat there in my booth a while, me practically a septuagenarian, who'd been congratulating himself just because he'd been able to climb up and down the stairs with all those kiddoes, and I said to myself, 'Felix, what do you think you're doing here with these champions? You'll never make it...' I can't tell you why, exactly, but it was just a very humiliating sort of thing, like it wasn't till that very moment that I felt, you know, *physically* handicapped: I'd had myself convinced that it was a matter of Brainpower and Discipline. "Brainpower: you got it, Gramp," my grandson had told me, and I'd fallen for his line...But now I was listening to these ladies, and I knew it was not going to be any shuffleboard game on a cruise ship, it was to going be an endurance test. What business had I going to school with young women who could swim like forever across an Olympic pool?

So as I poked my way through the crowds of kids to my next class, I almost whimpered. "Go ahead and shamble, you old dopehead," I said to myself dejectedly: "show your age." It was 4:30 in the afternoon and I felt like Rip van Winkle, ready to lie down for the next twenty years. Just the thought of staying awake for another hour and a half and then having to drive home on the freeway, and coming home to an empty house and having to fix myself dinner...suddenly the prospect of this coming *ordeal* made my whole body feel as if somebody had tossed it into a vegetable shredder.

So then I walk into my Social Change class, still feeling pretty put-down by the Olympics champ in the cafeteria and then I really *am* confused: something seems to have happened to the enrollment or else it had been true at the first meeting a week before and I hadn't even noticed it: this class was full of *women*, and at that time of day too: who ever heard of women going to school at 4:30 in the afternoon? There *was* one other man in the room but he looked to be a generation younger than me and somebody told me later he'd been some kind of officer in the army...Well, here I am already confused and feeling put-down, and I've hardly got to my seat when this week's Visiting Lecturer gets up (they have one every week), and *she's* a woman too—come to talk to us all about her work and her life. Everybody seems to know exactly who she is except me, and the ladies in the class are all eagerly, you might even say respectfully, taking notes. Me, I decided to give up on that: so I just listened while the lady talked.

And I tell you it was the strangest feeling in the world to hear somebody like that from your own time talking about her experiences as if they had somehow meant something to the whole world, not just to yourself alone. It seems this lady had written a book or something about herself and she had got to be pretty well known during the Depression, but "had fallen into obscurity when the Second World War was followed by the affluent Fifties," making what she had to say "seem no longer relevant." Then she told about how once she and a lot of other women had demonstrated in Washington, D.C. to protest the unemployment situation back then, and how she'd got arrested once, and how it was then that she had started writing articles, mostly her personal experiences about women in the Thirties, and during that time she had had three daughters and a son, who were also "in the struggle," and how she was glad not ever to have given up the fight, it had all been worth it, she said. She said she was especially gratified to see how "the Movement" was reviving "lost" writers like Davis, Smedley and Chopin.

And then she started to tell about her early life in northern Michigan, before she and her family moved to Cobden, Minnesota, about the farm they'd had there, and the harvesting of crops and driving a tractor and chopping wood for the stove. Well, you can imagine how I felt. Here was a lady who had grown up not too far from my very hometown, and had been through those things during the very same years as myself, and the stories she told were like stories from my own life. Like she told about how you could expect a couple of flat tires with those darned rubber inner tubes every time you went on a trip, and how awful the mud was in those rural parts, and how the snow would pile up in the school yards but the kids always went out for "recess" anyway, she said, and sometimes they had lunch and sometimes they didn't, "My kids ate many a banana sandwich in those days," she said. And then she started to tell about the lines: the Breadlines, the Souplines, the Unemployment lines, till I thought me, a grown man, would start bawling. It was like my whole entire past life had been building itself brick by brick till the moment when somebody like myself could walk into a classroom and see his life portrayed on the screen (she did have some moving pictures from that period, which she showed). Well, you know, if you could have resurrected some of the slaves to come and see a movie about their Middle Passage, that's about the way I felt watching these movies. But then she started talking (during the movie, that is) about how the women had worked as riveters and telephone operators and engineers and long hours in the factories of Detroit and Los Angeles and Birmingham, and then after the war were sent back to the cottage to nurse their babies, "preferably four or five, as we were instructed," she added, and here all the women laughed, it was like some secret joke. And this was when the trouble started. I suddenly began to resent this well-spoken lady who knew just the right line to feed her audience and I raised my hand to be recognized (I was still at the stage and I guess I'll never get over it, where I'd never interrupt a lady), and I said, "Mrs. Psalter, with all due respect, you ladies seem to have forgotten how hard your better halves...meaning folks like me...worked during those years. By golly, nobody can fault *me*," I continued, beginning to get hot under the collar in spite of myself, "for what I did...I worked like a horse. I raised my kids. I put in ten hours a day on the split shift, right up there on Michigan Avenue, and God knows when the war was over *I* didn't shove my wife back into the kitchen, no, she felt herself lucky and happy to be able to *get* a place to go, after all the years of the Depression."

There was a very long silence, like some Olympic-sized pool I had to swim across in order to reach this clever lady standing in front of the room dismissing my war effort and my fight for my kids' education like it was all a plot from beginning to end. Well, if it was a plot, it wasn't any of my doing.

Then, to add to my troubles, this ex-army officer started nodding his head in agreement with what I was saying, and somehow that made me madder than ever: here I was talking basics, the life and death of the family, the rise and fall of capitalism, the world being saved from the dictators and all, and somehow *his* hopping on the band wagon just seemed to reduce it all to a school yard squabble—Boys against Girls. I just threw my book down on the desk, put my hands in my pockets and growled, "Aw forget it. You're the teacher here, so speak your spiel—that's what they brought you here for, didn't they?"

There was a kind of gasp, as if I'd insulted the lady, though it was only meant for a sort of mixed-up apology, then she continued to show the movie and explain the events, without even once looking at me till the class was over.

Well, I was brought up to treat a teacher with respect, even if she is going like sixty about the wiles and wonders of womanhood like she'd invented her own sex and should get a medal for it. So after the class I went up to the front of the room to apologize to Mrs. Psalter. She was putting her things together in a kind of handbag that was made of burlap or fishnetting or something like that, and there was a group of women around her but when I came up they sort of drifted away, as if to say "Let Psalter handle him." Anyway, I'd rather they had stayed, I was a bit nervous, to tell the truth, and when I spoke to her my voice boomed out in the now-empty classroom so it seemed awkward, like I was still yelling at her when of course she could hear me well enough..."I'm sorry about that, Mrs. Psalter," I said. "I guess I shouldn't have lost my temper like that. But I've lived too long to take much of that kind of thing from anybody..." Now, there I was getting heated up again just at the thought, and it wasn't turning out like much of any apology after all but more like I was trying to continue the argument.

But Mrs. Psalter, Merle, her name is, Merle Psalter, she just smiled and kept on slipping papers and books into this fishnet bag with the long strap, which she now put over her shoulder. I suddenly got the impression that maybe she was just a little tired from all that talking and was no longer really interested in winning an argument—that is, if you could say that there *had* been an argument. So I just shut up and we started strolling down the hall together. When we got outdoors there was still some gauzy light in the sky, like it was not turned evening yet but just that the morning fog hadn't burned off. The grass was still dry and she just let herself down onto it a minute, resting herself after standing up so long talking, I guess. For a minute I stood there awkwardly, uncertain whether I was supposed to sit down too, but then I did, resting myself on one elbow and watching her closely to see had I done the right thing. By golly, I thought to myself, here I am lying on the grass like all the other students. And suddenly I didn't feel so bad about the whole thing.

"Are you retired, Mr. Mateo?" she asked.

"Felix. Yes. Retired a few years back. And it's such a good idea I wish I'd thought of it fifty years ago." I chuckled: imagine trying to retire from a couple of electro-shock treatments like the Depression and World War Two. "I still have my little store, though," I added. "Mostly my grand-children run it now. I'm too busy getting educated." I looked away, wondering if she thought I was making fun of her.

She sat watching me awhile. She had grey eyes set real deep in her head and I noticed how her eyebrows joined together as she squinted slightly in the sun. Her face had a lot of lines in it and since I had a pretty good idea of the kind of thing that puts lines into a face, it made her seem more familiar to me.

"You do a lot of travelling, I guess," I said.

"Yes, I do. A lot. It's not bad, though," she added quickly. "I mean, when the weather is nice like this, you don't mind much."

"You must get to meet a lot of interesting people, I bet."

She looked at me questioningly, then flicked a small green leaf from her lap. "Yes, a lot. People are wonderful to me—" Then she stopped, like struggling whether she should explain any further. "But it's tiring. Very tiring. I mean, you know how it is, there are bad days and good days on any job. Tonight, for instance, I have to get back to my hotel, get ready to leave for the airport. I'll hardly have time to change clothes, make a few phone calls..." her voice seemed to drift off.

I wasn't altogether sure that she wasn't letting me know that she was in a hurry and that I'd better buzz off, but something about the way she had said *job* made me think suddenly: well, all she's got is a *job*, she's not even retired like me: *she* doesn't even have time for a decent dinner, whereas I can spend the rest of the night wining and dining if I want to...I began to wonder if maybe she wasn't a little worn out from all that travelling around, talking to folks like me about her own life. Maybe she'd got to the point where she'd like a little more of her own life to live instead of just talking about it.

I said: "I suppose your family will be wanting you home." This was sort of pushing things, but I was real curious, and besides, we were running out of time.

"Oh no—my children are all quite grown now. They have their own lives, they don't need me." She laughed at the idea. Adding, "And that's the way it should be."

"And your husband?" I was too fast with this one too, I know, but here was the only Merle Psalter I had ever met literally getting ready to fly away: what would you have done?

"He had a heart attack while driving his tractor. He was only fifty-one. We'd bought a dairy farm, as I think I mentioned, in Cobden, Minnesota, during the McCarthy period."

I didn't ask what the McCarthy period had to do with dairy farming. I had my mind on something else. "So you've been alone a long time?"

"Yes, a long time." Then, kind of laughing at me, I think:

"That is, if you can call it alone—"

You can bet I latched onto that one. "If I can call *what* alone?"

"I had my four children with me, after all. I also had the dairy farm to run. And I had these personal memoirs I was going to write about..."

"And did you write them—the memoirs, I mean?" I was going to run out and buy the whole shebang, you better believe it!

She sort of blinked and looked away. "Well, not all... A lot of things...intervened."

I would surely have liked to know what it was that "intervened." But she looked at her watch then, and I saw how she'd begun to measure out her time, so I offered to walk her back to her hotel which was not far from the campus, and to my surprise she said she'd appreciate that. I even carried her books for her, a sure enough schoolboy, I was, that day.

In the lobby of the hotel we shook hands, and she said she'd send me some of her essays and articles and such. Which she did, she really did. She kept her promise and sent me six or seven pieces which, I tell you, I've got by heart.

Well, after Merle Psalter had gone, we had a lot of speakers come talk to us, but not one of them could hold a candle to Merle, to *my* way of thinking. Still, I did finish up that course and went on to register for some more subjects, and I tell *you* this education thing has been the best thing in the world for me. I've been learning like the dickens, every day something new: Economics, Western Civilization, Philosophy from Nietzsche to Sartre...In fact, I've been hitting the books so hard, keeping up with all the kiddoes and with Rinaldo, that I'm about ready for a rest.

So what I'm thinking now is this: I'm going to get rid of this little store altogether—sell it, I mean. And I'm going to get myself one of these what-they-call "recreation vehicles," and I'm going to take Rinaldo on a little trip with me. We've already mapped out our route, we'd go straight out to the West Coast first and see some of California—you know I've never *seen* the ocean—and maybe take in a little of Oregon and Washington by the way. Then we'd come home by way of Canada, the Northern route, dropping down maybe to see some of those places I've never been to, like Montana and Wisconsin and Minnesota. If we started out early enough we could be in Minnesota before the first snow fell, and you know Cobden's not far off our route, so why not stop off at Cobden and thank Mrs. Psalter for those articles she sent?—it'd be the gentlemanly thing to do, I think.

Main Street Morning

"Nor must you dream of opening any door
Until you have foreseen what lies beyond it."
Richard Wilbur, *Walking to Sleep*

You have come all this way to find out the truth about yourself, not the self you have carefully devised for over thirty-one years, but the self which split involuntarily into chromosomes, giving you his dark, curled hair but not her fern-green eyes—those mutual gifts which existed before you did, and which subsequently She gave away as if their love had not existed and therefore you, Marie, did not exist either.

A long search and a longer doubt have brought you to this ridiculous point, where you watch through your binoculars like a would-be assassin as *She* (Cecilia Roche née Cecilia Niall) goes to work, the woman who once either hated you or loved you, or both, but could not have been indifferent. She is about to leave Sears Roebuck where she is employed during the evening hours in Drapes & Fabrics, Custommade. She has gone in just now only to collect her check or perhaps to exchange a few words with her fellow employees and emerges, clutching her handbag. She does not trouble to straighten her skirt: perhaps she is indifferent to such

41

matters. A few doors down on Main Street, she pauses at the window of a shoe store where they are offering (you recall) two pairs for five dollars: you wonder if that means she still has no money: for long ago you decided that it was money and only money which could have wrenched you away from her, sobbing. Yes, sobbing: you will not have it any other way.

You'd be the first to admit that this is a crazy way for you to spend your vacation. Cooped up in a room of the Manor House, facing Main Street. Of course, every small town in the U.S. has its Main Street, but only this one has Cecilia Niall Roche in it. She has lived here for thirty years, ever since World War Two, as her generation refers to it—as if World War Three were already included in their plans. She (naturally) has had other children, though none of them could look like you, with that share of your genetic inheritance which belongs to Jules Blaine. Natural though it may be, the fact wrenches from you a spasm of loneliness, reminding you how quickly one's pendulum swings from being glorious Prince Hal to Falstaff snuffling in his bed. The moral of this comparison, Marie, you admonish yourself, is that a woman who plans to spy on her own mother ought to remain calm and not drink too much coffee. Already you're too nervous to handle the binoculars, which bear the sweating imprint of your fingers. But at least since you bought the binoculars you've been able to see her face, clearly framed like an antique portrait, and you accept the fact that she is (as they say) "lovely." (Suddenly you become "lovelier" to yourself.)

It's a round saucer of a face, with smooth puffed out cheeks, precisely the sort of face you would smile at for its Campbell Soup innocence, if she were someone else. If you were to meet that cherubic face at a party, would you ever imagine that she had lain in a ward, labored thirty-eight hours, and finally given birth to a nameless little gnome (yourself)? That, carefully adjusting her mask, she had gone back to Duluth, Boise, Davenport, Sheboygan—back to this very Main Street, the home of her fathers: absolved, pardoned, excused, by all except the main character of this drama, yourself? Nobody has yet asked your pardon.

Adjusting the binoculars like a telescopic sight, you think: suppose you were now to take the elevator, walk out the revolving door, and trap her as she emerges from, say, the bakery, and walking toward her, in face to face confrontation you say: "Mother?" you practice it a moment, repeating in various inflections: QUESTION: Mother?...EXCLAMATION; SHOCK OF RECOGNITION: Mother!!!!...SARDONIC: Motherrr! EXPLETIVE: Mother!

You turn away from the window, understanding very well that what you've tried to do is destroy your feelings. Good: you've destroyed them, Marie, how clever of you—now what are you going to do with the bits and pieces? You get up from your aching knees (you should have placed a pillow in front of the window but you were too nervous and you forgot). You decide to go out...to actually *see* her. You'll follow her, till you catch her metaphorically in the till. You'll then inform her she's under citizen's arrest. *J'accuse*, Cecilia Niall Roche...So you go down the hall which smells like a subway urinal: it's that roach killer thay use, an invisible fluid which destroys the nervous system, they paint it along the baseboards. In the elevator the elevator operator (no orange-eyed electronic robots in Main Street) looks warily down at his feet: you're a stranger here, he can tell that, but he doesn't want to be nosy, you've paid for your privacy and there've been no big-city habits, no men in your room, no strange activities—unless the long silences during which you are on your knees at the window waiting for her to come out have seemed to him portentous. It is a small local hotel where people know each other and are friendly; there's no protocol of deliberate silences separating Each from the Other, as in big cities. Still, you feel he'd like to penetrate your mystery. Not *my* mystery, you defend yourself sardonically; *my* life is a dull and open secret: *her* mystery.

But you think your bitterness may show on your face, so quickly you cross over the uneven step (he doesn't even say tonelessly, "Watch your step"—here on Main Street they

don't warn you every time of what's right before your eyes).
Out in the sun you're momentarily blinded. You've left your
binoculars upstairs and for a moment you panic, as if without
those defensive shields you'll not be able to bear the evidence
of your eyes.

Out here on the street—so quiet one wonders where all
the population explosion that demographers murmur about
has exploded to—there is no possibility you will lose sight of
her. There she is, walking very slowly this Monday morning.
Well, if she's not in a hurry, neither are you. You have the
advantage this time, there's no programmed period of
gestation, after which you must "show," willie-nillie. Now you
may show and be damned. The woman ahead of you is a bit
shorter and stouter than the one you spied upon from the
window: you take that in as though it's merely one more
response to a random sample you're doing on Main Street.

She's gone into a Rexall's. Although it's still early (10:30
a.m.) the three or four booths in the small drug store are
already filled except for the one nearest the cash register and
lunch counter: she takes it. Across the aisle from her sits an old
man, alone and unshaven. He's spread himself around the
booth with a newspaper borrowed from the rack, looking as
much at ease as if he were in the neighborhood library. She
checks the time with the red and black electric clock above the
lunch counter which reads, instead of the hours: S U N R I S E
B R E A D.

As for you, Marie, nearly a third of your face covered by
wide sunglasses, you head for the lunch counter, your back
turned to her. Actually, you see her quite clearly in the round
sign facing you which has a mirror finish and a Bicentennial
sticker glued like a bull's eye at the center, offering you
Homemade Apple Pie. You promptly order pie and coffee,
although you can see the bakery label on the pan, and you
know it will be too sweet and taste not at all of apples. Still, it's
something to shut your mouth on while waiting for the person
she is waiting for.

You've not long to wait—they're punctual on Main

Street, with no subway hang ups or traffic jams to slow them down—there she is. Her appointment is with no Jules Blaine, of course, no dashing young lover in khaki, but only another middle-aged woman like herself (wearing—somewhat to your surprise—real Indian moccasins such as are popular in the Southwest). Her housedress, however, is predictable—a pale blue cotton with some sort of trimming at the sleeves, a starched strand of which is coming loose near the rounded forearm. No matter: she's smiling a warm greeting and already they're into something you can't share, you've no idea what they're talking about. The occasional clink of money, the ring of the cash register or an eruption of news from a small radio on the counter chops up their conversation into secret semaphores and codes: you have to strain to hear them.

The woman in blue greets Cecilia with a sort of calm delight. You're somehow shocked to hear Her addressed so personally yet casually—rather like the *tu* instead of the *vous* coming from a street vendor once as you browsed among the bookstalls along the Seine. It had frightened you, as though someone had meant to insult you: it had in fact been only a boy about ten years old, selling plastic replicas of Notre Dame and Sacré Coeur: he'd stared at you, challengingly, enjoying his own insolence. Still, you'd bought one, pretending not to understand his rudeness.

Already Cecilia's begun to pull out some snapshots she's taken somewhere, and her friend of course thinks they're wonderful pictures. She even says it: "These are just wonderful."

"Neil took them. We said he shouldn't have to take pictures at his own wedding, but he insisted. He wanted some done by himself. He said he was the best wedding photographer in the State, he wasn't going to start married life by letting somebody else take pictures of his own wife!"

The woman in blue erupted into a delighted, mischievous laugh.

"But, Sandy, he's not at his own wedding!"

Sandy! Somehow you'd never thought of that. But peering into the mirror across from you, you imagine you do see a few faint freckles along the nose, rather like the vein of cinnamon deep in your apple pie. Well: so her hair has not always been corn-colored but rather (you now embellish the antique photo in your mind), a desert color, a sunset color, something Jules would certainly have preferred to his own coarse black hair cropped close by the Army so that one saw the pale olive skin against the hair, curling like knotholes.

"...so exciting, I thought I'd never make it...and not to cost me anything either."

"And what about?..." Her friend looks at her tentatively.

Sandy glances around to see if anyone is listening, sees only the rounded indifference of your back, hunched addictively over the apple pie. You hardly notice that in your excitement you have spilled hot coffee over your hand.

"Oh, I guess they'll be all right." Then defensively, "He might have done a lot worse, I guess. He might have married..." Her voice lowered, Sandy whispers the unmentionable. Then her tone changes. "But it'll work out, I'm sure. Besides, it's their affair, not mine. Why don't you take these and show them to Phil? I've got to do some more errands." She glances again at the red and black clock on the wall. Yourself, you have difficulty with the clock: it reads to you like a concrete poem:

BREAD
READ
AD

Or, if you blur your eyes a second, DAD, or even D EAD.

Sandy's friend murmurs something like "not losing a son but gaining a daughter." You strain your ears, you *think* you hear her say she knows what it's like to lose a daughter, but it must be your imagination, you can't pin the words down, Sandy's voice disappears into a kind of murmuring protest or enumeration, you're not sure which. Finally you hear it "...getting used to it, you know...daughters-in-law and one grandson."

You now experience a totally irrational pride in your sex.

But that she does actually have such an Item as a grandson is a bit of a shock to you: it puts her in danger of getting lost again just when you've "found" her, as if she could suddenly disappear at that point where the parallel lines between past and future meet. And now you're experiencing something else. Somehow the fact of her grandson is wrapped up like those Japanese *origami*, a design within a design, with the fact that you will soon be thirty-two years old. You feel suddenly hollow and wasted, as if the long struggle to resist entrapment by your own body (as Sandy was entrapped) has put you exactly there and nowhere else.

But now here she is: bright-yellow hair, and around her eyes criss-crosses, like those on your apple pie: lines so deeply slashed into the cheeks they might have been deliberately grooved there, as on some carefully crafted mask of clay about to be fired in the kiln. You try to imagine what she looked like back then—when you were presenting her with that historic moral choice: reject and survive or accept and be damned. In your now-corrected script of the Forties you see Sandy was "titian-haired": You even enjoy the cliche which at other times would have struck you as laughable.

In your new script Sandy is meeting her lover, your father Jules Blaine, in New York. She has told her parents that she is "taking a holiday" from the government office on Main Street (where several months ago she met Jules Blaine, who came to inquire about a friend of his who is missing in action). Part of Sandy's work at the big government office is typing up casualty reports: it's a job that fills her mind with nightmares and when Jules enters her office she already sees him as a casualty of the war.

But she has come to New York to be with him, with Jules. Where did she discover the cunning, the duplicity, during The Biggest War on Earth to escape from Main Street to do this? Impossible for you, in the Present, to understand how she managed it. Although for a while you helped run a radio program in New York, and have written television commercials, you've never had to make your audience understand why

they should purchase cars, curtains, cough syrups...all you had
to do was invent a catchy slogan, retain their attention.

Thus, it's difficult for you to imagine what she is saying to
Jules as they climb the Fifth Avenue bus. You understand the
feeling though: it's summer, they're sitting on "top-of-New
York," looking down. There is a slight breeze as they head
crosstown toward Riverside. Her hair is not coarse and curled
into knotholes like yours, like Jules', but soft and curved
around the ears like the mouth of a cream pitcher (they call it a
"page boy"). Jules is singing something from *Oklahoma*. If
you listen carefully, you can almost hear his voice: *People will
think we're in lo-ove...*There are tears in Sandy's eyes, perhaps
of joy?—no, of grief, because Jules is going down South before
being shipped overseas. "No," he says, he "doesn't know
which 'theater.'" They smile bitterly at the word *theater*. She
begs: won't she be able to be with him again before they send
him away? (Sitting in the drug store you almost urge them on:
yes, yes, they *must* see each other!)

All is quickly decided—ecstatically, spontaneously, as if
no lovers in time of war had ever thought of it before...She will
join him in a week. Not a word to Sandy's parents waiting on
Main Street of course: so far as they know she will still be in
New York, visiting Sandy's best friend. "Will Melissa cover
for you?" asks Jules. She nods; they are utterly delighted with
the conspiracy (Oh what a joy it is to fool one's parents, *isn't
it? isn't it? isn't it?*) They are as ecstatic as if there were not yet
to be endured in this war a Battle of the Bulge, an Iwo Jima, an
Okinawa.

They are on their way to Melissa's apartment: during the
summer Melissa's family are not there, they are at the Cape,
only Sandy is there with Jules—hour after hour, whenever he
can escape to her. After which he returns to the barracks,
where he becomes again the property of the State. He and
Sandy have a special arrangement for calls, so that when the
phone rings it can only be him: to the rest of the world the
occupants are permanently out of town. In a city of seven
million Sandy recognizes only one person. When one evening

while they are celebrating Jules' nineteenth birthday at Rockefeller Center they run into some of Jules' relatives, they brazen it out. Jules makes up a story on the spot: he is good at making up stories, as Sandy, obviously, is not.

Indeed Sandy is having trouble right now explaining to her friend in the booth how she feels about it all—about her daughter-in-law, or her former daughter-in-law, it's not clear which. "...it breaks my heart, though to see." and she goes on. It has something to do with the way her grandson is being treated or not treated, loved or not loved, ignored or spoiled or both. He's being deprived of something, that's obvious. And Sandy's grief is as keen as if it were her own child being singled out by fate for unjustifiable suffering. (You pause to wonder: is there *justifiable* suffering?) But no, what Sandy is protesting is not her grandson's suffering but her son's, his loneliness. You decide it must be the older son, not Neil, since Neil is the boy from whose wedding she's just returned.

While Sandy's present life continues under your ear like a pizzicato, you suck at the rim of your now-empty cup and gaze sideways at the clock which seems to your blurred vision to be reading the hour of D EAD. You continue to watch Sandy and Jules descend the Fifth Avenue bus. They are now returning to Melissa Levin's Riverside apartment. Again, there's an elevator—not much different from the one on Main Street, and they're going up, up, up: with your coffee cup in hand you are transfixed by the vision, which blurs as she steps quickly into the apartment. As they shut the door in your face, you can feel the melting of their bones.

It's been a long cup of coffee and you know you're beginning to look out of place, a young unmarried woman like you, having no job to go to on a Monday morning on Main Street. But you're afraid to get up, afraid your body will reveal how like a shuttlecock it's been tossed between two women, both of them Sandy. You now notice, with a combination of relief and panic, that Sandy's friend has gotten up to leave. That leaves you and her alone (at least from your point of view). Now would be the moment, the sweet and catastrophic moment to say...to say...Instantly you destroy your impulse by a rescuing gesture of absurdity...to say: *Mother come home. All is forgiven.* Love, Marie.

Fortunately for you Sandy has decided it's time to hurry on to her appointment. For a few moments you're too weak to move, you'll have to let her leave without you. But a faint grind of electricity from the BREAD clock reminds you that if you lose sight of her now you won't see her again till she goes back to work; and there you will be able to observe her only as she measures the fabrics, snipping away at yards of muslin, corduroy or denim like one of the Three Fates cutting away lives. So, leaving some money on the counter, you hurry out to the opposite side of Main Street. Ah, there she is, going into the local bank. So: she lives in the "real" world after all, complete with savings, mortgages, escrows and overdrawn accounts. You follow her inside. The bank is surprisingly crowded for such a small town and there're only two windows open for service. It's obvious that people are just as busy with banks in Main Street as everywhere in America...and what's this? Sandy is buying a U.S. Savings Bond for someone's birthday, for the grandson whose neglect she was protesting at the drug store.

You now get into a parallel line, ostensibly to cash a traveler's check and to get some small change for the parking meter. While waiting in line your mind wanders: waiting is for you (and for Sandy) one of the more draining rituals in our still unpredictable technology. It was to avoid Waiting that Sandy got on that train to the army base in Carolina (S.). You glance down at the modest hemline which presently hides her legs, and you contrast it with her appearance on that train in August of 1944. She is going to meet Jules, where she will sit in the sweltering heat (there is no air conditioning) for twenty-eight hours, the perspiration trickling down her back, while the train crawls along with its fantastic overload of servicemen (by this time next year the lists will be in the thousands who will never return).

It is the first train Sandy could get to—as the blue carbon share of her ticket assures her—CAROLINA (S.). There are no seats. All night long Sandy and about six other people sit on the suitcases piled between the cars, guarding their feet as the coupled trains grind again and again to a halt. At these stops a few teenagers called Soldiers climb down, their duffle bags on their shoulders. Always they have this dazed look, as if they do not recognize the town they have come to visit. Eventually Sandy's train does arrive in Carolina S., late in the afternoon. She is faint with sleeplessness and from the shock of the heat, which is something she has never experienced on Main Street. Jules cannot get away in time to meet her, so there she stands, feeling exhausted and lightheaded but also enjoying an odd excitement at the sight of a mule standing at the train station, its cart loaded with bales of hay. It stands patiently, only its ears flick in protest whenever there's a whoosh of steam from the locomotive (no diesel on this ancient train, though we are only a year away from Hiroshima).

Sandy takes a cab to the hotel Jules has instructed her to go to. She showers and changes her clothes, but she is too restless either to sleep or read (there is no radio in her room), so she goes out to the street. In spite of her fatigue and her awe at the sun which glowers down like some wrathful Jehovah making good His threat of destruction by fire, she strolls down their Main Street which is only a few blocks from the hotel. She is filled with a romantic curiosity about the town, which is exciting to her because Jules "lives" there. She presently notices a line of black people, extending all the way around the corner: they are waiting at the Colored entrance to see a film with Cary Grant. At the front of the movie house there is another ticket taker, sitting idly, waiting for the First Show to begin. Sandy does not wish to wander far from the hotel: what if Jules should arrive early and not find her? She begins—somewhat reluctantly, as she is enjoying her first stroll in a Southern town—to trace her steps. She is rewarded for her small sacrifice, because as the hotel comes again into view she sees Jules standing outside, obviously looking up and down the street for a slender girl with bare legs and honey-colored hair. They are at once in each other's arms: through the khaki shirt Sandy can feel the warm sweat of Jules' body.

The bank teller now holds the U.S. Savings Bond tentatively above her typewriter and asks Sandy, "Who should I make it out to?" Sandy replies, "Make it out to Jules B. Roche II."

Jules? You can scarcely believe the effrontery of it. What a cunning hypocrite, to name her firstborn son for her lover— to have this perpetual reminder of her love which is at the same time *her fault, her fault, her most grievous fault*...She has managed, apparently, to repress the memory of how she tried to destroy everyone and everything associated with Jules Blaine. How in late March of 1945 she rode out to the Armbruster Farm, which is about four miles south of Main Street: that is as far as the municipal bus line will go.

The bus driver looks at Sandy oddly as she descends—a girl of eighteen, with no shopping bags, no suitcase, no boots or scarf or gloves, nor (he glances down) stockings. And it is snowing, sleeting; a bruising March wind whips about the pools of water left by the boots of previous passengers standing at the driver's change box. He looks again, confirming his impression: the girl steps down one step at a time, bearing the heavy weight of her curving belly against herself as she grips the edge of the doorway, she makes her way clumsily out of the bus: the driver peers out the window on his side to see where she might be going. He sees only a weathered cowshed for somebody who may have a dairy animal or two and a water pump nobody uses any more. The old Armbruster farmhouse is still in use, though he does not presently see any smoke from their chimney: he has the impression that the Armbrusters are away visiting folks in Canada.

The driver watches while the girl whose honey-colored hair seems to be darkening as it becomes wet with sleet, makes her way to the farmhouse as if she knows where she's going and why. Certainly she must know the Armbrusters: she has a key and opens the front door easily. The driver is tempted to shrug away the incident, but the curve of the belly haunts him all the way back to the garage where he places a tentative call to the police. Not wanting to be nosy or cruel, "but not everyone who *looks* like a nut is crazy," he apologizes.

In the farmhouse Sandy does not bother to light a lamp or turn on the heat. Instead she goes methodically to the linen closet where she knows she will find all the sheets, dishtowels, bath towels and facecloths (she has been here many times, babysitting for the Armbrusters), and begins very expertly to lay the bath towels across the window sills, blocking out the air. She even admires the colorful towels, their creamy texture, towels which the Armbrusters received as a wedding present and which have lasted a decade: now they're soft and flannel-like, suited for swaddling bands. Every window plugged, Sandy now lays the folded sheets at the base of the doors, sealing up all drafts: the sheets are very white and glint in the semi-darkness like the eyes of animals. She is beginning to feel cold and at the same time somewhat feverish: yet it is not boring, this final domestic chore, there is even a tidiness about it: she opens the gas jets neatly so that their tiny porcelain arms all extend parallel to one another. Then she goes to a rocking chair where almost at once she achieves a slow rhythmical rock; the wood creaks slightly, gradually shading to a hum like a lullabye, to which she falls quietly asleep. When the screaming sirens stop in front of the farmhouse and the firemen smash the windows Sandy is sleeping soundly, her body soft, yielding to unconsciousness. At once she is carried out, given oxygen.

Well: she has made an attempt to get rid of you, Marie, and of herself too. But it's useless. After that fiasco, you grow and grow visibly, invincibly, for good or evil—until at last God repents of his wrath and washes you out with her blood.

You're glad you don't remember the trauma of your birth. It's bad enough reliving her trauma at the Home for Unwed Mothers. There's no such place on Main Street, they don't have unwed mothers on Main Street, so to spare Sandy the

pain of neighborly curiosity, Sandy is shipped off to a
benevolent institution in Philadelphia, where two months
after her failure at the Armbruster farm, you, Marie, are born.
Once in a sociology class you took part in a panel, along with
three other undergraduates on "The Unwed Mother." Eventually all four of you decided it would be an excellent idea to
visit the local hospital, where you taped interviews with the
women there, who made surprisingly fierce statements about
the right to keep their child.

Sandy's opinion on this subject, however, is not being
asked. Instead, now that she has carried "full term," she has
been lying all night covered by a coarse army blanket, her
hands on her belly, her eyes closed. She is praying, praying,
praying. For this ordeal to be over. For the wisdom and the
strength to know what to do. For some word from Jules who is
hidden away somewhere in Iwo Jima, hidden so well that he
will never be found except by Japanese children looking for
relics of the victorious invading army.

Finally a nun enters the room; it is dawn; she pulls the
curtains apart, and smiles at Sandy. Impossible to know
whether her cruelty is intentional when she says what she says
to all her girls every morning, "And how are you feeling
today?"

At last you have gotten through the line: it has taken, it
seems to you, an incredibly long time. But this is a small town;
what would have been a quick businesslike affair in any other
place is here a social event. You clutch your change, pocket the
money from your traveler's check and move slowly toward the
door.

"Put his father's name on it too, please," says Sandy.
"Jules A. Roche. I mean, not his mother's name. His
mother—"

"Yes, I know..." the teller says sadly. "It nearly broke my
heart to hear it. Like your son got to be a father and a widower
both at once. Like God didn't know which way to treat him,
hardly."

Sandy bows her head, pulls out a handkerchief which she

doesn't need but uses to conceal her pain at hearing her life counted out by the teller like so much small change.

The teller goes to type up the U.S. Bond while you loiter nearby, looking over some information about how the government is now insuring your savings up to $40,000.

Sandy now puts her grandson's gift into her handbag: you hear that he is six, going on seven, and the teller adds: "Well, you tell him 'Happy Birthday' for me, will you?" Sandy is perceptibly happier now that her list of woes, like the plagues of Egypt, have been named and numbered and she is momentarily free to forget them, including the one she will never forget and cannot share with anyone—not with the teller, nor with her husband, nor with her sons, nor with anybody but you, Marie. Who now share her sorrow as she leaves by the electronic door.

Outdoors she stands again in the August sun, squinting at the clock which is suitably cloistered in a church steeple. She feels the need to move quickly now, as the moment she has been planning for has arrived, and she must hurry to meet it. Ah...you see at once to whom she is hurrying. It is Jules B. Roche II, descending now from a bus, holding a sheet of paper on which you can see as he waves it at her whorled circles of dark blue fingerpaint. "It's a storm! A storm!" he informs her. Diffident, anxious to assure the artist that his success is clear and striking, she says simply, "Oh what a beautiful painting!"

You now apprehend that for Sandy love is always terminal, always something for her life to be lost in...Overcome by her failure to express her perfect admiration for his painting, she swoops down, capsizes the artist in her arms, covers him with kisses. "Did you have a nice day?" she asks at last: respectfully.

Your knees are weak as you lean against the freshly painted red, white and blue fire hydrant. Your impulse is to run toward them crying out, *me too! me too!* You can now taste your long denial; you want to run and tell her all about your thirty-one years without her and have her cry out with absolving certainty: *Oh what a beautiful daughter you are!*

have her insist with incontrovertible passion: *Oh what a beautiful life you have!* Which will give you the courage to go on, to go back to the ugliness of your century where life begins with television commericals and ends with nursing homes. But, as they pass you, Jules is trying to guess what they will do together to celebrate his birthday and Sandy is laughing. *Laughing.* It is the first time in all your imagined scripts that you have heard her laugh and it is real laughter, not something you have projected onto invented memories. Hearing it now for the first time, you lean weakly against the fire hydrant, standing aside to let them pass.

Lunching With Tenney

W hat Hirsch wanted was someone who could fix
his boots the way Manitello used to do them. First
Manitello would fit the leather around the soles,
then he would pluck the nails like tiny plants from his mouth
and with a single, perfectly aimed tap-tap, would place them
into the sole: shoe and leather would emerge welded by two
nearly-perfect parabolas. Maybe it was an impossible thing to
find nowadays, but on his way to lunch with Tenney, he'd give
the new repair shop another try.

It was always something to look forward to, meeting
Tenney, waiting around while Tenney dusted the bowling
lanes and set every pin in place. On Mondays (Tenney's one
afternoon off), the two of them would shoot a little pool, their
billiard balls making bright cricketing sounds still audible over
the fall and crash of pins. Not that Hirsch minded the noise:
he enjoyed it—the sound of wood against wood, the roll of
returning balls, people moving about in peaceful and meaningful ways. It was just the kind of activity Hirsch enjoyed
most, it gave him a reassuring sense of ongoing life in
Ginebra. Since his retirement, what he'd missed most were
the sounds of folks going to work, of traffic, of all the morning
music in his familiar neighborhood.

Now that he woke to long days of leisure, getting himself started in the morning had become as painful as probing some deep childhood wound. It was a matter of overcoming the silence—of his waking alone; of his Westclox, its luminous dial suggestive as an enemy's smile; of the dust-gathering silence of his French horn, which he'd meant to practice every day once he was retired. Even his phone was silent now, which was doubly strange, since it'd been Hirsch who—before Ginebra had become a summer resort and had been just another gas stop for the cars sliding down the muddy hillsides to the big city—had worked so hard on the telephone lines, helping to connect thousands of homes in the valley with telephones. Because of him and the other linemen he'd worked with, the rest of the town hummed with news from friends, relatives, jobs, banks, hospitals, vacation spas. People were no longer isolated or stranger to one another; they could ring each other up.

Of course his kids still phoned him regularly on birthdays and holidays. *Have a Merry Christmas*, they would say, or *Have a Happy Birthday*—as if they could give him one by saying so. They would repeatedly express concern about his spending the holidays alone; till finally Hirsch would end the conversation by assuring them—his son or his daughter, and the grandchildren he wouldn't recognize if he were to run into them in the street in Ginebra—that he was just fine all by himself, joking that he'd spent most of his life in Ginebra up in the air alone.

Hirsch used to be able to climb up the telephone pole like a monkey on its way to grab the big coconut at the top (nowadays the pole linemen used those van ladders, they were a lot safer and guys were unlikely to get scorched as had happened to some he'd known)....And a good worker he'd been too, he'd say that about himself: maybe a little overconscientious, never taking time to goof off and kibbitz with the other guys. Now, when at last he had all the time in the world to talk, he had to go out and hunt folks up to talk to.

Tenney Baeder was one of the best guys to visit with,

partly because he and Tenney had grown up together in Ginebra, but also because like himself Tenney had worked all his life, even during the Depression when it'd been hard as hell to get work: in fact, Tenney had probably been working the bowling alley more years than Hirsch had put in for the phone company—Hirsch had somehow lost track of the exact number of years.

So there was now a feeling of solid satisfaction in finding his friend exactly where he'd expected to, setting the duckpins. As he held up his boots for Tenney to see, Hirsch projected his voice down the lane so that his own echo came caromming back: "Taking these by to the shoe repair's..." Hirsch took in the slight shrug of Tenney's incredibly small shoulders. Sixty-two Tenney was and still built like a boy. Like he'd been born to be a pinboy, and knowing this, he'd stopped doing any growing that might have made it difficult for him to work back there at the lane's end.

Tenney's disembodied voice floated from behind the spread of duckpins: "Yeah? Where you taking them? Hardly nobody left can fix them right anymore. Tried that new place?"

Hirsch nodded, then remembered to speak out, since he was not always sure that Tenney could see him. "Yeah, tried them once. Had to throw the shoes away. They short on the leather, I think, then when the shoes get wet, they might's well be your baby brother's."

"Gonna be a big season," Tenney observed with satisfaction. "We got teams comin' in later today. Sorry, I got no time to eat right now...."

Hirsch now saw the head pause above the pins, fitting perfectly into its small guillotine of space. "Oh, that's all right. I'll just go down to The Dairy, see Buck awhile...till you're ready to go." He stifled the disappointment in his voice. Still busy men—most of his old friends couldn't just take off whenever they wanted to. But Hirsch wasn't going to start feeling guilty about it, as if he'd lost his job and was out of work: he'd earned every minute of his "free" time (why they called something "free" that you'd worked nearly forty years for was a mystery). His friends' free time would be coming up soon in a few years—men like Tenney and Mertz the Sandwich Boy, and the bartender at Perutti's, and Big Harry, the bricklayer. All these would soon be like him, lilies of the field, neither sowing nor reaping.

He sighed and gripped the boots: hightoppers they were, such as he used to wear in all weather. He pointed to the clock. "See you a little after one then?" Tenney nodded and bent to place a pin in the rack. The oak floors had recently been refinished, and Hirsch could just faintly see in their gleaming surface the shape of his own body following him as he left by a side door, heading for The Dairy.

He was pretty sure Buck would be there at this time of day. It was Friday, so Buck would probably be cleaning the ice chest and arranging his candy displays for the weekend. Hirsch strode past a nationally franchised ice cream parlor (he hoped Buck could see his disdainful glare into the window of the "big company") and strolled into The Dairy. "Dish of your best vanilla. Plenty of jimmies," he called out to Buck with authority. That the vanilla could possibly be anything but the best was a comradely joke. All the products at The Dairy were homemade: Hirsch knew exactly where Buck got his butter and cream. Yet all Hirsch had to do was suggest that maybe the flavor was a bit off, that maybe he'd switched to a different dairy farmer, and it was sure to set Buck off like a phonograph. Buck would be sure to object that he never used anything but the best, swearing there'd always be good honest farmers ready to sell their produce to people who were ready to drive out and pick it up themselves, that anybody who really wanted to could still give their customers good quality.... And Hirsch would sit back and listen as if Buck's voice were some familiar player piano music whose every rolling note he could antici-pate, absorbing it all with delight until, with a sudden spangle of notes the music was over, the player was silent: he and Buck together, they could play the music again and again anytime they wanted to....

But Buck was in a surly mood today: the local board had just raised the price of milk again, and sugar was getting like gold, he said, with the price of it fluctuating with the market. The chocolate chips were going to have to go—his wife couldn't afford to put all that butter in them anymore. Besides all this, he grumbled, the minimum wage increase was going to make it too expensive for him to hire kids from the nearby high school. "So here I am," Buck said, "washing my own glasses. How am I going to have time to make my own ice cream if I have to stand out here and scoop it out as well, besides cleaning the counter and washing dishes and filling the napkin holders, eh? They don't think of that, do they?" Hirsch glanced up at the list of flavors and noted that for the third time that year Buck had replaced the digits on the price list with new pieces of cardboard. This covering over old numbers with new seemed to suggest that the numbers were now infinitely changeable, they could be removed like bingo numbers and you could start all over again.

"Just one scoop today, Buck," Hirsch said apologetically. Cutting down on my calories."

"Yeah, pretty soon you'll be eating that plastic stuff they sell down the block, then you won't have to worry about calories—you'll never get fat from that junk...just cancer...." Buck muttered under his breath. "We've cut our butter content in half and still it's the best goddammed ice cream in Ginebra."

Hirsch nodded sympathetically. Into his heart stole a slow easing of pain. It was what he had come to hear.

Buck went on to complain about the vandalism—a couple of broken windows the night before. No reason for it, he grumbled: he never turned a beggar or a peddler down, he donated dollars to all the religious groups, commune groups, anti-defamation groups, to Moslem, Jew and Shinto, to Black power and white power and Indian power. It was good business, he admitted he did it for public relations, not because he was practicing Charity.

Through it all Hirsch nodded in agreement, trying not to be too enthusiastic. He rarely ever disagreed with anybody, though he'd learned not to be positively conniving in his enthusiasm: what he wanted was their voices, not their opinions...voices to fill up that part of his brain which lay awake at night courting memories with the kind of passion he'd felt once only for his wife and kids.

Only now, ironically, it was memories of his wife and kids that he mostly tried to avoid. Geraldine had not brought the kids up in such a way that he could even recognize his own share in them: even the rare visits from Tip or Eleanor were like photographs ruined by double exposure. He could see and hear them but while they were talking about "jet lag" or of "trading up" on some piece of property in Florida or Arizona or Hawaii, Hirsch was busy focussing them through a camera's eye—on a sled in the park, or in bathing suits at a summer cottage where their bare feet made deerlike tracks along the beach; or on the San Francisco cable cars—a very clear focus for this picture—where they'd all been together for their tenth and final wedding anniversary. When from time to time he talked to these sophisticated adults with their educated accents and fashionable clothes, he could no longer find the children whose voices he had longed to hear for so many years after the divorce. Rather, after one of these visits, instead of pride in what must surely be called his children's Success, he would be asking himself why The Marriage had failed and what these strangers-to-him would have been like if they had had Hirsch as a year-round father, instead of the men whom Geraldine had from time to time attached herself? And when they were separated from each other again—father and children—Hirsch would relive long into the night his private *Kristalnacht*, his shattering glass of memory and loss.

But Buck had begun moving restively, letting Hirsch know that he was about to withdraw into the back room to operate the ice cream freezer.

Hirsch shook his boots in a friendly way: "Got to be on my way. Takin' my boots in to the new place to be fixed."

"To Brindza's? No more Manitello, eh? Gone to Florida, that lucky sonofabitch, not like the rest of us, still breaking our backs here." But Buck laughed as he said it. He was not ready to quit. Why should he retire and go to Florida, he always said; he didn't like to fish, and besides it was too hot down there in the summer. He meant to stick it out till he'd reached the point where he lost money on every quart sold: he'd never give in to the franchisers, he said. Then he burst into a low hum as he retreated to the back room of The Dairy.

Hirsch sauntered in the early afternoon sun, his boots swinging from one hand. At Brindza's threshold he blinked, momentarily blinded by the banks of fluorescent light along the walls; then he stood quietly in line—not a long line, really, but just long enough to give him a feeling of not being in the right place. With Manitello he would have sung out, greeting him loudly in Manitello's own accent in such a way that his friend would have known it was a kind of cannon salute, meant to do him honor.... "Hey, Manitello, how about you fixa the shoes here, hah?" And Manitello would have retorted good-naturedly: "Hey yourself, old man, speak the English. We not in the old country anymore."

Now Hirsch stood silently while a bored young man in an olive drab jacket looked down at his boots. Good boots they were, crafted of Canadian leather, built high to protect Hirsch from snakebite and poisoned oak while he'd scrambled around in the underbrush connecting people into the greatest communications system ever invented.... Sometimes while repairing a line Hirsch had caught a few words rushing through the wind, and the sound had evoked in him powerful emotions for which one had no name. It'd been rather like watching one of those film clips where they threw out pieces of history at you that you had to understand quickly else the real meaning was lost: one shot of a concentration camp meant six and a half million dead, one head of Einstein or Roosevelt or Muhammed Ali meant a whole Era. And so it had been with the few words he would sometimes catch on the air: *But you never come home This is where it's at Doctor says if the chemotherapy doesn't work They gave him a breath analyzer afterwards but of course it was too I wouldn't*

*lie to you   What of the children?   Up for parole this
month   They ought to hang him   Don't care what they do so
long as they keep it to themselves   City is already fifty miles
wide   Expect two million by nineteen eighty-five.* Somehow
the very chaos of these sounds had always made a kind of sense
to Hirsch. It had been somehow reassuring that people should
be getting married, getting divorced, going to prison, burying
their dead, worrying about their health, moving to better
neighborhoods: it was as if something as big and unpredictable
as life itself was sure to go on forever.

The boy in the green jacket picked up Hirsch's boots and
shoved them to the end of the counter. At once the boots fell to
one side, their laces dangling. Hirsch managed to repress his
irritation, remarking mildly: "It's better to keep em up
straight. Helps keep em from crackin. Got any trees you can
put in em?"

The boy, who handled shoes all day for the minimum
wage, glanced down at the boots as if they were a traffic
accident he did not want to look at too closely: then, without
replying, he stamped the boots with a purple number (instead
of printing, as Manitello would have done with his dark stubby
pencil, *Sols & Hels*).

Hirsch made a final effort at communication: "When'll
they be ready?"

The boy shrugged, his reply was a denial of responsibility:
"Next week?"

Hirsch drifted back into the street, inexplicably annoyed
and depressed by the whole trivial business. Somehow the
purple tattoo had seemed the crowning insult. And it only
added to his depression that it had begun to drizzle. Great
clouds were suddenly forming overhead, and in a few minutes
there was certain to be a downpour: he'd have to run to the
new Mall for cover. He'd been really looking forward to his
afternoon stroll in the sunshine—past the barber shop
(waving at Jerry the barber), past the bakery, where he got a
sense of the events occurring in Ginebra ("Happy 29th
Birthday to Betty Johnson") and—for several months now—

past the construction company working on new Housing for Senior Citizens. Everybody was "senior" or "elderly" now, nobody ever got old anymore, Hirsch mused. Everything, even one's birthday ambiguously eroded, washed away.

Like this rain, washing everything away. It used to be they said rainwater was good for everything, good for crops, good for cleaning the air, that it brought fresh water into the lakes and rivers and ponds. But just yesterday he'd read in the paper that what they had now "in dangerously increasing percentages" was acidic rain; that what they had now, instead of rain that helped plants carry on their God-given job of giving folks oxygen was "precipitation-bearing nitric and sulfuric acids destroying the balance in our forests...." *Can you feature that?* demanded Hirsch of the louring heavens.

But the rain was beginning to come down heavily now, and the plain truth of it was, if he didn't start running, he'd get soaked. So he ran at a fast clip (*pretty good for a retired 'old man,'* he congratulated himself) into the new Mall they'd built several years back and which was now preparing itself for its annual flood of tourists. In a few weeks Ginebra's population would nearly double and tourists would be strolling through the carefully-laid imitation brick paths of the Mall, gazing up at the ceiling which drizzled artificial moonbeams and the light from pronged steel stars. One of the Mall's advertised features was its indoor Plaza, with curved benches (orange) and a small water fountain (bronzed) which was filled with perpetually hungry goldfish (carp). Still, people could actually sit on the benches, their backs against the advertisements paid for by the omnipresent shops which extended down either side of the Mall like a vast natural corridor, a Yosemite Valley of the twenty-first century.

It had never been advertised as a new Mall but always as Ye Olde Mall, as if Ginebra had thought about having one fifty years ago. *Which Ginebra hadn't,* Hirsch silently corrected, gazing around him. Ginebra back then had been near-wilderness, surrounded by lakes and rivers clear as diamonds. Back then even rich folks hadn't bothered to notice it because at that time rich folks went to Paris or Acapulco and not many would have thought of buying a second or third home in Ginebra. Now, because Ginebra had the luck of being only two or three hours away from several big cities, it had become a haven for escaping city-dwellers.

From where he sat in the Plaza he could see clearly into the interior of The Martha Washington Inne, its walls covered with wallpaper that resembled unfinished wood (Hirsch noted that the wallpaper had been hastily hung and one corner was licking its way down from the ceiling). On the walls hung glossy pasteboard globes punctured so as to look as if they'd been cut from tin: the kind of lantern Martha Washington might have used to shield her candle from the wind. The dining room had about a dozen small tables into which real nails had been driven, their heads left conspicuously exposed, their "wood" surfaces all cracked in exactly the same place so as to appear authentic. The restaurant itself lay wedged between a fast food place and a Rite Drug store whose window offered Hirsch the necessities of life: razor blades, mouthwash, shampoo (Hirsch reminded himself that he did need a few toilet articles, he ought to make a quick stop at Rite Drug).... And at the farthermost end of the corridor beamed a Pleiades of lights which announced the schedules for two theaters built back to back—one offering an X-rated movie, the other bringing back, by popular demand, *The Sound of Music*. Gazing around him, a melancholy gripped Hirsch, not unlike that helpless grief he'd felt when, while testing out a line, he'd overheard the news of a woman's loved one struck down in the street, and he'd stood poised in the air, helpless to assuage or heal her pain. The mere recollection of that grief was enough to bring tears to Hirsch's eyes...only he realized now, wincing at his own delusion, that his tears were not now for that remembered stranger but for himself—for his own loss: that what he felt was not grief but longing, as strong as first love, a longing to keep what he had; yet he dimly foresaw that it was a longing which could never be realized, but would only become more painful as time turned the town he loved into a consolidated mall offering toys and tinsel to a people who had learned to live without trees.

Hirsch cursed softly to himself, *Damn it all, why are they doing this to us?* and with a sudden angry growl he swore that he would accept nothing today from Ye Olde Mall, no, not even the necessities of life. All he wanted was to get the hell out of the Plaza as fast as he could, as if in some vague way he hoped to remove himself from his century merely by getting out of the Plaza; and he sprang so abruptly from the bench that its loosened bolts rattled absurdly beneath him. Hirsch shoved the bolts back into place and began walking as fast as he could to the electronic door. At the slight hesitation of the door, which seemed for a moment in conspiracy with the mall not to release him, Hirsch stomped angrily on the small square of carpeting. Fortunately no one had even noticed him, stamping with rage like Rumpelstiltskin...*No need to be so jittery*, it was just that he was in a hurry to get back to the bowling alley. It suddenly seemed strangely important to him that Tenney should be waiting for him and that they should eat their lunch together as usual; and in his eagerness Hirsch actually began to jog all the way back, weaving in and out of rain puddles till he arrived breathless but triumphant (as if he'd won out against some invisible foe), at the bowling alley.

To his joy (*but what did he think could have happened to the place while he was away?*) the bowling alley was just as he had left it. Hirsch stood at the threshold, breathing in as if for the first time the odor of floor polish and noting the grain of the oak floors glowing like veins in a human hand. The atmosphere was serene, almost monastic, and it was his friend Tenney who had done all this, setting each pin into its rack with enormous care as if he were creating a work which he meant to speak for him forever, creating this sanctuary which would soon be filled with people talking, laughing, competing in an undisguised effort to win their happiness and stay alive.

While Hirsch stood just outside the door of the bowling alley, still overcome by admiration for Tenney's work, Tenney gestured to him that he was going to his locker to get his raincoat, that he'd be out in five minutes.

Promptly in five minutes Tenney stepped out to the sidewalk to join him, checking his wallet at the same time to see if he had enough money, and complaining to Hirsch that he was exhausted, that his back hurt like hell, that the rack had torn his hand, that he'd found some gum on the floor and had had to spend fifteen minutes carefully scraping the floor clean, that people left their cigarette butts and ashes everywhere, that he was hungry, really starving and now he had only forty minutes instead of an hour and they would have to eat at that fast food place again, he hated it, he was going to start bringing his own lunches.... To all of which Hirsch nodded again and again, his eyes filled with sudden tears of gratitude, his throat constricted with silent love: *Complain, Tenney. Please complain. Long and loud. Dear God, let me go on hearing Tenney complain. Let there always be lunches with Tenney. Till the very end.*

Shopping

Eggs up again, tomatoes too. Amy could make a big one last three days, but if she took the whole package, she'd have to eat them all quickly (a pure waste), or eat them so slowly they'd spoil before they were gone. She took a cucumber instead, the biggest she could find. Then carefully she took three eggs out of their carton and put them in a brown paper bag (they'd grumble at the check-out counter, but Amy couldn't help that). If she boiled one and brought it to Gabrielle, who was having a real bad time of it, that'd leave her without eggs come Sunday, with four days yet before her check came. Still, it always did come on time, the government was good about that: she had her mind set on lunch with Gabrielle.

She paid for the cucumber and eggs—smiling steadily at the young cashier. No complaint about the eggs: in fact the girl seemed hardly aware of Amy: she could not know (Amy excused the girl's apparent insensibility) how much she resembled Antoinette (*Toni*, as she and Martin had always called her), could not realize that when Amy said to the unaware, unsmiling face, "Thank you, dear" she was really saying, "Thank you, Toni." "Wear your sweater, darling." "Turn off the stove now, be sure..." "How many are going, Toni, and will you have a safe ride home?"

69

Their baby, Toni...now a grey-haired divorcee fighting off cancer at the Medical Center in Houston. That oneself should get old, Amy no longer found surprising, but that one's children should get old was truly incredible. Of course none of all that could be understood from a mere smile: she knew that. She must simply have looked foolish to the cashier: one had to be careful with love, exposing it to a perfect stranger that way scared them: they thought you were senile if you smiled too much.

On her way out she suddenly bought a candy bar, pure chocolate, the kind Gabrielle used to love to break into a dozen dainty squares, offering them around...Along with the boiled egg she'd bring some biscuits and some tea, they'd share the chocolate: they'd have a real nice lunch the way they used to before all these troubles—before inflation and the oil and the gas and everything together.

Gas was the worst because there was no way to know for sure your own needs. It might be real cold, then again, maybe not. It was a matter of luck and the weather, it was like being a farmer: a streak of bad weather could wipe you out. If you took sick, or if your arthritis got bad, you had to have it warm, no two ways about it. So far she, Amy, had been fortunate: she could save on heat by staying away from home most of the day doing her shopping and little errands, then evenings she could keep her oven on till bedtime. For sleeping, she wore two sweaters over everything, and had knit herself a pair of warm socks. And of course hers was a small apartment—a blessing in a terrible February like this one, the worst (they said) in a hundred years—though stifling in the summer, it having but two windows, one facing Gabrielle's house on Aspinwall Ave. and the other in the bathroom. The man who had come to lay the new linoleum (this was before Martin died), had told her the place was a perfect rectangle. She liked it that way.

Gabrielle, on the other hand, still lived in the house she moved into as a bride forty-seven years ago. Had bought it with some insurance money after her folks had died, if Amy rightly remembered. And Gabrielle was stubborn, refusing to give up the house, though her boys were grown and gone and she lived all alone, cutting expenses to the bone, "cutting expenses to *my* bone," was the wry way Gabrielle had put it. She wouldn't even go to the supermarket or drugstore when the weather was bad for fear she'd catch cold, get sick, run up medical bills: and lose her house. Lately Gabrielle had started going to bed early, sometimes right after dark, depriving them both—Amy and herself—of the programs they so enjoyed, laughing delightedly whenever they recognized some long-forgotten actor reappearing on TV in a new role: as Wizened Villain or Noble Grandfather. Watching old movies was like rereading your adolescent diaries: with a knowledge of the future ahead of you, it made you laugh and cry at once. Gabrielle had used to be generous to all the Aspinwall Ave. neighbors—"generous to a fault"—Amy affirmed aloud, defending her friend. But now when she came to visit, Gabrielle sat huddled up in a blanket to keep warm, and served nothing, nothing at all: to Amy the lack of hot tea was the keenest blow of all. Still she easily excused Gabrielle: she knew what had happened. Amy had seen the symptoms before: beginning with some trifling economy, it became a disease ending only with the end they all dreaded and which they accelerated by their dread. One friend had got sick of malnutrition—they'd called it pneumonia—but poor Coretta had not had any resistance at all and had crumbled like a dry moth at the first winter wind. She, Amy, was not going to let that happen to Gabrielle.

At home in her apartment, Amy put their lunch together. She shook a little tea into a plastic bag, wrapped up the egg and biscuits and slipped them into her shopping bag: after the lunch with Gabrielle, she meant to do her day's shopping as usual. Not only did the many hours of bargain-hunting from store to store save money, Amy murmured to her interior audience, but it gave her needed exercise, kept her busy and tired her out so that she could often sleep till nearly four a.m. without needing those extra late-night snacks she used to indulge in, which (if you counted it all up), could pay for the light bill. When the weather was good she usually ate her lunchtime sandwich in the little park beside the Free Public Library, but this winter more than ever before, she ate her sandwich on the mezzanine (Women's Rest Rooms) of Krieg's Department Store (built 1886).

Amy locked her door and poked her small change purse and key into a pocket of her heavy wool coat, a coat Martin had bought for her one Christmas and which was still a pretty good coat considering...*Considering what?* she wondered in her own voice, which surprised her, it seemed to echo so loudly through the hallway: she turned to smile at any one within earshot who may have overheard her. But no one had heard. She was very private here at the top of Aspinwall Apartments. Hardly anyone saw her, except on her way in or out, mostly as she returned just before dark. For she was not so foolish as to wander about after dark these days, though Aspinwall was a "safe" building, and their neighborhood was not as bad as some. Mostly elderly people like herself, their children gone away to wars and marriages, leaving houses like Gabrielle's mortised between buildings. Muggers, addicts and prostitutes had not so much failed to invade Aspinwall Ave. as they had overlooked it. There were even a few fenced-in front yards left around, verandas like Gabrielle's trussed up by peeling wooden pillars, with a stringy rosebush or two. In the spring a streak of yellow forsythia would appear to flash in the sun.

The only time Gabrielle had been away from her house was when she had gone back to Baton Rouge to nurse somebody, Amy couldn't remember who: *you care more about your house than you do about yourself,* Amy grumbled silently to Gabrielle, resolving really to *say* this to her friend one of these days. Garielle's husband, Sam Gaines, had been a self-employed piano tuner until his death, and now Gabrielle lived on what her boys sent her—one son the former manager of a bankrupt Grant's store in Seattle, the other a landed immigrant who'd resettled in Alberta, Canada. When Amy had once tried, discreetly, to find out just what the boys did send her, Gabrielle had remarked emphatically: "You don't make *contracts* with your kids, Amy" while Amy had sat nodding apologetically, not wishing to say anything that sounded like a judgment, Lord knows everybody has their troubles. Still, the teacup had rattled in Amy's hand (Gabrielle was still serving tea back then) and Amy had been secretly glad she hadn't to depend on the sporadic affluence of children. She preferred her SS check, though most folks would have thought it'd barely support a child, much less a grown woman who might need...Amy stopped short of thinking of what she might need.

At the second floor landing a new tenant stepped aside to let her pass; he seemed surprised to see a woman come down from the top floor. Maybe he didn't even know there *was* a top floor; maybe he thought there was not but an attic up there. Amy smiled shyly at him, mostly to show she wasn't scared of every strange man on the premises: Gabrielle, for instance, never answered her front doorbell, no matter what. She said the friends *she* expected knew where to find her. And it was true—Amy always knocked on the kitchen door till Gabrielle opened the door a crack on her chain first, looking to see who it was even though Amy would have called out several times, "It's me, Amy. Gabrielle, it's me." The idea struck Amy with a sudden mingled surge of dread and anguish that maybe her friend was losing her hearing but didn't want anyone to know.

From Aspinwall's second floor to their hall was an easy descent. Though the walls of the building were deteriorating, the stairs were still in good condition. Amy had been climbing them effortlessly most of her life, and until Martin had died, they'd never given her any trouble. But it was as if the breath had got knocked out of her the night they carried him down and put him in an ambulance. After that, she'd discovered an obscure need—a need somehow unrelated to her real self—to pause on her way up, resting at every landing but always moving her shopping bag out of the way for other tenants coming and going.

She stopped at the mirror in the hallway in order to straighten her stockings: women didn't wear them with seams much anymore, but she did hate that wrinkled look around the ankles some tolerated. Amy's legs were not much swollen, and thank God she wasn't hammer-toed like some. She wouldn't brag, that was tempting God, but there was lots she could say she was thankful for: like never having been bad sick, even as a young mother. Always able to get around, to do her chores, and she didn't go to pieces if she lost her sleep either. Whereas some she knew had spent all their girlhood in and out of hospitals. There was Myra with one lung collapsed from the T.B. and Andree whose asthma had forced the whole family to move to Phoenix, and one of the Blake girls, Amy couldn't recollect how she called herself, who took fits. She, Amelia Buford, had been strong, straight-backed, smart in school, and had married well, so they said; and it was true, Martin had been good to her and had been from the same parish. Even Toni had had nothing serious, only the usual croup and chicken pox and teen-aged troubles, and she in her turn had married and "made-do" as Amy's mother used to say. Amy summed it all up with a faint nod at her mirror image, querying it at the same time, *Do you have too much powder on, do you think?* It did make one look old to be overpowdered. There was a letter (too soon for her check) on the small chipped table (it'd been a real nice marble back in the thirties—or was it the forties?—when the building had been owned by someone whose name she used to know). Now she never saw the people who owned Aspinwall Apartments. In the last decade she had not once appeared in the office of the Charles Street Realty though they were not two miles from Aspinwall. She had not asked for any service, nor made any complaint, nor suggested any improvement to walls, stairs, light, plumbing, stove or fire escape: what she prayed for was that Charles Street Realty should completely forget her existence, lose her as a bookkeeping error. For she knew only too well that if she were to telephone them or appear at the office to complain of anything—to ask, say, for an exterminator to come after the roaches who tore at her paper bags in the dark like school children—they would check her out, note with surprise how little rent she paid, and casually, automatically, they would increase it by 10%. It had happened once before. Once several years ago, her pocketbook had been stolen from her while she sat at the drugstore counter: with a long, silent knife, skillful as a surgeon removing flesh, the thief had simply cut away the straps. She'd been obliged to telephone the Realty Office to open her door with their passkey, and sure enough, she'd received a note in the mail the very next month informing her that her rent had gone up 10% "due to the rising costs of insurance and maintenance." One other time, while carrying out the trash, a gust of wind passing through the stairwell had slammed her door shut, the key idiotically safe in the lock on the other side. Fortunately the nice young woman, Louisa, who lived in the apartment just below hers, had heard her cry of dismay and had offered to climb the fire escape ladder to get into Amy's place through her open bathroom window. With mingled terror and admiration Amy had watched Louisa ascend the rusting metal ladder to her window and had burst into tears when Louisa safely reappeared in Amy's doorway: another letter from Charles Street would have cancelled out tea, sugar and eggs with a stroke of their pen.

She descended to Aspinwall Ave., her eyes momentarily blinded by the sunlight on the bastions of snow; then, spotting a runnel flattened by tire tracks, she picked her way across the street around to the rear of Gabrielle's house. The snow had piled up in drifts around the porch and the doorway was hard to get to. She stamped her feet as loudly as she could on the doormat so that Gabrielle would hear her, hallooing cheerfully at the same time so that Gabrielle would know it was just a friendly call, no emergency. She smiled into the crack of the door.

"Good. It's you," said Gabrielle, with more vigor than Amy had heard from her in a long while.

"You were expecting somebody else?"

"No, no, nobody comes. They used to phone first, and I'd have something ready by the time they got here. Now they don't bother. I don't call them, they don't call me." She looked away from Amy as she shifted the weight of her blanket which she wore like a Spanish shawl, tucked in at her elbows.

Amy rested her shopping bag on a chair. "Well, at least you have a phone. I...decided I could do without. I mean, who calls me anyway? If Toni got worse—"

"—they'd let you know that," said Gabrielle quickly, her voice neutral. Her dark eyes were very bright, but her hair looked as if it had not been washed in weeks. Gabrielle followed her glance.

"Too cold. Wash your hair with these drafts coming in, you catch your death."

Amy pretended that she hadn't heard, or that if she had heard, it was of no significance. Yet it mattered: the civilities mattered. She pulled the packet of tea from her shopping bag: Gabrielle accepted it without a word.

Both women stood beside the kitchen stove while Gabrielle boiled the water. Amy noticed that the rest of the house was now totally shut off, even the living room where Gabrielle had been sleeping on a sofa. There was now a daybed in the kitchen.

Amy sipped her tea, munched slowly on a biscuit. She declined any share in the egg, declaring she had cooked it expressly for Gabrielle, as if Gabrielle were convalescing and she alone had to have a special kind of diet.

Without troubling to get a plate, or a knife, Gabrielle merely cracked the egg and ate it, leaving the scattered shells on the table: somehow that disturbed Amy more than the unwashed hair or the daybed in the kitchen. The motion had the random quality of a forager, of a woman she'd seen once digging for food in the trash. Nervously Amy moistened her dry lips: *it mattered; hang on to the civilities.*

"Do you have a napkin? I mean a paper napkin?" Amy asked politely, as if it had been a mere oversight on Gabrielle's part. Lightly she touched the corners of her mouth with thumb and forefinger.

Gabrielle stared. A look of dismay crossed her face, then something like an inspiration. She rose from the chair and knelt down to a storage cabinet beside the sink. The blanket slid from her shoulders to the floor as she began turning over a few dishcloths, washcloths. "Ah, I knew I still had it!" She handed Amy a napkin with a finely crocheted edge: "I knew I still had some of these."

"Oh, nothing so fancy as all that. I meant..." But Amy accepted the napkin: where it had been folded the edges were still sharp; the cloth had turned a pale champagne color, rather like a yellow rose.

"Always meant to start using those things for everyday. They used to make such pretty ones, you remember?"

You remember was the signal for a game they could play endlessly. Like Scheherazade beguiling their listener, they could evoke countless stories from each other's repertoire, making the game last as long as they wanted...avoiding the present, not mentioning how long it had been since Gabrielle had been out of her house, the long illnesses of friends. For nearly an hour together they spoke of all the dead Down Home as though they were only in the other room, temporaily shut off for the winter. Then Amy remembered suddenly to bring out the candy bar for Gabrielle, tucking her own share into the pocket of her coat.

At last, with a sigh of reluctance, Amy rose to go. She wanted to get some new light bulbs, she explained. Also she meant to stop off at Krieg's Department Store to look over their patterns, maybe make herself a new blouse...Her voice faded away. No need to pretend with Gabrielle who knew very well that Amy sat looking at the patterns because her budget required that she stay warm somewhere till dark; that upon returning to her apartment, like Gabrielle she too would prepare for bed. And like Gabrielle her dinner tonight would again be what they jokingly referred to as Soup-plus. Soup-plus was (quite simply) one's favorite soup to which they added almost anything: bread, cheese, potatoes, eggs. Amy's favorite soup still came in the red and white cans even though there were several cheaper kinds under the supermarket label: an extravagance, but worth it. She could save on other things—like light bulbs. Today the kind she liked were on sale: a size giving her just enough light for her entire apartment (she left the bathroom door ajar).

Feeling better than she had in weeks, she kissed Gabrielle's cheek. Not frail and wrinkled like they're always describing us, thought Amy, but weathered, somewhat granular, the earlobes surprisingly oversized and pendant. She'd read somewhere that one's nose grew all one's life. The thought made her smile, so she shared it now with Gabrielle. "Gabrielle," she said with a spurt of mischief. "Do you know something? Our nose grows as long as we live."

"Good God!" Gabrielle laughed ruefully. "Don't I have enough trouble!"

Gabrielle watched her from the doorway as she inched her way across the snow. "Watch you don't fall. I can't get anybody to come shovel this snow." Amy didn't look back, she didn't need to translate "I can't get..." to "I can't afford..." She merely waved good bye, her own gloved hand before her face like some dark gull's wing over a sea of snow.

The lunch with Gabrielle had accelerated her day. After a brief stop for the light bulbs she went straight to the library to check out the advertised specials for tomorrow. She also wanted to read the latest Houston papers, as she planned to write to Toni again after supper. Gabrielle had once commented that Amy knew better what was going on in Houston than she did Aspinwall Ave; but after all when she wrote to Toni she liked to have something to tell her about besides shopping, like "I notice that they had a bad accident on your expressway, not far from the Clinic (Amy had traced it on the small insert map in the newspaper, or "I notice you folks have plenty of natural gas." The articles she paid most attention to were the articles about cancer treatments. She only wished she could cut out the articles on radium therapy and chemotherapy and operative therapy and cobalt treatment to send to Toni.

But the paper belonged to the Free Public Library, so she contented herself with copying out what she wanted to send to Toni.

It took more than an hour to write it all out in her small neat hand that Martin used to say was as good as print. By then half a dozen kids were skittering around the library (it was 3:30 and they made a rush into the library as though they preferred it to going home), giggling and holding hands to their mouths in mock terror, or whispering "Hush! Hush!" in a way that was louder than talking. One of them, a girl of about twelve, collided sharply with Amy as she rose to return the newspaper to its rack.

She stopped off at Krieg's Department Store, but without bothering to look at the patterns; instead she rode the escalator to the Women's Rest Room, checked her weight, on an old scale which she knew never gave her proper weight, but from which she enjoyed making interesting if inaccurate calculations: then headed homeward. The wind had risen by that time, and the clouds had taken on that smoky charcoal look that made the time between sunset and dark not quite real, like a picture of some other planet, like Mars maybe, where only the color of the silent sky mattered and there were no people at all. Her return was slow and difficult through the ice-packed streets, and by the time she turned into Aspinwall Apartments, the street lights were on.

All in all it had been a nice day, a day such as they were always telling you to have. "Have a nice day," they said tonelessly at the supermarket, at the drug store, whenever they handed you change for your money. Yet even as she came up the stairs she felt an odd weightlessness about her body, a premonition such as she got when she was about to come down with the flu, and as she stood before her apartment door, her legs still trembling from the long climb, she divined rather than felt that her coat pockets were empty, picked clean by some agile young thief, that schoolgirl perhaps who had seen something she wanted—maybe the candy bar—and had taken all: key, candy, coins.

Babbling her dismay, Amy moved down the stairs as quickly as she could to do the only thing she could do, she hated to do it, to ask that lovely Louisa to climb the ladder again, in this weather, oh God she wouldn't have let Toni do it, but now here she'd have to ask Louisa and of course she'd be angry with Amy, wouldn't she? "Doddering old fool," she'd think or even say..."you probably just forgot it again." She'd never believe Amy'd been done in by some cute little kid who thought it was O.K. to steal a candy bar...not a thief, actually, just a kid who wanted something and took it. *Please Louisa, just this once and I'll not ask you again.*

Her knock was not timid, but insistent, panicked, pleading—as loud a knock on anybody's door as Amy had ever given. It seemed to thunder through the hallway of Aspinwall Apartments, to rattle in her brain; it made her feel chilled and terrified, as if she were already enduring with Louisa her dangerous ascent into the air.

There was no answer to Amy's knocking. Desperate, she knelt down and tried to peer through the keyhole to see if a light were on: all was darkness within, the keyhole filled in or taped over. Of course: what woman would have a keyhole exposed to the hallway nowadays? Amy burst into tears. *Be calm. Stop trembling. You have to get in, that's all there is to it, you have to get in.*

She stepped outside. Odd how the charcoal sky had turned blind and black. All one could see now was the street light reflected in the snow, as if there were no more real light in the world, only this reflected glare between fields of dark.

She looked up and down the street. Perhaps she should wait, maybe Louisa would be getting home from work? Wasn't it about time for people to be getting home from work? But she had no time, even, for questions. It was getting darker by the minute, she'd scarcely be able to see the ladder. Better to do it now if at all...or call the fire department. Yes, she could call the fire department who would call Charles Street Realty who would "...due to rising costs of insurance and maintenance..." She dropped her shopping bag in the snow, pulled off her heavy coat and began to climb.

After the first step, it seemed easy. In spite of her terror at what seemed to be the swaying of the ladder in mid-air, she had actually gone up nearly half-way. When she reached the top rung outside her window, would the window be open? She could not remember; usually before leaving for the day she turned the hasp and locked it; now and then she forgot. The metal ladder seemed to stick to her gloves as, slowly, with fear but also with a certain elation at having overcome her fear, she pulled herself up. It was a matter of not looking down, that was the main thing, not to look down or at any other thing except at the window above her...She could make it, it wasn't the physical exertion, one didn't have to be physically strong to climb a ladder, one merely had to overcome...what one overcame every single day of one's life...one's fear. So she was doing it, she definitely was doing it, when she heard someone below on the sidewalk cry out, "My God! Look at that old woman up there!" Only then did Amy realize who was up there. Looking down she saw between the rungs at her feet three or four vaguely familiar faces: they loomed into her consciousness like faces in a dream, the fear she saw in them was greater than her own.

She believed that in spite of the gathering crowd she had worked up her will to ascend the last ten or twelve rungs—she even thought she could tell that the hasp of the bathroom window was turned at a slant: if she rattled the frame, she could shake it loose, the window would open—when she heard the roar of a siren and a fire truck pulled up beside Aspinwall Apartments. She glanced down, she saw her neighbor, the new tenant, signalling to the firemen. She saw them point upward at her, as if she were an escaped criminal. The people on the sidewalk now turned their heads from the fire truck upward toward her. The realization that her desperate climb could be labelled madness paralyzed her. She now wanted only to remove herself from their sight, as quickly as possible, she wanted only to get down. But she could not move.

It was not anything she had anticipated—this need of a rapid and immediate descent. She moaned with dismay; she was treed—just like a cat. Sobbing, she leaned her head against the ladder.

"Don't move," the fireman commanded. "We'll get you down." In a matter of moments a fireman had set up another ladder beside hers, and caught her in his arms—she was safe.

They began questioning her; their questions clearly indicated that they thought she had lost her mind.

"No, no," cried Amy. "I was just trying to get into my apartment. Just trying to get into my home. My key..." She stopped, her explanation interrupted by sobs—of rage, of fear that Toni might hear of this, think she had, in fact, gone crazy.

But some well-intentioned person had anticipated her needs: it was the new tenant who was offering her the familiar passkey with the long paper tag from Charles Street Realty.

Amy withheld her sobs: she stared at the key; then with a slight tremor held out her hand.

"Thank you," she said politely, remembering her manners; the civilities *mattered.*

A Love Letter To Peter Dalosso

Even before she spoke I found myself gripped with envy: I'd always wanted to have golden hair that would reflect the sunlight. Looking at her long, lovely hair, I was thrown back into adolescence: so difficult is it for us to forget our childhood losses: the bicycle, the electric train, the tresses of Rapunzel.

I hardly had time to wonder at this sick resurgence of old losses when, in a breathless, spilling voice, the girl told me why she had come: she was in love with my husband; my husband was in love with her. they wanted to get married.

She faltered once or twice as her conscience got caught between the urgent need for truth-telling and the fact of Rick's having deceived me. Her terrible urgency almost succeeded in making me her accomplice...She needed me to agree with her that Rick was a very lovable man: who would know better than I that Rick was inherently lovable?

Basically an honest person, I found myself thinking. By this I meant in the way we'd brought up our daughter Jody, to be honest: "Don't be fearful, tell the truth, be straightforward, there's nothing to be afraid of: you're as good as anybody." Daily infusions of courage by which we build children stronger than ourselves.

She said her name was Heather. (*Heather!* What poet could resist falling in love with a woman who bore the burden and promise of such a name?)

"You must have known," Heather said. "I felt you always *did* know..."

An explanation? An excuse?

"How long have you?..." I regretted the question at once and hoped she'd not tell me.

But again it was a question of honesty and so, looking directly into my face, she told me...(I now noticed with surprise or with some other emotion too complex for me to grasp, that she actually resembled me in a way I couldn't put my finger on.)

"And so now you've come to tell me...what? That maybe you want me to move out of here?" I managed a short laugh which may have sounded hysterical to her, but I was not hysterical; rather I felt remote and detached, as though I had already stepped onto an ice floe and was moving farther and farther away. "I mean, maybe you want this house too."

Shamed and reproachful, she looked at me. "Oh no, no. We wouldn't think of that. Rick understands his...responsibilities."

"Social security benefits, rather," I observed drily.

She was silent. She had come into the living room and was now toying with a paper clip she had found lying on the sofa. It was a place where Rick usually sat, reading students' papers. It occurred to me that she was much at ease there, that the sofa was familiar to her—that my entire house must be familiar to her: perhaps she knew where I put things—my underclothes, my contraceptives. This somehow seemed worse than the other things which one could have predicted: didn't more than half the marriages break up these days? Millions of people making vows, then realizing within a year or two that they were impossible to keep. Jody had already been through one of these accelerated episodes, and her attitude had been: cut your losses before they make you a lifetime bankrupt. But I was fifty: what lifetime? what losses?

Heather now began haltingly to tell me how they had not meant it to happen, she had been in his Workshop, she had written a few poems herself, etc. (I might have known that: it was the only kind he would have fallen in love with) and I shrugged with what must have seemed to her indifference, or even disdain. But it was meant to be—not generosity of spirit on my part, and certainly not "forgiveness"—who was I to forgive anyone at the moment?—I merely meant to convey a kind of understanding that this sort of thing had been happening since the first writer had begun addressing his Muse. Poets had to have new lovers, I knew that: it saved them from repeating the same poem.

Heather went on to tell me (did I ask her? did I imply?...) that she was not pregnant. No, that was not it. In fact, probably they would never have children, they didn't feel the need. It was their poetry that had brought them together. I smiled (at least I *think* I smiled, though it may have looked to her like a grimace), recalling how Rick had proposed to me shortly after reading my first novel.

She seemed to be waiting for me to say something—something more angry or more dramatic, perhaps. But I could say nothing. Nothing of the three children Rick and I had brought up—thirty years given over to shaping formless beings into real people. Nor did I speak of the books I had meant to write but had not, because Rick had been a graduate student and we had needed more money, or because Jody or Jim or Sara had been up during the night. Nor did I speak of the friends we had not visited, the places we had not seen, the opportunities let slip because Rick was in a crisis about his exams, or his job, or (lately) his health. Cooking heathful meals for him, I'd saved him for another decade so that he could make it with this girl. (Quickly I cut off that line of thought as demeaning: after all, I was a mature intellectual, wasn't I?)

Anyway, I said nothing to her of any of this. It would be like trying to explain what our lives had been like before the

Pill: the terror we had felt, the crushed career plans, the despair, the resignation, and finally, our theories of compensation.

"Does he know you're here?" I heard a tremor in my voice, as though Rick were not my husband but my child whom I'd perhaps failed to bring up properly, and now he had done something for which I was about to feel shame.

"No, of course not. He'd never have let me—"

"Well thank God for that!" I exclaimed softly, glancing at her with a kind of shared womanly bitterness. But she only looked puzzled. "What do you expect me to do now?" I presently asked, now wanting her to go and let me alone—and at the same time wildly hoping that Rick would suddenly appear at the door and we would have one of those dramatic denouements we knew so well how to set up in fiction.

He did not appear. Heather rose guiltily and moved toward the door.

She stood for a moment at the threshold, running her finger along the edge of the door. Her eyes took on a soft, worried look, the eyes of a loving person who was used to pleasing, and for whom my imagined hostility must have been very painful. "I don't know...I don't know that there's anything for *you* to do...I mean, is there? But I'll tell Rick tonight. That I've told you I mean. *Someone* had to!" she added, her face flushing with a sense of integrity or perhaps moral indignation.

" 'Tonight' " I repeated. I'd been under the impression that he was to be at a union meeting tonight.

Without looking back, she moved down the walk to her car. I waited till she had driven away, just to be sure she wouldn't turn again and say something. But she had nothing else to say: her courage was exhausted.

When she had gone, I immediately asked myself the unanswerable question: what had gone wrong? I had meant to follow all the rules. I had kept myself slim and "youthful." I had read interesting books, and had meant, at least, to have interesting conversations. Now and then I'd bought more fashionable clothes. I'd studied history, ceramics, Chinese—whatever would seem at the time to stimulate my mind and preserve me from Dullness. All this would have seemed to augur well for the future. Nothing had worked. I can't say I spent the day in turmoil. It was not like that at all. Perhaps the body takes over, protects one with a sort of coma. I can recall better what I did not do. I did not: answer the phone or bathe or pick up a newspaper or read a book. I did not work at all. Nor did I sleep. I must have sat and stared at the TV screen, but I have no recollection of what I saw. When I heard Rick's car in the garage, my arms, which had been crossed Indian-fashion on my chest, were so stiff that when he entered the living room I could not move them. After a moment I rose awkwardly and grotesquely flapped my arms. Moving my body seemed to restore other functions, and I managed to say: "Oh. You're home."

I knew at once that he knew Heather had been there. Looking now into his face I somehow expected to see the face of a stranger, a liar, a villain. But it was only the same familiar face, taut now with concern for me. It was so unusual for me to be sitting in the twilight, watching some mindless program.

I sat down again, as though exhausted. Without a word Rick came and sat down beside me. He took my hand, as though attending the bedside of a sick friend.

"I remember," I said, not looking at him, but into the fireplace, "that when I was eighteen, I was in love with a boy named Peter Dalosso."

Rick bent his head to listen. The good thing about Rick has always been that he listens. He's trained to use words, and he knows that in a true poem no sound is without its significance. We were now in a true poem.

"I met him in New York. I was visiting my aunt that summer. In '44...Did I ever tell you about him?" I went on without waiting for a reply. "He was very handsome, very young...He'd already lost a brother in the War. I don't know why I loved him," I explained apologetically—perhaps to assure Rick that I was not setting up some pathetic jealousy game. "Perhaps it was just that it was *that time.* Everybody needs to fall in love some time. How much more so during a war, when that's all you have to hang onto, being in love. So anyway, I met this sad-faced young boy—the same age actually as our Jim is now." (The fact startled us both for a moment, and Rick held my hand more tightly, as if Jim were being threatened by this fact). "The knowledge that you may never see someone again is somehow sufficient reason to make you fall in love with him. And this boy was a naval pilot...really dangerous, you know?"

I looked up and I saw tears of remorse had begun to form in Rick's eyes (he was no monster, my husband, he was a man of deep feeling: how else could he fall in love?) "Anyway, something went wrong. Peter got the wrong impression of me one night. He was very British in that way—you know, puritanical, really, we'd say now. Oh, did I never mention that? Yes, British, but of Italian descent, an Italian face, if you know what I mean. Anyway, that's neither here nor there. I mean, how people look." I shrugged. I knew it wasn't true. "But he got the wrong idea about me, I mean that's what I *think* happened—because of course I'll never know, really. When he came that night to take me to dinner, there were two college kids from Detroit at my place. They'd just dropped in, they'd come to New York to see some plays—just a couple of spoiled rich kids from Detroit—one of the plays they were going to see, I remember, was Robeson in *Othello...*" Rick shook his head solemnly, acknowledging how very long ago that was. "Anyway...I introduced them to Peter—they were *there*, after all, one could hardly *not*...and explained to my Detroit friends that Peter and I had this...prior engagement. Well, suddenly the two of them began putting on this horrible act, making sexual allusions, jokes, metaphors, reminding me of people we'd known together in high school, then bursting into suggestive laughter, as though they shared some secret together— God knows why they did it. Perhaps it was because they were young and they were *not* in service—both had been turned down for some reason or other. Maybe they immediately detested this handsome British officer, so romantically apparelled, headed for his encounter with Death; maybe it made for the War but seeing a few plays, at a time when everyone for the War but seeing a few plays at a time when everyone was dying?...Yes, it must have been guilt—I can't think else, why? Unless there is such a thing as Pure Evil?

"Anyway, Peter and I quarrelled about it; about their being there—not a very bitter quarrel, really. Not anything like the way you and I have quarrelled. God, the terrible quarrels we've had...the reconciliations."

Suddenly I'd forgotten all about Peter, and with a terrible wrench of pain I realized that it was not my old inexplicable loss for which I was grieving, but this new all too understandable loss. Our tears, Rick's and mine, ran down over our clasped hands. I looked down at our tears, at our hands; there was no way to disguise it: anyone would have recognized mine as the hands of a woman who had lived long and done much common labor. Somehow there seemed no more to say, since I did not know where in the wide world Peter Dalosso was, and Rick knew exactly where Heather Murray was. Waiting for him, no doubt, to hear what I'd "said."

Marriage, like politics, makes strange bedfellows. Rick and I walked upstairs to our bedroom, and he made love to me just as tenderly as if he did not intend the following morning to pack his bags and move in forever with Heather Murray. Tears ran down my face and I held him close, with as much love as if he had been an injured child.

And now my question is, why did it happen?

Women, we blame ourselves. We were too hot, too cold, we say; too fat, too slim, too spendthrift, too demanding. No, no—not true: all irrelevant.

It's just that one must grow or die and growth means knowledge, yes? Knowledge of something new...And for the poet whatever will cast him forth out of tranquility and into new knowledge is worth the cost: for silence to him is death.

Our tranquil lives, Rick's and mine, were a threat; for the poem rises upward from the Hegelian struggle: the poem survives on pain.

So let us not blame ourselves for what poetry has done to us. Let us not slash our wrists, nor turn on the gas, nor point the gun against ourselves. Let us not destroy the poem in the only way we know, by self-destruction. Let us simply go on...or go back.

Which brings me to the real purpose of this confession. This story is for Peter, wherever you are. I'm sorry you went away. I'm sorry your brother was killed. I'm sorry you did not stay and make love to me. I'm sorry I did not marry you and live an entirely different life with an entirely different set of children, exciting, revitalizing—a life in which I too would have written many poems. The fact is, Peter, I am writing this solely in the hope that somewhere in the world you will read it, and you will recognize me, and you will rescue me, rescue me, rescue me...

Why My Father's Birthday
Is Valentine's Day
(As Told By Himself)

The first thing they always ask you, Ori, is how old are you? Now, how should a Jew in those days know even that he's alive, much less what day exactly he was born? All I'm sure of is this: I told them I was twelve years old when they picked me up, a starving orphan in Paris. Imagine: I'd come all the way from Turkey alone, and then they sent me to Israel. Why *Israel?* What did I know from Zionism? And I was just learning there from a couple of pals how to roll cigarettes so that they looked, God himself couldn't tell the difference, like Turkish cigarettes. So I would go around Paris in my bare feet, making a good living. *Sure* I had shoes, a fine pair of boots, a soldier left them in a restaurant in Posillipo once. But I was saving them for winter because, first of all, they were big, like regular boats, I could sail in them; and second, in wintertime I could stuff them with old copies of *Le Monde.* Ha! I used to say: see I have "The World" at my feet! See how it's good to know languages?

So I had a good living for myself, no Ori? I could pick up plenty of tobacco in the street, and I would sit under one of the bridges along the Seine, and I would roll them exactly right, oval-shaped, and I sold them for ten francs. I could have been rich. But they had to go and send me to Israel—me, your father, an atheist. And then—did I know Hebrew? Where should a *goniff* like me have learned Hebrew? Spanish, Italian, French, even later English—but Hebrew? Did they take me for a Moses?

So in France, I was having a *succès du roi*. The first few nights it's true I slept under the bridges. It was cold, but after all when you're young, it's important to do things like that—it's a kind of initiation. After that I got a room near Les Halles—every morning at four o'clock an avalanche of cabbages rolled under my window into the cellar of the *brasserie* downstairs. What a smell, the smell of life. Nothing like a big marketplace to make you realize that you're made of flesh and bone, you have to be fed. I used to wander through Les Halles and dream about how one day I would be eating shrimp and fried eels and oysters and Malaga grapes.

So I was happy, I had a place to live, a career, and was gaining a knowledge of French girls which would have terrified your good mother, may her soul rest in peace. What are you smiling, Ori? I tell you a man is born with certain gifts. If he doesn't have them, he can't acquire them. It's like eyesight. And one thing, my Ori, I'll tell you this. I can tell a good face from a bad, especially in women. (Eh, didn't I do well by you?—what a mother I picked for you, a flower of womanhood. She was poor, but she came from a family of four generations of rabbis, and *that* counts!)

But then they had to go and make from me a Zionist. They had to save me from unhygienic conditions. Did they know yet that France would fall to the Germans? What excuse had they to pack off a nice Jewish boy with blonde curly hair (oh yes! all over my head, like this—you've seen the wedding pictures?) just when he was beginning to make a nice business for himself? In fact, I was expanding.

After many baths, injections, innoculations, who-knows-what, they put me on the ship to Israel, and within a month—just hear me!—I'm studying Hebrew at the *ulpan*. Did I ask them to make a scholar out of me? What did I care about their learned definitions? The Teacher told us himself, he said:

"There are three conditions for forming a society: common language (that was first), common habits, and common faith or religion." Now I *knew* my habits, particularly those I had picked up in Paris, were not like theirs; as for language, theirs was impossible. It made Spanish, Italian and French look primitive. I announced at once to the Teacher that I could never learn Hebrew, but he only smiled in a tired sort of way, as if I were telling him a joke he'd told himself many times. Then there was the matter of religion. I prided myself on having renounced God at the age of seven—when He refused to get a passport for my mother in Turkey. It was obviously a matter for the conscience. I was not going to accept their charity without telling them the truth: I was an atheist, I was practically *born* an atheist, and an atheist would I die, so help me...And so, the very first day, what did I do, what do you think? Hardly did the Teacher have his definitions out of his mouth when I stood up and gave him the big news. I felt a little bad I had to do this so soon, but after all I said to myself, if I start out now by being afraid to speak up, how will I end up?—a *nebesh*, afraid to open my mouth. So I stood up and announced to the Teacher that it was a big mistake my being here because I was an atheist.

This time the Teacher did not smile; he looked at me, I remember, a long time. He had brown eyes, soft, like a man gets who has spent years fasting. From the top of his desk he picked a piece of clean, white paper, held it in his hands a long time till the sheet began to tremble; then, turning his head to one side slightly, he blew a particle of dust from the parchment-like surface. Carefully he did it, as though it were a speck of eternity he was blowing off. I confess now, Ori, there was something almost holy about that paper, like a symbol of literacy, of civilization—and the way he stood there, his beard coarse and ragged, his *yarmulke* on his head in a silken cocoon—(All right, all right—so that's too poetical for you. Sometimes, Ori, I think you take after my cousin Itzik. And how is it that a son of mine has no poetry in him: do you think a word is a stone, a bridge?)

At last the Teacher answered me. "An atheist you cannot be. It's impossible—at your age. An eleven-year old cannot be a philosopher."

Naturally he was going to try to make me younger yet. "Twelve," I said stubbornly

"It's impossible. You are only a child. If you only knew— if you only knew how by God's grace it is that you are here at all..." Here his voice broke, and I began to feel sorry for the poor guy. After all, his business was God, wasn't it—he had to believe in Him.

"It's because God has pitied you—all of you—that you are even alive today." He bent down to pick up the paper which had fluttered to the floor like a bird. He pretended to grope at his desk for a long time before he stood up suddenly to his full height, which was not much—a ghetto height—and stood there, gripping the edge of his desk. Really, now I think of it, perhaps he was not well.

"Go read your Torah for ten years," he said sadly, as if that settled it between us. "Then come to me and we'll talk about God. Then tell me you are an atheist." He picked up his chalk then, and turned his back to us. On the board he wrote in Yiddish, while I sat back in my seat, silent, sullen and meditative.

(1) Jews (he wrote) are a monotheistic people who have no sacred image of their diety.

(2) Our first social law is to love others as we would love ourselves.

(3) In the Torah we are called the chosen people because we have been designated by the Lord—as it is stated in the Book of Isaiah the Prophet, "to bring Truth to all nations."

Well, Sonny, in my manly pride I was outraged. I had informed this anemic Chassidic skeleton that I was an atheist, and he gives me this spiel about God and the chosen people. I felt I had eaten gall, no less. I was intellectually insulted. (You know our people are very sensitive on this point.) Again I stood up. At first he pretended not to see me, but I was tall—much taller than he, and I was standing right in the front of the classroom; and he understood, too, that the others were waiting to see what would come of it all. I felt like a man on trial for his beliefs. I didn't care if they *had* saved my life. The truth is the truth, as Hillel says.

"Ben Levi," he finally acknowledged me, sighing heavily and crossing his arms into a bar, like a man who has learned how to hold himself together while he waits. "Well? And now what has the learned philosopher to say?" You see he was trying to be a little sarcastic, but he wasn't very good at it. I think, even now I remember it, he must have been a little scared: after all, a lot depended on his keeping his people together, helping them continue to believe what they had always believed.

"Teacher," I addressed him with that kind of politeness which is worse than outright insolence—you know? "Teacher, you have been speaking about Jews as they were in the time of Isaiah—as if they were a kind of homogeneous entity? (yes, that was the phrase I used—I had read it just that morning) "But I am deeply puzzled. I see here" (I turned around dramatically to the other students—*that's* the way to do things, isn't it?) "I see here many kinds of faces—German, Dutch, Slav, Armenian, French, Italian, Ethiopian: even American." (I could hear the American laugh.) "Now I have been reading Achad ha-Am (pseudonym for Asher Ginzberg) "and he has a plan to prevent the assimilation of world Jewry. I think, Teacher, you and this author use the word 'Jew' in the same sense" (there was a kind of stifled groan now in the classroom) "—maybe you can tell me: what is a Jew?"

Several busybodies raised their hands. There are always a few who think they know the answer to everything. But the Teacher just stood there silently a moment, his cinnamon-colored beard making the lower half of his head look wide and strangely open, vulnerable, while the top half was shrivelled and skull-like. Altogether, he was just skin and bones put together...He began to shake like a leaf, that fellow. At first I thought he was crying. Then I realized he was angry, furious— in a civilized sort of way, of course. He was the kind of guy who remains a school teacher all his life, eating himself up with rage because other people are blind.

Well, I didn't think I was blind; I thought I was honest, daring.

At last, from the bottom of a pit, he answered—his voice a loud dry whisper, his eyes burning with rage: "If you don't know what a Jew is, you have no business to be here." He waved his hand in a kind of bitter blessing on the congregation: "We're all Jews here," he added.

There came a great sigh of agreement. Fervent Jewish faces lifted themselves up to the teacher. Eyes filled with tears. I dared not look at them: they Believed. All at once I felt so lonely, Ori—I wanted to die. I didn't belong *there*, I didn't belong where? It was awful. They began nodding and whispering among themselves. I was the destroyer, the Moloch. Suddenly I felt myself the most unloved child in the world. Yes, a child, not a man. I think at that moment it was that I felt how terrible it was to be an orphan, to be unloved, unwanted. I was made an outcast by their sorrowful, accusing faces. Sometimes, Ori, my son—I think nobody in his youth had less love than I. Even my mother (may she rest in peace)—busy all day baking bread—all I can remember of her is seeing her facing me, each of us holding a long, shovel-ended pole for removing the bread, as we stood before the great brick oven which breathed dry heat like a monster, withering us in our basement room. But another time—when you're not leaving—I'll tell you about my mother. Only right now, where was my story?

Well, here I am, standing in front of the classroom: you can imagine me? About thirty students behind me; I'm looking into their anguished faces. They didn't want to reject one of their own: 'Come, be one of us. Will you always be alone, an orphan?' I tell you, Ori, at that moment I wished myself back in the little room by Les Halles, with the smell of vegetables rolling off the trucks making a taste in the air like smoke.

I stood there a minute, swallowing hard with nervousness, my mouth dry, though naturally I didn't show it, not even my voice. Was I going to let the power of numbers dissuade me from my convictions? Not Omar ben Levi.

I spoke very loud and clear: "If I must believe in your God to be a Jew, then I'm not a Jew." And when I'd said this, I really did start shaking, not like the kid almost six feet tall that I was, but like a starved beggar in the streets, selling stolen goods...After all, Ori, I knew there was a time when I might have been stoned to death for this.

The Teacher was calmer now, as he saw I'd defeated myself by my own iconoclasm, at least in the eyes of my classmates.

"If you feel that way," he said with intense but quiet scorn, "you should go to America. There, all the Jews are atheists. There the God is business, and there's no concern for your immortal soul. Go, go—you'll be happy there!" (The American student was denying all this loudly, but it was not a moment for complete justice to Americans.)

He spoke to me with contempt, as if I were being exiled from ancient Israel for sodomy. But what he said struck me to the roots: he had given me the role I sought. I put down my pencil, laying it carefully in the ridge of the desk, so it shouldn't slip and roll to the floor and make me look ridiculous; and mustering twelve years of empirical doubt and dignity, I left the classroom.

Within three months they had me on board a ship for the States, they were so clever: the Jews are the cleverest people in the world, I tell you. They found for me somebody who I had always thought was a mythological beast—that's my cousin Itzik in Texas. I ask you, who has *mazel?* Yours truly, Omar ben Levi. More luck than brains, they say in America, and I was an example. We had to go a long, long way, stopping everywhere to let off a few Jews here, a few Jews there— C.O.D. show your papers, show your cousin—Africa, Greece, Montivedeo, Buenos Aires, Santa Domingo, Haiti, Cuba, Florida—at last to Boston, so that by the time I arrived here, well, I won't boast—I already knew enough English to take a job in Itzik's store. Because that's what my cousin Itzik had for me.

But like everywhere, in Boston, the first question they asked me is: "When were you born?" My passport *had* a date, an invented date, but I thought maybe they weren't satisfied with that for some reason. As it turned out, they never looked at the date of birth as registered on the passport. They were used to asking this question, that's all: "When were you born?"

Now Ori, would you believe it, for the first time in my life I was really scared. I didn't know what to say. I had some idea in my head that if I don't even know for sure when I was born, they won't let me in, papers or no papers. And God knows I didn't want to go back to that Teacher.

"1926," I said.

"What day? What day?"

I looked around in desperation. At this time I was not very certain of the months of the year though I knew "Important Things Immigrants Should Know" like: How is the President of the United States elected to office? How old must he be? In the event of an electoral tie between two candidates, who determines who shall be inaugurated? What is the procedure for reporting an automobile accident? How many people in the United States carry Life Insurance? What is the distance between San Francisco and Los Angeles? Between New York and Boston? You see? *important* things.

"What day is today?" I said calmly, like an actor, you should have seen me. But I was so scared, I didn't dare try to pronounce FeBREWary—extremely difficult word, that.

"I'm asking *you*, Sammy. What is your date of birth?"

"My name is not Sammy. My name is Omar Ben Levi. And my birthday is—today."

The youthful assistant at his side, with a ruddy face and huge thick hands, his nails cut to the quick like the broken shells of almond, wrote it all down, chortling wildly.

"Today? Well, if that ain't the luck of the Irish! And I wish me own mother had thought of givin' *me* St. Valentine's

for a birthday. Think of the lovin' I'd have got—and all for
gettin' born along of a Saint."

"You're keeping good company there, Charley," the
immigration officer assured me, grinning.

"*À votre service, monsieur,*"—I have no idea why I found
myself suddenly saluting him respectfully in French—I guess I
was pretty nervous. "But my name is Omar, not Charley.
Here—" I made a gesture, indicating I would write it down for
him, thinking it perhaps a difficult name for Americans to
spell.

"For the love of Gawd, man, any high school kid can spell
Omar—but how in the bloody blazes do you go after writin'
Khayyám?"

For a few minutes both immigration men were weak
with laughter. I had brightened up a long, unpleasant day for
them—a day perhaps filled with inadvertent cruelties, over-
sights, deportations for the dozens of immigrants awaiting
salvation. Behind me, in fact, two troubled, nearly empty-
handed immigrants from Russia looked at me bitterly,
distrustful of all the merriment I had brought down on my
head. You could see it in their eyes: the *goyim,* they seemed to
be saying, they start out by making jokes about your name,
and—you'll see—it'll end with a *pogrom.*

The assistant slapped his thigh with happy inspiration:
"Samuel Omar Khayyam ben Levi," he entoned. "Born Feb-
you-wary fourteen, nineteen hundred and twenty-six. Well, if
that don't bring down the wrath of Gawd! What a monicker!
By all that's holy, you'll surely be the Valentino of them all,
with a double-header like *that* one!"

Suddenly the elder officer lost patience; perhaps he felt it
was beneath his dignity to cavort with his young assistant.

"O.K. lover-boy. Let's get moving. This is the U.S.A., not
the Taj-Mahal." (Later, Ori, I looked up that reference to the
Taj-Mahal, and I rejoiced to see that officer couldn't have
known where the Taj-Mahal was any more than I did.)

I confess, and it was natural, that I hardly understood a
word of their strange gibberish; and as I picked up my duffel

bag and moved along in line, I heard the young assistant chanting:

> "A loaf of bread, a jug of wine
> And thou, Kathleen, beside me
> In the wilderness..."

"Ah, cut it out. This is the Back Bay, not a pub in County Cork."

Cut it out; lover-boy, monicker, double-header, Valentino— these were not words I had learned on board ship; I was depressed at my ignorance; but I knew at least that I had an enchanted name, a name that would bring me luck. How should I have known that I was carrying on the glory of two Catholic saints, no less?

But the *mazel* that birthday has brought me! First of all, let me tell you, without me, Sonny, your cousin Itzik's store would have been a nothing. He had at first a little hole-in-the-wall five and dime in San Marcos (I used to say to him, "A five-and-dime you call this? A penny-and-a-plug nickel, *that's* your store-kele") and the first thing I taught him to do was to *expand*.

Why San Marcos? How do I know? All I know is this—if a town needs a business, a Jew will come all the way from Turkey to put it there. Ha! You don't think that's funny, eh?

No—serious now, Ori—I turned that Shop-with-rooms-in-the-back into an A-number-One department store! Your mother always used to say of me (may she rest in peace) that I had *goldene* hands. Yes, the hands of Midas I used to answer, but she didn't mean it that way. *I* meant, like the story says, whatever I touched turned to gold. Either you have it or you don't: some people are born with three hands, as the saying goes—they get in their own way. Me, I worked like an artist. Where there was no gold, I made it. To create something out of nothing, that's Art, no? But your mother thought I was meant to be a builder—an architect or something, a maker of cities, that was *her* idea of my talents.

So I used my golden talents to expand. "Every birthday a

holiday, every holiday a birthday" was the motto for my
greeting card display. And on Valentine's Day I was my own
best advertising man. I sang "Happy Birthday to Me" over and
over again in my baritone voice—no cigarette cough in those
days, Ori. And I wore a big cardboard heart on my shirt with
the name of nearly every girl in town, I knew them all...And
you know, I received birthday and Valentine cards from nearly
all of them: they ate it up. It was their favorite sport. They
came right to my own counter to buy me a card and I'd find it in
the evening in my mailbox. The girls from high school and the
girls from college used to come in sometimes, buy a card, read
it aloud, blush like roses, crimson—and run out like a flock of
geese. You see what a marginal profit I had...One girl, I
remember, a sweet little girl with eyes like plums, wet and
shining, read to me once:

> "Roses are red, violets are blue,
> Sugar is sweet, and so is a Jew."

And when I snatched the card from her hand she ran
away, neighing like a filly. Of course she'd made it up...

My best luck came on Valentine's Day, my twentieth
birthday. Itzik had been married three years already and his
wife Ruthie said it was time I settled down. They had moved to
Austin, and poor Itzik commuted thirty miles to the store
every day, but they said "at least in Austin we have a 1%
Jewish population, while in San Marcos the only other Jew is a
male hairdresser—and who ever heard of a Jew homosexual?"
(Your cousin Ruthie was convinced that all male hairdressers
were homosexuals.)

So...You know the rest, Ori. They had for me the most
wonderful party—it was all mixed up with the Sabbath, I
remember the candles and the *chaleh* on the table. And then,
Ruthie, who had been reading up on how the Romans used to
do it at the Feast of Lupercalia, arranged the match-making by
putting the names of "lovers" in the jar, so that no matter how
I picked it, your mother was to be my "partner" for the
evening.

"Naomi," I read out loud from the sheet of paper. And she came to me right out of the darkest corner, where she'd been hiding. She was very pale and very sad, and as she told me later, shocked at the luxury and frivolity of the Jew in America.

"In France we were hungry," she used to say. "In England we were hungry; in Israel we were still hungry..." It was weeks before I saw her smile, and when you were born, Ori, she wept because all your grandparents were dead.

Like I say, we prospered, Itzik and I. We worked hard, keeping the store open till eight every night six days a week, and at the Christmas season till ten and eleven. Just Itzik and I, we worked like slaves, with one high school boy to clean up. Every time I'd say to Itzik: "It's time to expand," he'd kibbitz around and agree: "O.K. Khayyám, with a monicker like yours they'll love you in San Antone." And they did. They loved me in San Antonio, in Kyle, in Killeen, in El Paso...Our problem was not success but where to get managers we could trust...We needed more sons. (And that's why I say, Ori, don't turn away a good chance: the business is already started—all it needs is somebody like you, somebody with a good head on his shoulders...)

So after your mother married me, she never was hungry again, God is my witness. I bought her the best. We had a fifty thousand dollar home in Austin; we could go to Miami, to Puerto Rico, to Hong Kong if she wanted. But she went only once to France (to visit her parents' graves) and after that every other year to Israel, a pilgrimage...One year, she was gone all summer into the fall; the letters stopped coming. I thought I'm going to lose her to that bloody Teacher after all; she'll never come home. You know she was a Believer, Ori, and you can never really trust a Believer—at any moment, maybe, they'll give up husband, home, fortune, their life, and follow after some Fanatic. But she came home at last, not at the end of the summer, like always, but after five long months, I thought I will go mad—I thought, even, I will go to get her.

Well, five months is a long time not to see your loved ones, to be away from home. I hope you'll feel that, Ori. I hope when you come back from Europe you'll have a new view on things. You'll see, you'll see—business is not so bad after all, there are good guys and bad guys, no?—just like anywhere, good and bad—and you'll find it's nice to have a few dollars in your pocket, to go to a good hotel. And I need you, Ori, I need you like I need my right arm.

Now only one thing more, and then I'll let you go—drink up, Son, and then I'll walk with you to the ship. I know you're going to be very busy—after all, all those wonderful places, Westminster Abbey, the Eiffel Tower, St. Peter's—don't forget to see the statue of Moses! And then, too, all those pretty girls in Paris—with that curly blonde hair and built like a Cossack, don't kid me, my son, my birthday isn't Valentine's Day for *nothing*—so you won't have much extra time for side trips, I know—but would you mind, Ori, as a special favor for you father, just for a few days—why don't you stop off at Israel?

By The Sweat of Your Brow

U sually when Morrie left his cabin and showed up at the sawmill for a few hours, it was because the winter had lasted too long and he felt a sudden need to be with folks: it was not for the money—so long as he had his tobacco and enough to buy seeds, he could get by on his VA check plus county assistance. But today he'd packed himself a lunch, resolving to work a full day for Tucker at the mill: the caseworker had assured him again and again that it'd be good for him to take steady work, it'd help him reestablish contact with the community; besides, (she'd added), it was a necessity: every year it was getting harder to justify supplemental assistance to an able-bodied man like himself.

Morrie, sensing that there was no real choice, had nodded his agreement and they'd turned him over to Tucker because (they said) Tucker had the right attitude. Again Morrie had agreed: he had known Tucker as a boy, and experience told him that anyone he had known that long would be preferable to a stranger in Knox Township who would not remember Morrie when he was young, before he had ever been up in a plane or seen Japanese islands many times bigger than Knox puff up like parti-colored balloons and burst into flames at his feet.

"Ready to work, are you?" Tucker now moved his pipe to the side of his mouth and appeared to be examining Morrie's Norfolk jacket.

With a talismanic gesture Morrie removed his gloves and began buttoning and unbuttoning his jacket: when it was winter and the ground still frozen, Morrie kept his jacket buttoned to his throat; when it was nearly Spring, and warm enough for planting, he wore his jacket casually open, the pockets filled with seeds to be pushed into the earth even while the snow melted. But this year, though it was already March, he kept the seeds buried in his pockets, and he wore his jacket as close to his body as he could.

He'd worn gloves today too, but only because the caseworker had insisted: when he worked on the grounds he liked to feel the earth on his hands; the sweet smell of the soil evoked in him that awe most folks felt for the blooming flower only. Now as his fingers moved along the seam of his jacket, he became aware that a button was missing and it bothered him that he had not seen it fall. He was thoughtfully fingering the fiber where his loss had left a small scarlike knot when he heard Tucker say (*for the second time?*):

"Guess they want you to work for a livin' like the rest of us. How'll that set with you?" Tucker was ironic, sad—but he was not smiling the way others sometimes smiled when they said it. He stared down somberly at Morrie's jacket, as though the jacket were a healing scab he didn't want to touch or even look at. And in fact Tucker did look away, down at the whorls of shavings spangling the ground like great curled ear rings carved from trees. When Morrie did not reply, his voice rose slightly: "You gonna be all right?"

This time Morrie nodded, and Tucker sighed. When the caseworker had asked Tucker to put Morrie to work, Tucker had sighed just like that, saying, "Well, I've known Morrie ever since we were in Civics class together...*Civics*," he repeated mildly, looking at the caseworker with an odd expression. "They don't teach that anymore, do they?" as if this somehow explained why he had to help put Morrie to work.

Anyway, he was here, he wouldn't cause Tucker any worry.

"There's plenty to sweep up," Tucker said.

Morrie nodded again, trying to smile; he smiled so rarely that it felt strained, yet he smiled now more than he used to. He knew that people had said of him that Morrie had not smiled or shown any what they called "affect" for more than a year after coming back to Knox Township. Then after that, there were months, perhaps five or six, when he did have responses, mostly weeping or choking. But that had passed; he had got well, even Deirdre had acknowledged that he had got well. All that was past, Japanese cities were no longer exploding, and the only harsh words he ever heard were from workers who complained that Japan overproduced and sold things too cheap, cheaper than anybody else could.

He did manage now to smile at Tucker in a way that he hoped would assure him that everything was O.K. He now only wanted Tucker to stop talking and let him, Morrie, commence work, so that the sole solitary consolation which came from the work might begin. Not the pleasure of the work itself, but the dreaming of Deirdre which the work sometimes evoked in him. For often, in the fetching of barrels, in the sweeping of shavings, in the drone of the machinery which he could hear as he moved to and fro under the eaves of the sheds, he could dissolve into the past while remembering Deirdre. It was a comfortable enchantment, like music. Though it was not true as the caseworker had once implied, that he came to work merely to dream: he enjoyed the company of the other workers, who though they sometimes laughed at him, reflected in their voices a thwarted affection which he prized because it, too, was rare. But then, he had known these men a long time, and Morrie understood that they were therefore more willing to forgive him for having left Knox Township while some of them were still children and returned to them a "dependent," who lived off their own bodies' power to work, to work continuously, day after day, season after season, as if work, too, were a kind of seed which one planted and harvested: as though work could be a grateful, growing thing and not merely a punishment to be endured.

As he prepared now to work, Morrie noticed that Tucker, though standing aside as inconspicuously as he could, was still watching him. Morrie wished he could overcome their long habits of silence and explain to Tucker that there was nothing to worry about; that he understood himself very well: it was simply the long winter; here it was already so late in March, and when Morrie had put a few seedlings in window boxes to help them overcome the late start, they had frozen overnight. And on the North wall of his cabin there was still a thin but solid layer of frost—a poor prognosis. Above all, it was because the pond in front of his cabin was still a solid floe of ice. That was always the worst sign: he hated the pond when it was frozen over, hated it precisely because—unlike himself—Deirdre had loved it, had learned to skate outside his cabin door, to skate so wonderfully well that they had lured her away from him with her skating, like some enchanted snow princess who could not live anywhere save on ice...As he dreamed his past, he could see Deirdre with perfect clarity—barely sixteen, and skimming the pond like some shimmering sea anemone that thrived on water and light—an artist on ice, etching leaves, flowers and figures-of-eight into perfect mandalas. Wherever there had been a frozen pond, Deirdre, like some mythic force of Nature had planted herself and blossomed, creating from her own energy showers of ice which flew upward and fell like rain.

But then it had all become very serious business and not merely sport for kids; she'd become so very good at it that they'd first sent her around the U.S. with a bus load of kids, and then, after the war, even while Morrie had been recovering in the VA hospital, they'd sent her abroad, skating for international goodwill in places as improbable as Reykjavik and Moscow.

Morrie was working hard enough now to work up a sweat. He loosened his jacket just enough to cool his chest: with his bare hands (he had shoved the gloves deep into his pockets, in part to prevent the seeds from spilling out), he began pushing the shavings into neat pyramidic piles, while considering at the same time what a remarkable thing it had been back then for a girl like Deirdre to travel to such faraway places. And indeed, it had been part of the mystery of their lives, like some mystic balancing of the heavenly books, that while he lay in the hospital, his body scarred, his conscience burning, Deirdre had been skating around the world on symmetrical arenas—a Celtic princess with absolute self-control and a flawless sense of direction.

His own long loss of direction after his discharge must have seemed to her a weakness of will: she had been reared by a struggling immigrant family who believed in greater control of one's fate, not less. So even before he'd been released from the hospital, she had perhaps decided she didn't really want or need him anymore, she had just wanted, perhaps, to help rehabilitate him. He could accept that view of her now, he'd certainly not been the same handsome young man she'd married before his first flight; and although afterwards she had flown to the hospital to be near him for a few weeks and had encouraged him to get "well," he'd sensed that he'd lost her, that she could hardly wait to go skimming off on the ice ponds of the world forever.

In spite of his resolve to put in a full day's work, his self-confidence was now beginning to waver: his back had begun to hurt (there was a lot of scar tissue in places he never looked at anymore), and in order to relieve the tightness of the puckered skin, he began to crawl around on his hands and knees while he picked up stones, bits of wood and broken tree limbs lying around between the sheds. Again and again he returned to the central shed where he assembled it all in an orderly way, as though he were creating something instead of merely toting trash. He did like things to be orderly, that much Deirdre always praised him for. Even at the hospital she'd praised him for the way he kept his room, especially admiring the arrangement of the plants he had growing in his room. Indeed, she'd spent more time looking at his plants and admiring his room (which was anyway, as she said, in perfect order) than in looking at him; she had hardly looked up at him at all, maybe he had hardly resembled himself anymore, so much of him pleated and seamed and scarred, though everyone said the doctors had done a marvelous job. Probably even later, when she'd come back from her tour and found him much improved (he was then visiting the therapist on an outpatient basis only), probably even then she was just helping him out so that she could be free without guilt: she probably hadn't wanted to be with him anymore, it was just her way of saying thanks for all those allotment checks she'd used to pay for her lessons.

But for just this moment, at least, he preferred to dream that she'd really loved him. It was just that it had all been so painful to her because, as she said, he was so confused, he couldn't settle down to a job, because he didn't know what he wanted or if he wanted anything at all; because it seemed as if all he wanted to do was drop seeds into the ground and wait for a miracle; but unless he studied, she said, *really* studied, and became a botanist or horticulturist, or even a florist, well, what was the point? The way he went about it (she said), lifting herself on her toes slightly, as though she were about to leap into a perfect figure eight, there was no control, there was just this aimless *puttering*—or at best, she'd added hurriedly, perhaps noting his anguished look, mere gentleman farming.

But no gentleman farmer, he: Morrie knew that much at least. Nor no gentleman either. He understood well enough what they were saying of him—that the war had stolen his head as well as his good looks...But warming to her exhortation, he'd tried for steadiness and security for a while, he'd understood that she needed someone to be stable and fixed if she herself was to launch like a great flying bird into the Ice Frolics, the Icecapades, and the Ice Shows of the Western World. So Morrie had first tried for stability within the limited range of campus life, he stuck to his books, he studied an entire year preparing himself for his engineering exams. But when Spring finally came (it had been very late that year), suddenly the walls of the classroom had seemed as fiercely repressive as the prison camp in which he'd spent the last thirty-eight days of the war: just a day or two before his exams, he'd gone out to plant seeds. The earth had been as moist and yielding as a lover, the soft soil taking up his seed at the merest touch of his hand: or so it had seemed that lovely Spring afternoon, which he could so clearly remember now, or believed he could remember, when the sun had melted the icicles and he could hear the *drip drip* on the concrete walk he had built from his cabin to the pond, and the pond itself was no longer frozen but breaking up into lines like some ancient map recording places in another world than this because the cartographers in their sublime ignorance had not yet known the exact shape of things to come and had erred slightly in their measurements, leaving these misguided charts they had dreamed. Then, as the ice on the pond had broken up, it had been an orchestration: the birds had come out to bathe in the pools of water guttering down from his eaves. Warmed by the sun, they had behaved like school children on a holiday. Recklessly singing and calling, they had indulged in a twittering so joyful it had seemed a kind of madness—the madness of bruised hopes, as it had turned out, because the pond had frozen up again, the seeds had died, the examinations had been plundered as if by vandals (himself), and Deirdre had left with the International Ice World, a new touring company.

He paused a moment to look down at his work: from bits of wood, stone and tree limb he had constructed a sort of pueblo where by climbing a ladder of twigs one could enter through the flat roof built facing the sky...not like being perpetually locked in a room to study. *Locked in* was the way he always thought of schools and study after that Spring of failed exams. Any locked door could evoke in him the same despair—though of course this symptom was a mere projection, as the VA therapist told him, of lying in prison awaiting the end of the war...Awed by the therapist's insight, Morrie had agreed with an intensity he dared not reveal. For it had become blindingly clear to him then that *of course*, everybody wanted to lock him up somehow. More than that: they wanted to lock everybody up—from nine to five, and even if a man had a nice job like being a doctor or lawyer, he couldn't get away from it all, the sick and anxious folk lay in wait for him from one day to the next—somebody's troubles became his troubles, all the troubles of the world carried on, endured somewhere behind locked doors. Folks locked the cars they drove off in in the morning, the elevator doors shut on them as they went into their prestigious asylum of work; then they shut the door so that no one could intrude on them (or rescue them either).... Where, after shutting the door, the phone which was wired to the desk began to ring, and then they were locked into the day, all the hours of their lives in a safety deposit box, not to be unlocked except with permission of the bank officers.

Nevertheless, he had tried it, for Deirdre's sake and for the sake of her parents and for his own parents who pleaded, cajoled and even prayed for him. On this very property here— couldn't remember the name of the man who'd been in charge back then—they'd hired him to do the bookkeeping. "You ought to be able to do that, I guess," old Shamus had said (*yes, Shamus, that had been his name*), "'cause I know for a fact you were the smartest kid in 'rithmetic I ever saw." Old Shamus' confidence in him had encouraged Morrie to try. Again it had been nearly Spring, the small bookkeeping office, stifling. He'd wanted to open the windows, but everything had been painted shut to protect the firm from a rash of postwar burglaries (the company's small green safe was also locked in with him in the bookkeeper's room). Morrie recalled how the smell of the new wax they were laying down everywhere rose from the floors; the door leading to the main corridor had refused to open. Sobbing with rage and fear, Morrie had picked up his office chair and smashed the window in order to get some air and put his feet back on the earth. On that day dozens of people—workers at the mill and even their wives and children—had gathered around him watching him with shocked, mournful expressions.

As he was about to lay another stone upon the pueblo, Morrie's hand paused in mid-air; either there was something from the past event with Shamus which had carried over to his present dreaming, or else there was something frighteningly familiar in the expressions of the people now watching him that reminded him of the old event with Shamus. Whichever event had triggered the other, it was clear to him that the workers were now watching him, either out of concern or curiosity...or perhaps simply because they could not believe that he, Morrie, was doing a day's work, living by the sweat of his brow.

He stood up, straightening his back, his fingers pressed against the old scar tissue. He must remain calm and not confuse old times with new. Still, the people did seem to be watching him and murmuring among themselves (he was now certain of it), though of course it could be some advice they wanted to offer, some encouragement. Morrie turned away, trying to disguise his nervousness: if he ignored them, maybe they'd go away.

But they didn't budge, they continued to stand there, staring with mild motionless surprise at his neat piles of wood shavings, at his carefully constructed pueblo with its ladder to the sky. Morrie felt the sweat burst out on his body; with spasmodic but dextrous movements he began buttoning and unbuttoning his jacket; he touched the seeds in his pockets. Without exactly turning his head, he smiled reassuringly at the people, but they did not smile back: with a desperate show of courage Morrie turned to face them, his eyes questioning: *was anything wrong?* It was then that he noticed as if for the first time how the trees were silhouetted against the sky, their black branches limned with snow as though sealed like wax to their limbs. New snowflakes had begun to fall—heavy, ragged flakes like flying white paper. The silent, motionless workers who were watching Morrie seemed oddly collapsed, one-dimensional, as though they were about to turn into paper dolls or snowflakes flying through the air.... A nausea gripped

Morrie at this vision, and he recognized it: it was his old sickness, only it was the reverse of the jungle burnings; instead of the earth turning to flames at his feet, the land now lay enveloped in this eternal white stasis. Like the dead at Pompeii, he and his friends would remain trapped in this scene forever while the snow fell endlessly, camouflaging the death of the planet. Tears sprang to Morrie's eyes: it was not something one should accept. One must resist....

Morrie bent again to the frozen ground and with his bare hands began to scrape together piles of snow. Then, with great care he separated the piles into furrows, using his hand as a hoe. From out of his pockets he took fistfuls of seeds and swiftly but expertly let them slide from his cupped hand into the icy runnels. Then he gently covered them with snow.

He sensed now how the other workers, keen with interest, had drawn near for a closer view of his work; but he no longer minded—what was important was that they must see at last that the planting was not just a Spring ceremony, but a serious thing, a matter of survival. He was still kneeling, contemplating his work, when he felt his friends come forward to assist him to his feet and he looked with pride into their familiar faces which told him that he had done his work well, that Spring would come and the seeds would not be locked up in the earth forever.

The Man With The Pinto Bean Hair

Sophía watched as Inés put the kittens into a brown paper sack, aimed carefully and knocked their brains out: they did not even mew. Inés at once threw the sack under a bush and kicked dirt over it. As it was August, this action was perfectly sensible, but Sophía began to cry anyway: she did not want to be sensible, she wanted the kittens back. She clutched the two survivors of Brígida's litter and stood defiantly before Inés: she was furious with herself for letting Inés see her cry.

"Tomás," murmured Inés. "See your daughter." With a gesture of indifference Inés lifted her heavy coil of hair to let the morning breeze lick at her neck (and also, as Sophía knew, to show off her breasts to Tomás).

"Quit the cryin' " said Tomás. "A big girl like you." But he said it without anger, his eyes followed Inés' arms. He shifted his weight and leaned back against the wooden steps as if he were out of breath. Beneath his head a loose board jiggled; with a burst of energy he wrenched it loose, tossing the splintered wood into the front yard. He looked up at Inés. "To hell with it. 'Stead of to kill the kittens, you should get rid of the cat."

"Ah *no*. Brígida's mine, I keep her." Inés' voice suddenly changed; her eyes gleamed like olives in a tin of oil: "One thing I know for sure: a Tom that can't buy beans, he better stay down from the fence."

They were caught up in one of their games. Sophía had seen their games many times before, ever since Inés had followed her father home from the fields one day. Beginning with a cheerful taunt or challenge, their pace quickened into a pinch or slap; but they ended always in the same way. At least they had now lost interest in the kittens.

"Sell em. Don't kill em," her father shrewdly advised Ines. "Send her to the market, she can make a dollar on em." He looked expectantly at Inés whose hands paused in mid-air, palms outward as if testing for rain. For a while they pretended to haggle over the price Sophía would ask for the kittens; but they were in plain agreement, their tone implied that it was a case of two birds with one stone. Sophía listened, she knew that in this subtle pantomime acted out by the adults (Inés was sixteen), her future was being arranged. From time to time Sophía had caught other glimpses of her future: to hear one of them say *Sophía should* was like being again on the small fishing boat at Vera Cruz where once, when she'd been too small to see overboard, Tomás had lifted her to the rail· terrified, Sophía had seen nothing but the dark, while at their feet the fins of the great fish flowed like silk.

"Yeah," Tomás repeated, enjoying his joke. "Sell em, don't kill em. Take em to market. Lotta people like kittens. And people like to *pay* for something—you believe it? Give it to em free, they don't appreciate it. Even an apple got a worm in it, they'll buy it." He shook with silent laughter. "Make em pay extra for the worm." He grinned up at Inés, who turned her back, feigning offense at something. To Sophía he said: "Take some apples. I pick em yesterday, they still look good. It don't take any more room in the stall to sell apples."

Sophía wanted to go at once before they changed their minds, because if she got to the market early enough, she could make two or three dollars and still get to the carnival before dusk. Sophía adored carnivals, she wished they had them in every town, like schools. A few years ago, when her mother and Tomás had been picking oranges in Florida, she'd gone to Orlando, she'd won a kewpie and a transistor radio on the same day: it had been a revelation to her, that one could get these things wholly by luck, merely by having the wheel of fortune stop at one's coin. But she'd felt guilty about it because her mother had been livid with rage at Sophía's being out so late. She'd wondered later whether it'd been the rages that had killed her mother and not, as Tomás said, the great purple bulge like an eggplant which grew in her ear. Of late, she'd decided that when anger was called for, she preferred Inés' style: there was a coolness at the heart of it that was somehow reassuring, she'd like to have caught the knack of it.

Quickly now she found a box for the kittens. They were almost identical in size, rather like those thin-skinned potatoes she and Tomás had picked by the thousands one season (it'd been either after Florida or before McAllen, Texas, she couldn't remember which). To placate Tomás, she now filled a sack full of apples, though she didn't think people would buy any, they were slightly bruised. Then she banged the screen door after her, not bothering to say goodbye (they weren't looking at her anyway).

At the market, she had no difficulty persuading a young farmer to let her stand near his stall (she saved a rental fee that way). She was sure he thought her older than she was, she was nearly as big as Inés. She knew that what Inés repeated over and over, as though it were a proverb, was true: that in a year or two she'd have to move fast to get away from the men in the fields. But Sophía didn't worry about it, it created rather a heightened picture of herself when she'd have a kind of bargaining power: for the present she was both neuter and voiceless. But there were times when she thought she'd never go back to the fields: she'd go to work at Orlando, perhaps, she'd heard of several girls who'd gone there and now rode real horses in a ring.

Somewhat to her surprise, people had bought nearly all

her apples, which she'd assembled in a pyramid, their bruises turned inward. By noon, she had nearly a dollar. If she could make another dollar on the kittens, she'd get two slices of pizza and spend the rest at the booths. She'd try her luck at throwing those rings round a stake, she was good at that. But if she won, she'd not get a kewpie this time, she'd get one of those make-up kits with a reversible mirror: one side enlarged your face so you could see how it was made up of tiny bits and pieces, the skin flung loosely together, like sand.

The thought of winning something inspired her to showmanship, and she began calling out, *Kittens! Kittens for sale!* But her voice didn't carry far, it sounded as if she were shy and scared, even when she wasn't, it hadn't developed like the rest of her. After about an hour of this, she felt hungry and bored. The kittens looked shopworn too—threadbare, as though being taken from Brigída and exposed to the air had worn them thin: raw spots showed through the scant fur; they looked more like guinea pigs than kittens. Sophía had a moment's trepidation: they could die on her. She was thinking Inés was right, what was the use of standing here, one might just as well have got rid of the litter all at once, when a tall, well-dressed man stopped by her stall. She keenly wanted him to take the kittens so that she could go, go quickly before it was too late for the carnival: so she smiled invitingly.

The man looked at her sharply, then leaned over as if to peer into the box; his eyes, she noticed, were so deeply embedded in his face that at first she could not tell whether he was looking at her or at the kittens. She took in at once however that his hair, the color of pinto beans, was all one shade, as though it needed sunlight. His face was grey and the skin coarse-grained, like canvas, but his hands were smooth, with a whiteness at the quick, like a twig peeled down to the flesh.

Sophía poked the kittens, stirring their listless bodies so that they would be attractive to the man. But they merely opened their eyes, mewed plaintively, and burrowed closer to one another.

The man rested his hand under his chin, as if deliberating on the price; then, after a pause, he said he'd take both kittens, to keep each other company. Sophía was delighted and at once held up the box. But she lowered it again with a sigh when she saw the crisp twenty dollar bill. "Oh," she murmured: it was a complication, and she'd learned to fear complications, one never knew where they would end. Meanwhile, the man stood holding out the new bill. He meant to buy the kittens, the gesture implied, but if she didn't want to...His stance seemed to show contempt for her lack of foresight. Nervously, Sophía whispered to the young farmer nearby, who made a show of going through his pockets. He shot a look of anger and envy at Sophía's customer. Finally he said that he had to keep his singles for himself.

But now the man became gracious, showing no irritation with the farmer. "The little lady and I will find some change," he said, and pointed to a drug store across from the market-place. He even smiled at the farmer who turned his back on them. Sophía noted, as they walked away from the stall, that when he smiled his teeth were white and identical, like small ice cubes. Outside the drug store, he said: "Do you want to run in and get some change...or shall I...?" He opened his wallet again; this time she saw dozens of bills wedged in like a folded newspaper. "Wait a minute," he said. "I've a better idea. Come with me and I'll show you the kittens' new home. Here—give me the box, I'll carry it."

She understood that she was to follow him. Obediently she handed him the box: before taking it he slipped on his gloves, which were fawn-colored, and covered his hands like another skin. He cleared his throat: "Now *march!*" He ordered theatrically.

She smiled happily, not so much at the game, but at the man. He was like an impresario, he might have come right out of the carnival. Best of all, she knew that he was playing this game to put her at her ease. So she began to laugh, enjoying herself, it was pleasant to have someone try to please her, however oddly.

Still, at his doorway she lingered, not quite ready to follow him into the apartment. She stood uncertainly a moment, embarrassed by the dirt on her shoes: she could see that there was an oval carpet in the center of the polished floor, with something like animals or Aztec gods rising as though carved from the surface. She moved slowly forward: he was smiling at her, he was friendly and benevolent. There was a fragrance everywhere, heavy but sweet, rather like Inés' thick coil of hair when she let it fall loose to her waist. In Spanish she knew the word for the fragrance, it was not peyote, but *incienso*. From the very walls there issued forth soft plucking sounds of strange music, sounds between pangs of pleasure and a wail; but strangest of all was that the man had not troubled to turn off his music before going out, it was not something she could imagine anyone neglecting to do.

"Here," he said. "Let's put the kittens in the bathroom. My name is Jones, what's yours?" She did not know whether he heard her reply, for he had already turned away with the kittens.

Sophía followed him to the bathroom. She felt no surprise at the thick blue towels, the commode covered with the same cloth as the blue towels, or at the wall paper which matched the towels. Metal faucets gleamed, bright as polished knives, everything was so flawlessly clean, she would not have hesitated to have slept on the pile rug where Jones now laid the kittens: at once they burrowed into it for warmth.

They've found a home," said Jones.

"*Sí.* I mean yes." She smiled apologetically; it was not always easy to remember. They stood in the bathroom watching the kittens for a few moments. Then Jones put his arm around her shoulder.

She knew her breasts were small, she feared he would be disappointed in her; but if so, he did not show it. They went into the living room and Jones sat in a rocking chair. This puzzled her. She knew that in the movies, that was not the way it was done. In the movies the man sat on a wide sofa, one arm flung across the back; then the girl sat down beside him. Then his arms came round her, down from the sofa, and rested on her body.

Jones rose quickly, and Sophia followed his movements with her eyes, then looked away: she could tell nothing. With Inés and Tomás she could always tell when they were about to disappear into the next room, sometimes whispering together, more often forgetting themselves and shouting their oblivion. But Jones was merely removing his jacket. Then he said:

"Come here."

She came. He tried to pick her up and put her on his lap. But she was heavier than he expected and they staggered slightly. She was afraid he would be offended, it was so awkward, she had not meant to be awkward but she could not help it, she was big for her age, she knew it. But he smiled and did not seem to be displeased at the bulk of her across his thighs. He even said, as if admiringly, "You're a big girl." She nodded, not knowing what to say.

Then he put his hands between her legs, she had known he would do that, she had seen it done lots of times; but she had not expected his face to turn to stone as if he were angry. He frightened her for a moment. Then he whispered something in her ear, she expected it also to frighten her, and she was so relieved not to be frightened that she giggled: it was only a figure, a fortune, really, he could not mean it, perhaps he was only testing her, then he would begin to haggle, like Tomás and Inés.

"What would you do with all that money?" he asked. He was rocking her as if she were a baby; it made her slightly nauseous, but she realized it was necessary, it was what he wanted.

"I—" So many things crossed her mind at once, she was not sure she knew all the words, even in Spanish. How did you say you wanted a big house with servants and clothes that cling to your body like skin? And that she'd like to go in a boat straight from Vera Cruz across the ocean to everywhere; only, of course, Up Here, she'd go sailing on the lakes instead and have two houses, one in the summer and one in the winter; she'd be cool in the summer and hot in the winter: the idea made her giggle.

"Would you like something to eat?" he said. "Are you hungry?"

She was not sure it would be polite for her to eat alone, with him watching her, so she merely leaned against his chest in a gesture of assent, which seemed to please him so much he whispered again in her ear, something so incredible she could not believe it, even Tomás and Inés could not have imagined it: she stared up at him in amazement. She noticed for the first time that the wrinkles round his eyes were filled with white powder and that his hair was not really the color of pinto beans, she could see another color, like lead, coming through the sweating scalp. Maybe he was one of the other kind, the kind Tomás laughed at, but if so, why was he so insistent? No, he was not the other kind, she decided almost at once: for he had softly unzipped himself and he offered it to her now like a gift. She knew that she was to accept it in her cupped hands: but what he had whispered to her, that she still did not believe.

She understood now that he was, after all, haggling, he had raised the price, it was confusing: he apparently misunderstood her silence as demanding more money, but she was only trying, clumsily, to do what she thought he wanted. He tried to help her, but his eyes were moist and from time to time he dropped his head weakly to one side. Suddenly he cried out as if she had hurt him, and pulled a handkerchief from his pocket as if to cover his wound: she became terrified, but she was reassured when he began sucking her fingertips like the kittens at Brigída's belly. "Sugar, you're going to be great," he said.

Then he abruptly eased her off his lap. Sophía politely averted her eyes while he regained his composure, patting down his colored hair. He reached to a bowl on a nearby table and gave her an apple (she noticed at once that it was a Delicious, not bruised like the ones she'd sold earlier): and was now leading her to the door. He was polite and encouraging, he said she would do, she should come back tomorrow.

At the door, Sophía lingered, not wanting to insist, but knowing her rights.

"*Oh!*" he exclaimed softly, but with something of grudging admiration in his voice. "*Of course,*" and he handed her the crisp clean bill which she took without a word of thanks. "Come back tomorrow," he instructed her pleasantly, but he did not touch her again. Sophía nodded, and tucked the money away before he should change his mind and take it back.

When she returned the next day, he greeted her with a smile, but sent her at once, curtly and abruptly, into the bathroom to wash up first—giving her explicit instructions how to do so. In the bathroom she looked for the kittens, but they were gone. When she asked about the kittens, where he had put them , he laughed long and silently. Then at the look of dismay on her face, he took her again to his lap, as if to console her: they were gone, he said, somebody had stolen them.

The Emperors of Ice Cream

B y nine o'clock Maggie's arm felt as if it were caught in a roller, yet there would be three more hours to go; the dipper would begin to slip from her grasp, she would feel her arm growing painful, swollen: the flavors would begin to turn before her eyes—orange, pink, blue, rainbow. By eleven she could not make the scoops round enough to please the patrons of Dipper Doc; grimaces of discontent would appear on their faces. She dreaded this look as though they were the face of her father who, having stopped at every bar along the way, would finally arrive home, lurching his way to the top of the stairs, his face already contorted with rage. What they, the customers, wanted was a fat, round, ice cream cone, a cone whose sweetness dripped lightly, like the languors of summer, from all sides. Then they would lick it, at first gently and sensuously, then eagerly, insistently—smiling and talking and curling their tongues around the cream as it melted, melted like love in their mouths.

Dipper Doc's ice cream was twenty cents a dip, thick and rich, the best that money could buy; it was a thing perfect in itself, the one perfect thing they could have, if only for a moment. But Maggie had discovered that the customers were never satisfied with it. What they liked one week, they wearied of the next. It didn't matter whether Dipper mixed the six basic colors with pistachio, pecan, walnut, pignolia, cashew, or peanut: they were insatiable, there would never be flavors enough in the world for them. As she watched their faces over the melting sweetness, she grew to hate ice cream with that special hatred one reserves for lost causes; for it seemed to her, as she watched, that in their lust for sweets all the passion of their youth had been dissipated to this idle whimsy. Sometimes at night, in her little room on West Warren, she would lie awake at night calculating the dimes people paid out for their distraction from Reality each week. Yea, verily, a sea of dimes, enough to keep Dipper's flotilla afloat forever.

Her "cousin," Dipper Doc, twenty years her senior, owned the place. He was not really her cousin, though he did seem at times some remote prehistoric ancestor. The truth was he had been whelped by a sister of one of her stepmothers. Whenever the kids she knew from the university came in and teased her about working for the boss, she emphasized that he was not in her blood line, that he was a cousin at *least* once or twice removed. "Twice removed from what?" they would laugh. "From penury," would come her reply. For though he was "family," he worked her as hard as he did the black girl on the day shift, Lola, paying them both, with fulsome democracy, precisely the minimum wage.

It was not a job noted for its bright future: in fact, she would have preferred nearly any other kind of work. But there were no summer jobs for students this year, and she needed money so that she could return to Wayne State in the fall. The entire summer she had kept her eyes on college the way a prisoner watches doorways. She declared she would stand anything for three and a half months: the assinine circus uniforms, the scum of milk that stuck to one's skin like plastic, even the flamboyant students who arrived in dozens, pacing the floor impatiently in their bare feet, calling out for "triple-deckers" before piling back into somebody's overloaded convertible, red and arrogant as a rooster's crown.

The worst thing about working for Dipper Doc was that her routine was never allowed to become automatic; for no sooner had she mastered the thirty-two flavors and their arrangement along the counters than Dipper would change the labels, ingeniously assimilating the moods of the students. When their cause had been panty-raids, the ice cream had been promptly relabelled Bikini-haven, Lorelei-briefs, Playtex-pink. Lately, because the spirit was revolution, Dipper, dumb as a fox, had spun the gallon cans around as though in a mystic trance and rewritten the labels with black or red borders: People's Park Pistachio, Conspiracy Blue, Mao's Mousse, Panthers' Peanuts, and a new honeycomb flavor the color of burnt toast which capitalized on the whole youth movement: Peace and Love. It was the ultimate in petty larceny—peace and love *ice cream*, for Chrissake. It made Maggie writhe with rage; but silent, gnawing at her insides, she put in her fifty-four hours a week and collected her minimum wage.

The minimum wage, as anyone knew who had ever worked for it, meant somewhat less than minimum survival, especially if you wanted to buy something real, like an operation or a trip to Canada. But out of every week's envelope she took two twenty-dollar bills and hid them away in a drawer. There was nothing of sacrifice or virtue in it; she would never have thought of herself as thrifty: it was a case of obsession over desire. For her room on West Warren she paid eight dollars a week—too much for what they gave her, but she was allowed to cook on a gas burner that had somehow got left behind when the house got chopped up into smaller, more profitable pieces. The stove, a triple-burner, took up too much space, but was useful for heat in the winter. This past summer she had cooked two meals on it every day—cereal in the morning and some variation of rice for lunch: she had found that abstinence from meat, though it did not convert her to non-violence, did wonders for the pocketbook. Shortly after midnight, on her way home from the ice cream parlor and feeling too tired to cook anything, Maggie would buy herself a pizza and eat it sitting on the bed in her room, watching the neon sign flash Taystee Bar BQ in red, white and blue. Sometimes before closing the parlor, after Dipper had put his wife and kids to sleep, he would return to the ice cream parlor, count up the night's receipts, then run out to get them some hamburgers and french fries, or even a Kentucky Fried Chicken which he would spread around with an air of great lavishness. But in spite of her natural desire to enjoy the marginal rewards, so to speak, of her position, Maggie had always remained wary of these gifts without knowing why. Perhaps it was because, though Dipper was supposed to be "family," he was, nevertheless, a man with a man's propensities and she could never forget *that* (she had not grown up with six brothers, some half, some step, some good, some bad, without having learned what she thought were a few basic truths about men). But more than likely it was simply that he had plenty of money and she didn't. This gave him a real if invisible edge of superiority. His face reflected the calm which came from a night's repose and the detachment that was without need. It made his round, black eyes glisten as though with secret knowledge (later she was to recognize this as the lacquered stare of ruthess ease). His clothes were of a kind whose cost she could not tally, only it was clear that they fit him well, that they were pale and cool in the summer, thick and warm in the winter. Altogether, he would have been called a good-looking man, with that slash of sideburn on either side of his face, and a mouth with that extra stitch of cruelty which held it together and which many women craved (there were many nights, she knew, when Dipper did not go home to bed at all).

Thus she looked at Dipper inquiringly when one night before closing he brought in not only a basket of chicken but a bottle of wine. "Celebrating?" "No, what's to celebrate?" He shrugged. "Business is bad." She knew he was lying. About business there was nothing to say lest she ask for more money. *Yea, a veritable sea of dimes...*So she said ambiguously: "I didn't know you cared for that kind of stuff."

"Sit down and eat," he ordered. "It's a whole chicken. Lola

can finish sweeping in the morning."

She felt, in fact, painfully hungry. She decided to eat: he couldn't very well hold it against her, it was his own idea. Yet at the same time she felt inexplicably nervous. She had decided that it was a perfectly normal thing for them to have wine when Dipper explained softly:

"Besides, I've heard you *like* wine. Or is it maybe you don't like my brand?"

She forced herself to move her head so that his eyes met hers. "What do you mean, 'heard?' You heard *I* liked wine. And who told you that? I mean who had the right to tell you *any*thing? About me." She had managed not to emphasize *you*.

"*Shah, shah,*" he said with a shrug. "Why so touchy? Who's accusing you of anything? So, sit..." He pointed to the chair beside him. With a blandness which she somehow found insulting, she noticed that he had already popped the cork.

She sat down on the edge of the chair which Dipper had painted gold, then wound round with red and white ribbons: it was supposed to represent a Maypole or something.

"I didn't say anybody was accusing me. I just want to know: who said anything about me? To *you*. I just want to know what you heard." She found she was flexing and unflexing her fingers, opening and shutting them like a drawbridge over her lap.

"Why're you so anxious if you've nothing to hide?"

She gasped, unable to answer; she felt as if some ugliness were about to be forced down her throat: the smell of the fried chicken rose sickeningly sweet. She found herself unable to eat.

Dipper took a piece of chicken and bit into it tenderly. He seemed to be trying to eat delicately in her presence, but she had seen him when he thought no one was watching, when he tore his meat like a predator. Now, by the third bite, in spite of his effort at restraint, he had to wash the chicken down with wine before he could say, with a kind of fierce gentleness:

"Well, for instance...How much do you make here?"

"You know goddamned well how much I make!" she exclaimed with exasperation.

"And it's enough, is it? To buy clothes, I mean. Pay for movies, stockings, underwear..." he glanced down at her skirt as though he knew what luxuries lay hidden there. Then with a visible effort he managed to widen his gaze in a kind of parabola, taking in other details: "You have to buy books. Students need books." He emphasized every syllable as though it were a slogan or a new delicious flavor. "Then there're medical expenses, dental work, that kind of thing— you have very good teeth, by the way," he added abruptly. "You take good care of them, eh? Who's your dentist?"

"Marivaux," she said, her lips tightening with resentment at this invasion of her privacy.

"Ah, he's my dentist too. He's a won-der-ful dentist..." He strung out the words as though she were unconvinced and he meant to persuade her. "How could you afford such a dentist? But then—" he added, as if with an air of collusion "—for a good product no price is too high. Is it?" He waited a split-second, absorbing her shocked silence; then still holding her gaze with his own, he said softly: "Let me see...your teeth." He touched his thumb to her lower lip and began stroking it tenderly. "A *beautiful* smile it would be...Only you never smile. Why is it you never smile? 'Smile and the world—' "

Maggie sprang to her feet. "I'm not paid to smile!" she exclaimed fiercely.

He caught her hand. " 'Not paid to smile!' " He seemed to laugh. "That's a good one. And it's true, it's true that everything has its price. Even a smile. So how much would it cost me for a smile? For a smile...for me alone?"

A hot flush surged across her face. "You bastard!" she growled, moving away.

But he would not release her hand; she felt the hot licking insult of his thumb as it flicked across the center of her palm.

She wrenched herself loose, breathless with rage: "Why you worthless son of a bitch, do you think I'd let *you* lay a hand on me—at *any* price?" Savagely she kicked the broom which lay in her path, and without stopping to cover her uniform with the poplin raincoat she usually wore, she banged the door so that the blinds cracked loudly against the glass. She did not turn to see if she splintered the glass.

Dipper had followed her out toward the street; he stood on the threshold as she moved swiftly into the darkness. She could hear the tremor in his voice, of self-love swollen into a passion keener than lust as he called to her: "Not me, eh? I'm not good enough for you. Anybody you'll take, but not me eh? A blow job for twenty dollars, I hear. For anybody else, cheap enough. But for me nothing. A call girl with high-class tastes. So O.K. It's your right. A *curveh* has rights. A *curveh* with im—peccable taste." Suddenly he raised his voice to a new pitch, comical, hysterical: "Nothing personal about it. You got a job here. I got no grudges."

She knew that she ought not to return to the ice cream parlor, but she leaned heavily on the theory that now that Dipper knew what the score was, he'd let her alone; that, moreover, he was no different from other employers, only more stupid and more obvious. She would put the whole thing out of her mind and return to work: she needed the money. What had shocked her was not so much that cousin Dipper was lecherous—that came as no surprise—but rather the realization that there were yet lower depths into which the judging eye of the Establishment could plunge her. When she had abandoned the dubious sanctuary of a family who had kept her perpetually torn between pity and contempt, a family she could not even laugh at lest she be destroyed by hysteria, she had had no notion of what middle-class respectability was, never having seen it. Nor was it a concept she had had time to learn much about, till one day she had discovered that for some reason she did not have it. Then she had realized that it was because she lived alone; worse, she worked at night. *A priori*, a girl who worked at night could never be respectable. The year before last she had been on the point of marrying a Nice-Jewish-boy, whom she had met at somebody's *bar mitzvah*. She had thought they were both free to marry each other if they wanted to; but one day the mother had drawn her aside and told her she had a lot of *chuztpah* wanting to marry her son, Meyer, when not only was her father a drunk (as everyone knew) but she herself was a penniless nothing (and probably no virgin at that). Worst of all, Meyer's mother said, she—Maggie—*didn't even have a college education:* whereas her son would be a lawyer, a Congressman, a Senator, a Supreme Court Justice. Agreeing with her adversary quickly, Maggie had acknowledged that she was a poor risk (why she barely read any language other than her own, she had confessed irrelevantly, staring at the mother as if *this* were somehow her Ultimate Degradation). Maggie had surrendered her property rights in Meyer quickly, breaking things off before she should become pregnant and therefore ruthless. After all, Meyer's Mama had a right to Respectability as a material asset: the wife of a future Supreme Court Justice should be above suspicion. Only Maggie had never been sure what it was she was suspicioned of: of having loved that dopey son of hers? A mistake she would never repeat.

What she had carried away with her from the encounter—however mistakenly—was the conviction that a college degree was a symbol of such importance to the Establishment that by its sanctification one could be exempted from the armed services, acquitted for manslaughter, freed from the scarlet letter, absolved from mortal sin. What The Meyer Period, as she scoffingly called it, had taught her was that the ritualistic forms surrounding middle class marriage were pure, conscious deceptions: if she had been willing to lie, deceive, twinkle her twat, she could, by means of this slender, slick little security-piece have purchased white sheets and security for life. If she had kept her mouth shut about her drunken father, her gutless stepbrothers, her retarded half-sister, her lonely miscalculations in the frenzied world where dollars exorcized evil, she could right now be rolling in private property and legitimate orgasm. But in her ignorance she had thought that her chief merit lay in her transcendence over these things: she had not thought they contaminated her, since she had steered as wide and clear as from a dog's vomit. She had been wrong. O.K. She was willing, now, to admit it. Lying achieved, purity paid, twittering and twatting gave eternal life. She had used to pretend that what she had instead of Meyer was freedom. But could anyone be free on a dollar-sixty an hour? It was like the fulsome emancipation of slaves, left free to die in the cotton fields on fifty cents a day. No, in a world where it was absolutely necessary to have thirty-two delicious flavors available day and night, she would never be free from the whimsy of those who had absolute power over her life.

Nevertheless she had returned to the ice cream parlor, tasting defeat like bile. Now, Monday night, as she swept up the store before closing, she stared down at the refuse she had created. She felt so tired and dirty the pile might have been her own personal leavings, the product of her working day. And not only was she exhausted but she had to admit she was lonely, and *that*, she thought, was a sure sign of spiritual defeat. She should have got herself pregnant and married that rich bastard who was already a lawyer. Meyer's father had "dealt" in ladies' wear, and on their first date Meyer had murmured appealingly: "Do you mind my asking just why, for tonight you picked out this dress that I've seen a dozen times on our *schwartze?*"

Since the night of their quarrel (or misunderstanding), Dipper had not been around checking out the ice cream cases as he usually did. He must be avoiding her, she reasoned, and a good thing too. But no: she could hear him now puttering around in the basement as usual, sliding ice cream cans across the concrete floor. He would have to come upstairs to lock up the parlor for the night. In spite of herself, Maggie began to hurry with the sweeping.

When, finally, he came up the basement stairs, slowly and heavily, as though carrying a great burden, she was surprised to find him looking grim and surly—not sheepish nor grinning as she might have expected. She had planned to act as if nothing had happened, as if she were a kind of dependent relative to whom he had been generously offering employment; and he, of course, quite guiltless...But it was as if he himself had forgotten it all. Far from seeming sheepish or apologetic, he nodded at her coldly as he passed behind the ice cream cases. She sucked in her breath at his cool aplomb; the man had a nerve all right: rigid and ruthless as the hard wall of a firing squad at your back. Determined to be as silent as he, she swept up the dust with a kind of controlled fury; then she pulled her sweater over her uniform, prepared to leave.

She saw him counting the bills. He counted them twice, his back turned toward her. Then, moving his body as upon a fulcrum, he turned toward her, took all the bills and laid them carefully across the ice cream cases, spread-eagling his fingers in a wide span of protectiveness. "That's funny..." he murmured softly. She pretended not to hear. A conversation with him on any subject at that hour was beyond her: she could ignore him, but she felt she could not *talk* to him.

"I could have sworn," he pronounced carefully, "I would have *sworn* there were five twenties in here when I checked in this afternoon."

That caught her ear. "Oh? I didn't know you'd been in this afternoon. Lola didn't mention it."

"And why should she mention it?"

"What do you mean, why should she mention it? She doesn't—not deliberately—she just lets me know something about what you did, like change the flavors, or run an ad, so I'll know..."

"You two girls have a pretty nice set up. Between the two of you, you could keep your eye on me pretty good."

She stared, wanting to smile but afraid to.

He looked at her sternly, his mouth a set puzzle: "There were five twenties in here when I came in at 4:30. Counting the rest of it there should be..." He spread the money out before her eyes as if the sight of it were explanation enough. "There should be, altogether, four hundred dollars here."

"How the hell should I know how much there's supposed to be. *I* don't count the money except to make change. You set and lock the register yourself, opening and closing. Except to make change for a customer, I never touch the stuff—"

"So you never touch the stuff. You're very fussy. Never tough *any*thing, do you? But it sticks to you somehow. Just natural." He was not sneering; he had not the facial resilience to sneer; there was something compact, immobile, righteous about his face that terrified. It was a face that believed in witchcraft, therefore a face capable of believing it had found a true witch.

Somehow she already knew what he had in mind for her; but skillfully practicing disbelief, she headed for the door. If she refused to believe that he was going to say it, perhaps he could not say it.

"And where are you going? You'll just hand over the money before you go."

There. He had done it. She felt as if his axe had struck her head at last, and though her head was rolling in the basket, dead, her now-useless, stupified head, as Carlyle had speculated, went on thinking, went on feeling terror.

"You're mad. Do you think I'd stoop—?"

"Oh you'd never stoop. Who's saying you stoop? Stealing is not stooping."

"Goddam you, Dipper, if you accuse me of stealing your filthy money, I'll—" she looked around desperately for some weapon to throw at his head, a broom, a brick—or a lightning bolt.

"So now you're threatening *me*. I want you to know, I'll have you arrested for this. I've known for a long time what you've been getting away with... So I've talked to Brady already. He says a search warrant is all I need. Or maybe not even that, he says. He says we can use the *no-knock*..."

"You mean, like for *drugs?*" She thought she was screaming with fury, but the words had come out in an inarticulate whisper.

Dipper shrugged.

So she had to throw the broom, even though she knew at the time it was useless. But she had to throw something at him, hit him with something even if it was only a straw, to show her utter contempt for his transparent tactics. But the broom merely sailed like an African spear straight into the glass counter; there was a loud crack and the glass split down the middle without coming apart.

"You goddam bitch! I give you a job and this is what you do. Rob me—destroy my property. I'll bust your ass for you, that's what I'll do, you cheap tramp, nobody's good enough for you but blacks and cocksuckers."

Instead of running toward the door, she stood terrified and calm. She believed she had the ultimate weapon: "You lay a hand on me, you hypocrite, and I'll tell the whole world about you. I'll go to the university. I'll tell every kid in the street. I'll tell your family—your wife, your kids, just what a son of a bitch you really are—"

She thought she heard him snarl: *Shut up. Shut up or I'll shut you up.* If so, it would have been his only warning as his fist came crashing down on her. She thought idiotically, as the pain burst in her forehead, that he would have to turn out the lights, certainly he could not kill her with every light in the shop blazing away. She intended also, somewhere along the road of consciousness, to scream; but found that those who have the will to destroy also have the cunning to silence their victims. After her own first stifled groan, she heard nothing, not her own voice, not even his furious, "Bitch! Liar! Thief!" but only a far-removed thumping, as of someone chopping wood in the distance.

She found out later, after she had been hustled off to Detroit Receiving in a police car, that Dipper had accused her of assault with intent to kill, producing a sharp knife from somewhere to prove it. He pointed out that she had been stealing from him all summer, but that since she was his cousin, he had tried to be patient. When she was discharged from the hospital, there was a brief trial. Her family, shocked and humiliated at their forced association with a bona fide criminal, refused to come to the court to say a word in her defense: they had always known, they said, that she would come to no good, stubborn and hot-tempered since she could talk.

Maggie was never afterwards able to remember exactly what took place at the trial; only that she was guilty and they sent her to the Women's House of Detention. There, for several weeks she lay on her bunk in her cell, talking to no one, letting the sounds of the radio, the screams of the other women—their curses, their occasional laughter—wash over her like a violent film in which she had no part. Then, one evening at dinner, almost against her will, her mind began taking it all in: the hideous prison garb; the clatter of metal plates; above all, the faces of the other women, so distorted by grief, rage, fear and defiance that they appeared for a moment like some other species, some mutant intended for survival after the flood or the bomb. Suddenly, a gust of compassion, of identification with these others—so unlike herself, swept through her, and when supper was over, she staggered, still blind with tears, back to her cell. There, crushed, annihilated, humiliated, she continued to weep for hours, days...till at last, reason returned. Instead of sobbing over her injuries, over her lost money (which was "returned" to Dipper), she began to concentrate on Dipper himself: his face, his hands, above all whatever it was that had given him the superior force over her. And she discovered, after much brooding, that she had in her something even stronger than that force, which was growing and strengthening and building itself to a vast energy, and that was her hate. She took over hate as she would have the Holy Ghost, it was a conversion. Hate was to become her life style, her personal strategy of defense, her welfare program, her free lunches, her Great Books Program, her afternoon tennis. A truly great hatred had liberated her from mere dislike of trifles. She could even enjoy eating ice cream again, for she had learned that the first step in the coming struggle was to know your enemy.

Ericka

Find someone? *Here?* Ericka's raincoat leaked slowly down to the island of carpet in the brilliantly lit hallway while her hostess stood smiling a gentle smile, as if it were her fault and not Ericka's that the rug was there to be dripped on. Nevertheless, Mrs. Ascher stood a polite distance away, her fingertips resting like those of the virgin in a tripdych on the soft mound protruding delicately from her womb. In the gilt mirror, magnificent as a Borghese landscape, Ericka took in the spectacle: the patterned carpet, the collected art works—statues on marble mounts and abstracts framed into the walls as if into their own bodies—and above all, the glittering clusters of couples who stood, palms resting under elbows, tinkling the ice in their glasses. For a moment the refracted light of the mirror seemed to fuse the vision, first into a melting collage, then into an explosive psychedelic glare: Ericka busied herself with her coat, burying her terror in its plastic pockets as she put away her scarf.

Mrs. Ascher was already murmuring in a casual way, as if it were only a public and not a private request: *would* she, Ericka, mind taking her coat upstairs? She'd find a room with the other coats on the bed, the room next to the children's. "Roderick's not here yet," Mrs. Ascher went on to explain, as if this momentous breach of custom needed an apology. "He's out picking up a few guests...students without cars." Mrs. Ascher's awareness of her husband's kindness seemed to grow heady on her lips; she flushed as if with pleasure. Ericka could sense in her hostess a controlled excitement as she swung her swelling body toward the doorbell which was ringing now in rising tones, like the questioning voice of an intelligent child: anybody *innnnnn?*

As she climbed the carpeted staircase Ericka glanced over her shoulder at the couples below, all, it seemed to her wearing a look of cultivated differences—a heterogeneity achieved by a culture first carefully instilled, then just as carefully plucked up and idled into Personality. She was already sorry she had come. She had accepted the invitation upon the insistence of her roommate, Susan Hallam. Sue's view of the world was so simple that Ericka had been beguiled into sharing the divorcee's apartment simply for comic relief. "A pair of divorcees. We'll have group therapy sessions," Sue had said. But the last thing Ericka had wanted was anything *groupy.* After two years of the pervasive family "love" of eight other people, leaving the commune and living by herself with baby Jonathan had been like cutting off some intravenous flow of survival. It had at first amused Ericka to hear her roommate, a great believer in private ownership, exclaim impatiently, "Would you mind just *not* sticking these things in *my* books," as she shook out a band aid or pencil or postcard Ericka had carelessly stuck between the pages. Ownership, order, ritual: Susan's books, *her* son. Exactly what Shelley would have execrated in the commune. Except, of course, that it had been Ericka alone who had cushioned and creatured Jonathan for nine months like a slowly exploding star; and during his birth, it had been *her* private world that had cracked and splintered for forty-two hours. But those hours had been her single claim to Jonathan for months afterwards: for the rest of the time, until she had left Shelley's Commune, he had belonged to The Family: odd how in the very dissolution of the family as a social institution, they clung to the counterpane of old words—the sisters, the brothers, the word *commune* itself. Yet, altogether an experience she would not have missed; for genuine love had permeated their household—genuine hate too: elements never quite assimilable. As for Shelley, it had been a cosmogony of Love, available from any of the women in their house, because as Shelley said, they did not "own" each other. So they had had their Love. She had found that keeping your cool in a houseful of Love could be as dangerous as sitting near an open window in an overheated room. You got cool, but you could die of it. What had died had been her love for Shelley.

Upstairs, in what appeared to be a guest room, Ericka folded her coat beside a pile-up of fake furs and jaunty capes. Her shoes were wet and she stood gratefully against the hot air register, assuring herself that it was a good idea to get dry; but she knew she was only delaying the moment when she would have to face the knotted cords of cocktail conversation, each one powerful, swift and unexpected as your own private case of whiplash. She could plainly hear someone querying the Ascher children, whose hot air register adjoined her own: "You have your pajamas in that bag? Good. And take Binks with you. He'd be lonely sleeping here all by himself." And to something the twin girls murmured, something not quite audible, as the furnace with a faint sigh suddenly wound itself to an intenser blast of heat, "Oh, yes, *all* bears love divinity fudge. Did you say goodnight to your daddy before he left? So...we can go...Just leaving, Gertrude," the voice added in a higher pitch, to Mrs. Ascher. Obviously an old family retainer, Ericka decided, or a friend with plenty of room in her house, chauffering the kids away from the noise and hubbub to a paradise of TV, teddy bears and divinity fudge. At Mrs. Ascher's approach—to kiss the children goodbye—there came faintly through the register a dark wave of perfume which Ericka recognized. Called Always Autumn, it had been the favorite of one of the girls at the commune whom they had named, simply, *Ping* (their repeated failure to learn her real name had been the subject of a long lecture by Shelley who called it subconscious racism) an oriental girl with eyes so perpetually bright, beautiful and intransigent, one would have said a taxidermist had carefully positioned them in her flax-colored face. Shelley had doubtless slept with her, Ericka now admitted to herself, with a spasm not of jealousy but of exhaustion, as if the sheer attrition of her twenty-three and one half years of life had begun to bear down sandpaper-like, rasping away layer after layer of sensibility, leaving her raw and vulnerable to every slight—past as well as present: even in retrospect she could dredge up new insults to her self-esteem.

In a rush of self-discipline—she couldn't very well stand drying her toes all night—she slipped out of the bedroom to the hall, where she met Mrs. Ascher on the stairs. "Quite dry now?" smiled her hostess and explained, without waiting for Ericka's reply: "The children were so excited! They love to sleep away from home. Tessie and Beth pack their own bag. They never forget a thing. But Arthur, on the other hand, always manages to leave something behind—so he can come back for it, I suppose. The girls are—," Mrs. Ascher just faintly hesitated, "...secure, whereas Arthur is...is the only boy," she concluded, vaguely inconsequent. Ericka smiled politely, accustomed to the ordered world of psychiatrists' wives where everything one did really meant something else. But it made conversation a one-way street, so she asked, instead, the question she had grown to learn was pure ritual: "And how old are they?" It was a question renewable forever; grandmothers were still asking each other names, dates, births, baptisms, schools: it was a mindless, solipsistic game, like solitaire.

Mrs. Ascher now politely began to describe her children to her guest. Ericka's mind wandered, a fault she knew was unpardonable, like blurting out some awful truth in public. "And you?" asked Mrs. Ascher, stopping suddenly as if she had programmed herself to say just so much and no more.

"Oh. Me? I've only Jonathan..."

"Oh but don't say it like that!" protested her hostess softly. "You'll get married again. But of course you will," she added with an odd intensity. "You're too young to think of your life as *over.*"

"I don't think I really *believe* in marriage," Ericka tried hesitatingly to explain, more to herself than to Mrs. Ascher.

Mrs. Ascher looked puzzled, even pained. Then she interpreted Ericka's words, apparently, from what she had heard about her, perhaps from Dr. Ascher. "Ah, but you're one of the new women...the liberated women," she added haltingly, as if the word were far too weighty and significant for the lightness of their conversation.

Who me? Liberated? thought Ericka as they descended the stairs together; and just managed not to strike her forehead in comic despair. Liberated, as Sue Hallam, always sticky with cliche, repeatedly informed her, was to be liberated *from* something. And what the hell was she, Ericka, liberated from anyway? Nothing at all, so far as she could see. A dreary typist in an airless office at three hundred a month (take-home pay). No graduate assistantship for her because Ascher said she wasn't qualified: a B.A. in English didn't qualify a girl for anything in *his* psychology department, he had said, smiling genially. Not that graduate students earned any more money working in the very bowels of the beast (in fact, they earned less) but at least they were saved the hassle of traveling into the inner city to take courses, and the 9-5 claustrophobia: there were times when the mere smell of her office gave her something akin to morning sickness. The only reason she had enrolled in Roderick Ascher's course, *Ego Identity in Urban Crisis,* was that it came at the right time of day and because it was supposed to be a snap course—one could fill the void of the term paper with flocculent phrases signifying ego-and-identity till the cows came home (still, it hadn't turned out to be a snap course at all: fraudulence, she had found, by the very vagueness of its criteria, can be as demanding as truth). Fortunately Ericka was not required to assess the value of the university system, but merely to hang on to what it might all mean to her when Jonathan was a grown-up man of twenty, and *she?*...But she realized with a start that Mrs. Ascher was already clutching the newel at the bottom of the staircase, while gesturing with her other hand to a young man with a beautiful honey-colored beard (he must spend as much time on it, Ericka thought, as she used to spend on her eyebrows). He stood uncertainly in the hallway, dazzled by the lighted hallway. "And where's Dr. Ascher?" inquired Mrs. Ascher, her voice charged with a sudden rush of tension, as though she feared the students might have somehow mislaid him. Rather ungraciously the young man jerked his thumb toward the portico under which headlights were shining. "They'll be here in a minute...I guess."

"Miss...Mrs. Stein, Mr. Gehan." In her desire to make it clear that they were meant to speak to each other (two young people, after all), and not to her, Mrs. Ascher was tugging Gehan by the arm. Ericka glanced at him, wanting to give the poor guy a break by striking out for herself, straight into the undertow of conversation; but for the present there was nothing to do but comply with their hostess' insistency and set themselves afloat in a tub of conversation.

"Student of Dr. Ascher's, I presume," Ericka asked lightly, trying to make it sound as if she had just come upon him in Darkest Africa. But her intonation perhaps was not just right, because his reply came back, grave and factual.

"Well, not exactly. I grade for him—Dr. Ascher. I'm in computer science. And you?"

"Sociology. Social *welfare*, that is." Should she bother to explain the difference? He was already glancing over her shoulder at the doorway, and she decided to save her energy: he was clearly not even interested enough for polite games-manship.

He blurted abruptly, his gaze returning to her with a sharp owl-like twist of the head: "Say, I've seen you before. I know where it was. I heard you speak. The other evening. At the discussion."

"Heard *me*?" Was he confusing her with someone else? She went out so rarely at night that she thought she must have some record for anonymity: one stupefying movie-date since leaving *Sheldon's Commune*. Besides, she had never made a public speech in her life. Ericka stepped back restlessly, feeling her identity threatened: to be unknown was one thing, but to be so commonplace as to be confused with others was sheer annihilation.

But Gehan was explaining rapidly; he seemed nervous and guilty about something, and was still watching the doorway. She saw him glance down at her left hand as if to look for a wedding ring. "It was that book discussion," he said. "And you asked the author...authoress..actually, you *told* her, that you didn't think there was any such thing as freedom. For either men or women. You seemed kind of *upset*, and you said..." out of consideration for their surroundings he lowered his voice "...you wanted to know how the hell—your words—" he apologized quickly, "—how the hell a woman with a kid to take care of could ever be free—you said that you couldn't even stand there and *listen* to her...the authoress...because you had to pick your kid up before six o'clock." He faltered and checked the crowd again as though he hoped someone would rescue him from his recitative. He seemed startled at his invasion of her privacy, as if it indemnified him toward her somehow.

Ericka pondered. Had she really said all that? She remembered now that she had had a bowl of chili at the cafeteria to save herself the trouble of cooking when she got home. Then, on her way out, she had noticed a lot of women sitting around the Student Union, rapping with Cynthia Carpenter, who had just published a book on the New Woman. With her eye on the clock she had paused for a minute to listen. Some of the women's answers had irritated her—perhaps she had been merely resentful that Jon's demands (he was always hungry and irritable if she arrived late) prevented her from feeling free to stay—and she had demanded of the writer to explain freedom to *her*, Ericka Stein, mother of two-year-old Jonathan, invoice-lackey to a pseudo-insurance company, daughter of a poor postman who had walked twenty thousand miles and didn't have a nickel to his name, and whose skin cancer was now slowly killing him. "Jesus Christ," she had added, hot tears of self-pity springing to her eyes, "I'm not concerned about whether somebody's daughter gets into metallurgy class. What I want to know is, how am I going to *survive?*" There had been absolute silence in the group; then several older women had begun whispering among themselves, and a black woman—the only one present —had murmured in antiphony, "Teach, sister, teach!"

Ericka felt embarrassed now as she stared into Gehan's clear grey eyes—he was obviously sympathetic, but also more at ease with her now that he had forced her to admit her pain (it had given him the uncontested upper hand). She could only stare at him in silence, declaring a truce, beseeching him to stop: O.K., O.K. He had won the Battle of the Sexes before it had even begun between them. Nor did she feel obliged to explain her silence. He knew everything, didn't he, if he knew what she had scarcely admitted to herself: that she was lonely and terrified and never had enough money and the responsibility of Jonathan was too much and she would surely break under the strain of it all and then they'd take away her child, and they'd put her away, away, *oi wei*...Even now, in a very rational way, she knew her nerves were frayed, that her feet were still cold, and that after the party she would either have to walk home, wait for a bus, or spend two dollars for a taxi (punitive choices, all three), and that Jon would certainly wake up when she came in—he was really getting too big to sleep in the same room: and Christ, what was she to do about it all?

She took advantage of a surge of arrivals to duck Gehan. She couldn't take the image of herself she received from his eyes. Alone at 3:00 a.m. she could confess her misery, cry out *"God, this is unbearable!,"* not sure to whom she was speaking. But not here; it was as if she suddenly found herself the only one naked. Perspiring with nervousness, she eased away toward the refreshments, hanging over the delicacies of cheese and ham and chicken as over a funeral pyre onto which shortly she too would be thrown and consumed.

But she was relieved, for the moment, to be alone. A few more such encounters and they could tie her up and carry her home in a body bag. She bagan to ply herself with food, forcing herself to feign *bon appetit* while fumbling with the cheese cutter, which was an odd-shaped clever thing, like a genteel guillotine...

"...help you with that?" It was Ascher. He had apparently arrived at last, alive and well, with his convoy of students. Beside him, as he showed Ericka how to manipulate the little guillotine which pared cheese as thin as a veil, stood a stunning girl whom he introduced to her as Deborah. A foreign student, apparently, but Ericka couldn't place her accent. Ascher began slicing the cheese for them, holding down the wooden board with one hand, while making manly lunges at the rounded cheese with the other. Deborah stood beside him, smiling down with pleasure at the curling whorls of cheese. Ascher then began entertaining them, his manners pervasively democratic, as though it were definitely his prerogative as well as responsibility to entertain students, not the other way around. Before Ascher could finish his sentences, Deborah would begin laughing, an interruption which Ascher took in his stride, adding the punch line after the laugh. Then they would both laugh simultaneously, while Ericka managed what she felt must be a very tired smile. She began to wonder whether she should stay, but felt it would be rude to leave; it would look slanderously as though she mistook their public laughter for private; so she stayed. She was slightly shorter than Deborah, and Ericka's line of vision fell exactly parallel with the girl's cleavage—a fact which was somehow disconcerting as Deborah swayed toward them in animated conversation. The girl was very intelligent—indeed, so witty and beautiful she made Ericka feel like a cabbage. But in spite of her gifts, Deborah seemed troubled by an unnatural tension; her breasts loomed like weapons, her earrings glittered. One felt in a moment how those agitated breasts might brush up against a man in some initiatory rite. Ericka suddenly remembered that there was an unmended rip in the seam of her dress—over the shoulder where she herself could not see it—which exposed like an unsutured wound her poverty, her haste, her reluctance to come to this party at all, and which exposed, above all, her indifference to all those roles into which "they" wished to cast her: "sexpot, mother symbol, husband catcher." Choose your Procrustean bed and die on it. And now she felt a headache beginning, one of those like a medieval torture in which that part of her which had refused to accept something would be slowly, horribly crushed in The Boot of her brain.

She definitely ought to go home. But first, for good form, she would join her hostess. A circle of guests had gathered around the physical security of Mrs. Ascher's pregnant body as around an ancient fertility goddess. It was a group, Ericka sensed, which like herself had been glad to surrender sprightliness and grace for the solid honesty of sitting down. Sitting down was an admission that you were dead-tired. And having arrived at that moment of truth, other truths naturally followed. You at once dropped the sealed mask of attentiveness, Ericka reflected; and conversation was allowed to languish. For to sit was an honest and quintessential act of nature: one sat beside the sick and dying; one sat at a wake, at a peace pow-wow; one sat at dinner and sat to evacuate. Sitting was akin to squatting, a modified form of hunkering down in the cave: it reminded you that you were a mere body, and mortal.

Having lifted her fatigue to a social philosophy, Ericka sank with a groan into a chair beside two women who seemed to be sorting out courage and cliches like hired poker hands in a card game. Ericka decided she would merely listen. She felt exorcised of any personal vanity or greed that might ever again propel her into speech. Let others shine, she was willing to vanish, to disappear into silences. The talk shambled for a while like a clever clown taking in the needs of its audience. This film, that film; within five minutes they had reviewed five films; Ericka thought wryly that they must attend movies like Browning's Bishop eating God daily. But she became more attentive as she realized that they were discussing what "their" group was planning to do Again and Again Against the War. She began immediately asking herself whom she could find to keep Jon for the weekend; for she felt obliged to go along to protest the war the way one might feel obliged to give blood to the dying. Though the disease might be terminal, it was an act of expiation, fending off a jealous god who had jurisdiction over her ultimate right to survive. Ericka was about to break her self-imposed silence, to make inquiry about buses, transportation, sleeping arrangements, when Mrs. Ascher observed that several women had been arrested in a mêlée outside the State Capitol while picketing, she said, " 'for the right over their own bodies.' " A look of melancholy invaded Mrs. Ascher's eyes. Then an argument began between Mrs. Ascher and a young girl with long blonde hair, a very polite argument; for after all Mrs. Ascher was Dr. Ascher's wife and, besides, was so plainly and helplessly pregnant that a consciousness of it rang through everyone's speech like a clapper in a bell. Ericka listened as the girl—only a freshman, she explained as though it were somehow relevant—argued for what she called Absolute Freedom. Then suddenly the blonde girl became more emotional, she began citing personal facts—a love affair, an abortion, a father who had run off to join the circus—as if by confessing these personal crises she might persuade Mrs. Ascher of their right to Absolute Freedom. Through it all her hostess sat, surprisingly un-moved, only turning from time to time to regard the group sitting around her. Ericka averted her eyes, feeling herself unable to take sides. She knew she had never—no, not once,—been "free." Freedom, like sex and money, were painlessly discussed at leisure by those who had the most of them. Those who did not have these things were silent—ashamed of their lack, as if by the power of their wills they might have wrested from the havoc of their lives, A Beautiful Life—well-loved and rich, and chock-full of the four freedoms. Ericka's despair, her conviction that she would never have this freedom, drove her deep into self-abasement. She allowed herself to envy Mrs. Ascher, in a veritable orgy of covetousness. She admitted to herself with disgust that she envied everything her hostess had: her composure, her home, her love, her friends, her exquisite frock, her vaginal orgasms: envied her, in fact, down to her very shoes which, glossy and neat, rested side by side on the rug like a pair of expensive and well-trained pets. Then abruptly, Ericka's gaze flickered, she wearied of her own apostasy, of her own cringing admiration, the very depth of which had left her exhausted, cleansed, purged—momentarily, at least—of envy. She said to herself that she had sat courteously enough, and now she would try to leave. Her head was twinging like a rotting tooth and she felt morally justified in improvising a strategy of escape. She would, she decided, excuse herself and go upstairs to the bedroom where she had left some aspirin in her coat pocket; then, she might perhaps drift slowly downstairs, and drift slowly homeward, if it were —say—anywhere near ten o'clock. But what was the time now? she wondered, with a glance at Mrs. Ascher's watch. Her attention was at once rivetted to Mrs. Ascher's anomalous timepiece, as she realized with a shock that she would never find out the time from that strangely incoherent watch: it had only one hand.

Ericka looked up at her hostess in surprise; she and Gertrude Ascher exchanged oddly meaningful looks—Gertrude's, as it seemed to her, intensely pleased, as though she were somehow gratified that her odd secret was out... "Excuse me," said Ericka, determined to outface this enigma. She leaned toward Gertrude's wrist with curiosity, "But can you tell me the time?"

Gertrude laughed. A flush of pleasure crept over her face. "It's five minutes," she announced mysteriously.

"Five minutes to what? I mean after what?" Ericka found herself absurdly correcting herself, as if to force it all into chronological good sense.

Gertrude laughed again, lifting the back of her hand to her mouth. Just faintly, Ericka could see the imprint of Gertrude's teeth on her hand.

"That's all. Five minutes. Five minutes before, after, during *any*thing. It's not necessary to know the hour. That way you always have enough time. You're never rushed. For instance," she went on to exclain with a logical air, "let's say

you're taking Roderick's clothes to be pressed." She glanced
around as if looking to see if Roderick were present, her voice
slightly breathless as if with laughter: but she was not smiling
at all. "You allow fifteen minutes in all: five for parking the
car—just outside the cleaners. Five for taking the clothes into
the store, getting your receipt, that kind of thing. And five for
your return."

Ericka set her face into an attitude of polite curiosity; but
her head throbbed; her own pain was rapidly becoming
excruciating, but she was held to her place by a consciousness
that some other pain—a pain deeper and incurable—was
being revealed to her.

"Think of it this way," said Mrs. Ascher amiably, looking
down at her watch as if she were a magician about to make all
her rabbits disappear at a single whisk of her handkerchief.
"When I wake up in the morning, nothing is changed. It's all
exactly as the day before. I still have...*yesterday*. I begin: one
minute to brush my teeth, a half an hour for breakfast, thirty
minutes on the phone. The rule is, I never consume an entire
hour for any one thing...Then I begin again. Say, I'm on my
way to the library. The freeway is no excuse," she added
harshly, her face suddenly all sternness and self-discipline.
"You can't allow yourself extra time just because of a crowded
freeway—or because the tunnels are loaded with traffic. *All
this has to be taken into consideration beforehand.* It should
never take more than twenty minutes to take books back to the
library. Allow for a maximum of seven red lights if, instead of
the freeway, you're going by way of Mercy Avenue. If you don't
allow for the red lights, you're trapped," she warned them
with a fierceness which revealed to them all her dedication to
her ideal: to consume her life in meaningless pastimes and yet
to have it, to waste it, and yet to possess it. It was like an
endless game of crossword puzzles, each word fitting perfectly, yet all of it making no sense in the aggregate and
leaving one again—and again—with inexhaustible but untiring
stretches of achievement. A self-induced labor of Sysiphus.

The blonde-haired girl who had been arguing with her

hostess about freedom looked frightened; then she laughed, or pretended to, as if Mrs. Ascher were being terribly witty; the others followed suit, and it was as if the loud ticking of hysteria were washed over in good-natured joking. Mrs. Ascher removed her watch and looked at Ericka, smiling. Ericka had not laughed, and had not ceased staring; Mrs. Ascher bent toward her with a mysterious air of complicity. "Sometimes," she added, "it's best to stop things altogether. Then I wear it inside out." Mrs. Ascher then fastidiously attached the faceless leather band to her other wrist, after which she leaned back with a fatigued but satisfied smile.

Without bothering to apologize, Ericka rose and ran up the staircase to the bedroom full of coats. She had trouble locating her own folded-up raincoat; in its commonplaceness it seemed to have disappeared beneath the vast pile of clothes. As she struggled with furs and alpacas, not wanting to dislodge the entire mass so that it all came crashing down, she heard through the hot air register, Ascher murmuring with exasperation: "What *difference* does it make? You don't really think she doesn't?" Followed by Deborah's strongly accented whisper: "Yes, but what about *me*." "*You!*" echoed Ascher, and there was a long silence. "What is it you *want* then?" Ascher exclaimed presently, forgetting to lower his voice. "But you're mad," protested Deborah in a whisper. "Suppose she comes in?" "Here?" "*Now?*" Ascher retorted. "She'd never dare..."

Trembling as if she were guilty of some secret crime, Ericka clutched her plastic raincoat, trying to keep it from rustling. "Wait..." whispered Deborah. Ericka's heart pounded with fear. She sped through the doorway, in such terror of being discovered by Ascher that she actually flipped off the lights in the hallway as she flew downstairs. She had safely reached the foot of the staircase when she found herself face to face with Mrs. Ascher. She believed now the entire household would surely explode into pieces, but to her surprise Gertrude said softly, her voice rising and falling with a mechanical regularity, as if some internal device had sanctioned these measured crises: "Oh, it's you, Ericka. Going already? I thought I heard Arthur cry out. I thought the children were awake. I thought they might want something."

"But they're spending the night..." began a well-meaning guest, looking hesitantly at Ericka. But Ericka did not exchange the look. Instead she bent over hastily and kissed her hostess. She discovered to her surprise that it was all she could do to refrain from throwing her arms around the woman and begging her pardon, begging her forgiveness for something she, Ericka, and all of them present, had somehow done to her. But she said only, with an intensity which frightened herself as she looked directly at her hostess, "Thank you, Mrs. Ascher. Thank you very much. It was a lovely party."

"So glad you enjoyed it. But I did think I heard the children," Mrs. Ascher added, as if irrelevantly. "Isn't that strange?" she asked, smiling at them—maternal, fond, collusive.

The Assassins

Les extrêmes se touchent.
— *Pascal*

In the middle of the deserted room you pause: there is no one, nothing. Did Alain never live here? You stand like a compass, equidistant from the four dark rings on the floor where only a month before, the bed—his and yours—stirred with your love. If you shut your eyes, Alain will at once be murmuring his litany, an elixir of love like honey running down the walls. You lift your head in response: you could sink to the floor and relive the act if you wished. But it would be childish; your problem is not sexual but psychic. Any fool or knave, as you have learned, can give you pleasure; but Alain's absence here is more than physical, it is total, psychic, annihilating.

It is possible they have assassinated him. Anything is possible, that is the terror of possibility. It is possible to see his hands tied behind his back, his body curved, a mute prenatal bow; his ankles bound: there is silence. Three men—no four, counting the one who is wearing black leather gloves as in old gangster films—surround him, pointing pistols at his head. There is an explosion, as in a Manet painting. Alain vanishes in a volley of smoke. The men climb into their ridiculous little black car which they have chosen because it is like hundreds of thousands scuttling through the streets—not like a car chosen by assassins. They leave Alain's head eyeless, a spilled dummy's. There is nothing, now, to distinguish him from any other victim; from, say, those murdered by the madman who attacks only drunken old men on park benches. Nothing, except that Alain is young, and in his wallet there are snapshots of yourself, one in shorts standing on the beach, the other taken as you emerged from the shower. For a moment you are torn between the terror of their recognizing you by your pictures and the conviction that your imagination is not being, as one says, overactive.

Your pulse pounding, you begin to search in the apartment for vital signs. There are no strong smells, only the odor of linoleum. No apple cores, cigarette butts or even, say, a broken mercurochrome bottle (Alain frequently cut himself shaving).

He has cut himself shaving and he is asking if you have seen his styptic pencil. You say, yes you have, you saw it roll under the tub. You hurry to help him find it before he leaves blood on the towels. He too dreads the sight of blood and you are always careful, during your period, not to probe but merely to dab between your legs. You bump into each other in the small bathroom while you kneel together to search under the claw-legged tub (a fleck of peeling paint falls on Alain's face and he complains, as always, about the landlord). Under the tub you find the relics—a candy wrapper, a band-aid preserved from the bathtub drain but which has now landed on the floor; also this time, an earring, made of two circles of gold, rather like those toys children play with, made of two bent nails. You have been missing the earring ever since the evening Peter was suddenly released from jail, the evening of the party at which you ended up with Pete, who used to be Greta's lover, and who abruptly became your lover (you were only trying to prove that you were free).

You are not to be thinking about freedom, however. You

are wasting time, what is needed is a systematic search. You are in this "vacated" apartment, you have found the apartment ruthlessly stripped of everything, though not by vandals. You are (you feel certain) about to come upon some message from Alain, which will be hidden in an obvious place overlooked by the three—no four—men in their eagerness to climb back into the ridiculous black car which they have chosen because it is like hundreds of thousands. From your central position amid black circles left by the legs of the bed, you can see the cabinet in the bathroom. The mirror is slowly swinging to and fro, and the scrawled letters mirrored from the wall are momentarily suspended in air, then slowly swing again: OT HTAED. But DEATH TO whom? Not to yourself, Caroline. Alain would not have left you such a message, so it can mean nothing to you, it is mere rhetoric, not a message of love which would be assuring you as it slowly returned on the pendulum of the mirror: .NIALA UOY EVOL I ENILORAC. Still, you tell yourself that your view of the systematically-ransacked apartment does not prove anything, it is not conclusive; you tell yourself that it is only your fear, your love, which is distorting Chaos into perfidies, executions, assassinations.

You will not think about that. In a moment you will find the message. Alain *has* left one, you say aloud—unless he does not wish you to know where he is, where they are. But that would be preposterous.

However: you have been away over a month, since shortly after the party which they (Greta and Koko and Deirdre and Liz and Moonface and Alain) gave for Peter on the evening he was unexpectedly released from jail; and Alain has many friends, friends you do not even see or know, cloistered as you are in the Children's Reading Room, where you resort to passive resistance in exhibits under glass: HERSTORY: A New Look for the Bi-Centennial; BOOKS ABOUT WOMEN: *Abigail Adams, Sojourner Truth, Martha Washington.* Coming here to this apartment, trying to blend invisibly into Alain's life and those of his friends—lives which seemed to you at once austere and exotic, full of secret activity and open hardship—you were like a leaf fallen accidentally into a raft heading for white water. Perhaps from among these friends, known and unknown, Alain has found someone who...Never mind. That will not be relevant here in this search where something more than hypotheses, suspicions, speculations, is needed.

At last, in the naked apartment you have found something—Alain's pipe, a favorite of his, he would not have left it behind. Unless (your scenario begins again) he was lying in bed, the pipe beside him on the floor when they arrived, those three—no four—men surrounding him, pointing pistols at his head. Fortunately, as on television, your scene is interrupted and the phone is ringing. It must be Alain, who else? He wishes to assure you all is well. You rush to the phone, breathe *hello*. For the first time in your life you are struck by the complete idiocy of saying *hello* to every random ring of the telephone. When you are expecting your lover's voice, what does *hello* mean? Does *hello* say anything? Does it express tenderness, concern, terror, jealousy? Does it ask, where are you? are you alone? why didn't you tell me? The emotions with which you pick up the phone resemble those of an anxious parent who has found her lost child and is now uncertain whether to caress him with relief or to punish him in anger. The need to caress is overwhelming: *Hello?* you breathe into the mouthpiece; and at the silence—a silence of thorns, of knives, of poison, of hatred which is patient, cunning and resourceful and which will wait any length for its revenge—at this silence which does not even breathe because it is not an obscene phone call, you realize that it is a trap : they are taping your voice, your easily identifiable voice. Now you know that Alain will not be here, will never be here again. Because Alain does not leave telephones connected (*fool! fool!*) when he abandons ("vacates"?) an apartment. Still, since it is already too late—like a gambler becoming reckless, risking all —you say again *Hello? Hello?* and slam the receiver down as if you are angry. You are not angry, you are terrified.

There it is again, that feeling of utter disgust which you felt upon finding yourself in Pete's bed, followed by anxious questions from Alain: What did Pete ask you? What did you tell him? Don't you remember anything? Jealous? Me? Don't be a fool! This is serious. I don't have time to be jealous. Jealousy is for people still playing games.

Like me, I suppose.

Yes, like you. What did you need him for? Did you need a good—?

Don't say it.

Well, what else was it?

I did it to be free. You are trying now to make it sound grand: you will never admit to him that you thought that he and Greta, who was really Pete's lover, were about "to become sexual partners" (as your friends say). That you wished to prove that you too can have "relationships" with another person without possessing him: neither your owning him, nor his owning you. You will not confess to the sadness and guilt you felt while with Pete—and certainly will never admit to having wished all the time Pete was caressing you that Pete would do what Alain did so well, but Pete did not know how. You do not explain this to Alain; you do not want to have to use the word "love" in explaining to Alain what Pete does not know.

Of course Pete knows other things very well. He is perhaps the most intellectual, the most articulate person in their circle. Really philosophically *aware,* you remember thinking before the two of you, as if by silent consent, moved to the kitchen. Before you chose freedom. While you were all sitting together on the floor.

You are all sitting together cross-legged, Indian style: Koko & Deirdre, Liz & Moonface, Alain & Caroline (yourself) and Pete & Greta. But Greta, who has been Pete's lover for two years—until this month when he was arrested and now suddenly released—now refuses to sit beside Pete and moves herself instead so that she is sitting beside Alain. A slight tremor begins within you as her bare toes touch Alain's arms;

and at times his elbows (accidently?) touch her bare toes as he speaks. He speaks almost as frequently as Pete. He is arguing with Pete who appears contemptuous of others, of all of us, for their/our pacifism.

A luxury of the intellectual middle class, he says.

A moral principle, says Alain.

A cop-out, retorts Pete. One thing he knows, he says, is that the other side is *not* nonviolent. While we're running our collective ass off trying to raise money, trying to get people to sign A Petition Against Torture in Greece, A Petition Against Torture in Spain, A Petition Against Torture in Chile, the other side is rattling their chains, collecting their dumdum bullets, firing with all their artillery. What you ought to face up to, he says, is that you're too chicken for a real job with real risks. He argues that they are very naive, that they don't understand the difference between Social Change in industrialized nations and Social change which must take place in a country of peasants.

You feel stirrings of guilt. For Pete is right, you are unwilling to break the law, you know that. You know also that it is a moral weakness on your part, that you ought to be willing to but you aren't, you're all hung up: having school teachers and ministers in your family did it to you: as a child you couldn't even break a window without offering to pay for it.

Alain and Greta exchange glances. Greta gets up to change the record, and when she sits down again it seems to you that she has moved imperceptibly closer to Alain: soon they will appear to you like a motorcycle couple. Greta's balance on the floor maintained only by her grasp around his waist. But not yet. Greta is merely rhythmically tapping Alain's thin, green-striped shirt (under which you know the skin is bare); the bottoms of her feet are grimy, as though she is determined to leave her imprint on the curve of Alain's back. Then, for a moment, Alain catches her bare foot in mid-air and steers it like a tiller till it rests on the floor. Peacefully he does it, without irritation, his eyes showing a touch of surprise at the smoothness of the scalloped arch. It is as if he expected Greta's soft skin to have been coarse and roughened as the hands with which Greta cleans house, and takes care of three children (two of them her own). Greta lives in a garage, she says, with three children, two cats, and a printing press which she inherited from her ex-husband who is now selling real estate in California.

While Alain is holding Greta's bare foot you turn your head away, the guilt of not being able to break a window without paying for it has merged with the guilt of your jealousy: a jealousy monogamous, elitist, possessive: You are guilty of wanting to "own" Alain—only you, only for yourself. It is involuntary, this jealousy, it is like saliva, a saliva of acid which corrodes your voice so that you can barely reply as Pete asks you

What do you think?

What do I think? Of what?

Of what we're talking about, for Chrissake. He looks at you as if you are an idiot.

Oh I agree. I agree. Anything to be distracted from the fact that Greta has now plainly moved slightly behind Alain, their legs forming a pair of V's, an elegant, graceful chevron. Alain's hips fit perfectly into the vise of space.

Rapidly you begin to tell Pete about the library, what days you work there, what the children are like, etc. But he wants to know about your commitment. Commitment to what? You are not sure. His eyes narrow with contempt, and you struggle to talk about something you think you are committed to. You are in the Movement, the Women's Movement, that is, you add inexplicably, as his eyes widen. Yes, you spend three hours a week answering the telephone and "cataloguing" the reading materials at the Center: yes, you do feel that what Pete says has some justification. He tries to pin you down, asks exactly what you mean, but the truth is you barely remember what he has said, and clearly his moral pulse demands that you do remember. But you can remember only that he has testified that you, all of you, are moral cowards because you are letting people die of torture merely because you won't get off your collective ass and do something. You are still not quite certain just how you are guilty of complicity in this torture, but Pete says never mind, forget it. And it is about then that he pats his shirt pocket and nods toward the kitchen, and you welcome now the opportunity to show that you are really free from middle-class hang-ups (your glance at Alain and Greta tells them—if they see you—to go ahead and do it right there on the floor if they want to, you won't care, they too are free). And sure enough you do not have to wait long to prove that you are free.

Pete is perhaps the most intellectual, articulate person among you, the most philosophically *aware*. You are more certain than ever of this as he points out that we're all friends here, nobody owns anybody. Only to prove it, you have to do it, otherwise what do you prove? Only that you're scared. So, after sharing his joint (rich, powerful stuff, Pete says, not for your ordinary pot-smoker), you assert that it's best not to own anybody, you want to give everybody their freedom, their... You forget what it is you want to give them, you float, you laugh, you giggle, you love everybody, there is not a mean bone in your body, you say. Except *moi-ine*, says Pete, with a cockney accent meant to be funny, and it is funny, wildly so, and you both slip to the floor helpless with laughter, and Pete is ineffectually trying to loosen his belt when Koko looks into the kitchen and says, hey you horny devils why don't you get into the bed? I need to get to the refrigerator. So still giggling, silently, helplessly, you and Pete go to bed together, the bed from whose four circles you now stand equidistant, wondering whether the phone will ring again and if—

But when Alain asks you, did he ask you any questions, you really, no, really cannot remember.

What questions? Why would he ask me questions? We were—

Cut that out. I know how you were, I don't need a blow by blow description. All I want to know is, did you tell him anything?

What could I tell him? What do I know? It is not meant to be facetious, you are genuinely troubled by the notion that you might know something you ought not to know, that others might want to know. Thoughtfully you touch your ear as if considering what you might have said, but the truth is you haven't a clear recollection of much except the rush of a velvet curtain brushing across your ear as you lay laughing helplessly on the kitchen floor, and now as you touch your ear, you are also aware that you have lost an earring.

You were so stoned he could have yanked it right out of your ear, you wouldn't have felt a thing.

You suspect that Alain is hoping that truly you did not feel a thing, but you are not going to let him off that easy, you want him to feel what you feel, a wretched guilty mouthful of jealousy, bitter as bile, so you say that's not true, you weren't so stoned as all that, that you knew what you were doing and you would have felt it, would *definitely* have felt it if someone—

Then why can't you remember what you said? Alain asks.

Finally you are reduced to lying. He didn't ask me anything (did he? you ask yourself).

Alain rests his head in the palm of his hand, as if weighing it. Then, exactly as in your present scenario, the telephone rings. It is Greta, and Alain explains to her that you are O.K., there is nothing to worry about, and he will call her back later. Take care, he says.

You are enormously relieved that everything is O.K. And you and Alain make love to prove that everything is as before: everything is O.K., you say, no hard feelings, you sleep with Greta, I sleep with Peter, maybe later Caroline (yourself) will sleep with Greta, and Koko and Deirdre will also realize how easy it is to be loving and comradely and sharing and we will all regularly switch partners. Your addled tongue runs on: we will be a regular non-profit organization for Loving...But your voice, which has begun with philosophical conviction, has risen to shrill complaint, accusation. This is partly because Alain, after an exhausting effort, has not achieved the reassuring climax you needed to rend from him because of your body's unreconstructed belief, in spite of your philosophical conviction, that it is yours alone to give him, not anybody else's. He lies quietly looking at you, listening to you, still alert and excited, but somehow he has managed not to share himself with you. And now he is asking you to do them all a great favor.

Them all? You don't want me to rob a bank, do you? You both know you are being funny, you couldn't take a cheap ballpoint pen from the bank, when you go to the teller's window you are always careful to lay down the pen after using it, if only to avoid the embarrassment of someone calling after you, *pardon me miss*—

I want you to go away—for a while, he adds, when he sees that in spite of your every effort at control, the tears have sprung to your eyes. You are utterly stunned. Is it a command or a tender, bitter love-push intended to turn you around in the right direction, back to him?

You mean—

I want you out of the way. I can't have you just messing around...

Me? *Messing?* You try to sound indignant, to point out that it is he who started it all, with Greta. But you're not sure you're both talking about the same thing. Does he mean that about...with Pete? You decide not to ask, you prefer to have even his indictment ambiguous, clinging to your confusion as if it were a veil which might suddenly part and reveal to you, very clearly, Alain's love.

Take a vacation. It's *time* for you to have a vacation. Good time of year and all that. School out, not so many kids at the library. Demand it. You can arrange it. If not, play sick. But it's time for us to get away from each other...so we can think things through...A vacation...in Mexico, maybe. You've always wanted to see—

But Alain, why are you doing this to me? The anguish is choking you; but you try to remain calm, he likes you to be calm—not "vulnerable."

Because...I love you.

You are distrustful of this answer, it is too easy. But if you love me, why are you punishing me? Why are you sending me away? Can't I know why you are doing this to me?

He hesitates, then says softly, like a litany, There is no need for you to know.

The phone is ringing again, and this time you do not answer it. You understand who it is, though you do not understand why. It is not Alain whom you still see in your mind's eye as bound hand and foot, his eyeless sockets speaking to you, assuring you that it has always been this way, that there have always been three—no four—men, one wearing black leather gloves, that it is not anything he cannot bear, he is inured to suffering, and now go back to your library, Caroline, where you will be safe.

But you cannot bear this image. You turn your back on the phone which is ringing through the apartment like a fire alarm, and you abandon the room with the four circles annealed to the floor like ancient scars. Slowly, avoiding the clattering sound your sandals usually make, you descend the stairs. Directly below Alain's apartment you notice that someone new has moved in: a man, who leaves his door ajar as you make your way down, an ordinary man with a clean-shaven face so anonymous that afterwards you cannot recall his features but only that you glimpsed on the floor (the apartment was unfurnished) a newly-installed telephone, bright and black, the receiver off the hook. Upstairs you can hear the telephone ringing through the deserted apartment, and you know that it will not stop ringing until the anonymous unmemorable man in the doorway has replaced his receiver.

Thus you are neither totally surprised nor entirely unprepared when they come to your new address to question you. You are sufficiently intelligent to know that you need not say a word to them, that they are neither judge nor jury but only an insinuating, intimidating and invisible force. You know now that you should not have returned, that you would be better off strolling along the *avenidas*, looking just like any other tourist. But here you are, Alain's woman—and where is he? It is true that you do not have to tell them anything, but it is also true that they will never tell you anything about Alain—and where is he?. When the subpoena arrives a few hours before you are summoned to appear, you feel, in spite of your trepidation, an excitement: perhaps now at last you will learn what they have done to Alain, those four men who have dicovered your snapshots in Alain's wallet, one of you in shorts standing on the beach, the other taken as you emerged from the shower. You dress nervously but impeccably for the grand jury, you are not going to let them use your appearance against you; and you are glad you have done so when, in the anteroom, you see the Judge, for you see that neatness and modesty are not irrelevant here. The Judge speaks to you gently, confidentially, as though you are his own daughter, assuring you that your testimony is (probably) not even of sufficient importance to warrant your taking the Fifth, so he has granted you immunity, so now you are free to say what you like, nothing to be afraid of.

But you are more afraid of this courteous, kindly, ruddy-faced interpreter of Solon than any mugger, and you thread your voice carefully with deference, as if he were your minister-father, your schoolteacher aunts and uncles. You do not know what Alain has done and you do not care; according to your scenario he has already paid for it, lying somewhere bound hand and foot, his head exploding beneath the white dust of—

But now a friendly-looking matron, a court aide, touches you on the sleeve of your respectable seersucker suit, remarking that you look to be a decent sort, not the kind to get mixed up with a bunch of bandits. Bandits? Alain? Pete? Koko? You feel you will faint but instead you take a deep breath as the matron points the way into the courtroom, where it is being explained to someone that this is not a criminal trial but merely an investigation and that is why the witness (that is, you, Caroline) does not need a lawyer present, though you might have had one (outside the courtroom) if you had wished, and you would have wished, but there was no time, and now you are so confused, all you can rely on is...

You asked to be seated.

And now all the figures in your scenario have vanished and in their places are the Judge, the Court Stenographer (Male), the Prosecuting Attorney—and Pete. Pete is standing slightly behind the Prosecuting Attorney, and between his fingers he is turning slowly, very slowly, as if he wishes to be certain you have recognized it, your missing earring. Then he quietly turns to leave the courtroom, abandoning you to the Judge, the Prosecuting Attorney, to Yourself, and to the Stenographer whose broad fingers on the black stenotype machine are still tapping out Pete's long list of credentials: in Greece, in Spain, in Chile...And in this simple tableau you now perceive who they are, the three men—no four, counting the man at the small black stenotype machine—who have bound Alain hand and foot and are now pointing pistols at his head. And you know at last what you did not need to know, only thank God, you do not really know, thank God, you did not need to know, and will never know. Never.

The Exile

I f one of those Mexican or Negro girls answered the door, Giersche knew she would not buy any needles from him; the maids never bought any, but merely looked at him, helpless and consolatory. They were obviously bewildered by the apparition of a clabber-voiced old man, his hair tasselled in whitish strands around the naked crown, sweating like a dray horse, and dry-mouthed from the Texas dust—selling needles. The maids naturally could not afford to buy his needles, but once a compassionate hand, daguerreotyped in brown and white, had reached out to him with a glass of water, the girl herself not asking him in, but standing uneasily on the other side of the screen door while gusts of air conditioning in a veritable ocean gale blew impotently upon the summer heat. When he had begun selling needles a couple of months ago, during those first panicked hours when the clerk had handed him the remains of his social security check fatally reduced by his drug bills for digitalis, he had at first maintained a mildly ironic view: he had seen, with something of amusement, that he had made a strong impression upon the women at the door; and his sense of the dramatic had been sharpened by his consciousness of having risen, successfully, to a crisis.

164

But now the humor, however grotesque, had vanished and he grimly awaited the passage of two more broiling months before he would be able to receive sixty-three dollars a month under the state classification: "Totally and Permanently Disabled." The golden prospect had been marred somewhat by his friend Tom-the-Antique-Man's mordant prophecy:

"Boy, you couldn't tag that title on me for *no* amount of money. Why Ben, *everybody* around here knows you can't get that money unless you ready to die for it. My own daughter-in-law, she worked at the State Capitol, she told me that ninety per cent of those guys die first year they get it. Now is sixty-three dollars worth that much to you?"

After that whenever he passed Tom's secondhand junk store, his friend would yell at him: "Buyin' anything, today, Ben? Say, how about this nice secondhand tombstone here—I'll give you a good price on 'im."

"Naw, I'm too young to die," Giersche would retort. The date on the cracked stone alongside a German lady's name in Gothic letters was 1879.

"I'll change the date for you!" Tom would yell after him...

He was no longer certain now as he had been in April that he could earn about two dollars a day canvassing. The first box of needles, which he had purchased for a quarter from the desperately shaking hand of an alcoholic, had seemed an economic inspiration. They were portable, very cheap, and his stock could easily be replenished from McCrory's Variety Store. The big trouble, he allowed himself to complain as he waited for an answer to his ring, was that people just weren't used to vendors any more. After the First War, a lot of veterans had had little suitcase-style kits and shoe horns; and they would even give you a Free Weather Almanac. Nowadays people preferred to do all their shopping in a basket at the supermarket.

"Miz Ritchie, she ain't never home on Tuesday afternoons and besides, she don't use none of that stuff. She mostly has all her clothes made for her down by that Petite Maison, you know there on Nueces Avenue?" The way she said it, his north Michigan mind had noted, sounded like "wazes av-nooo?" and he found himself resting pleasurably, like a dozing fly caught in the web of her speech, smiling at her as if he were an accomplice, in spite of the tremor of exhaustion passing through his body as the heat boiled up around him from the flagstones. He wondered whether the girl would offer him a glass of water, but before he had time to articulate his thought, the door had closed upon him and he turned to face Hillcrest Road alone. For a moment he envied the Negro girl her luxurious servitude—a cool place and plenty to eat in a well-furnished house (he had glimpsed the modish Danish chairs and the womblike silences of wall-to-wall carpeting). A quick but experienced glance at the house allowed him to estimate the number of rooms, and he found himself calculating the air-conditioning costs for a house this size. It must cost them over fifty dollars a month just to keep cool, or nearly the whole of his social security check every month. The startling fact had for him the effect of a drug to his brain. It made income, expenses, luxuries, all dovetail into a standard of living that was like a glimpse of paradise. Within him, physical weariness, coupled with a longing for a paradise of his own, merged momentarily—lethean as the summer sun—melting his will. What he felt was an unexpected craving for sleep, the desire to return to his barren room and sink into its dark lonely heat as into a dream. Even hunger held not so deep a pang as this, the longing to escape...Then after a long, dark sleep he would wake, drenched in sweat, but brought back to life by the sound of the New Orleans saxophone several blocks north on Red River; and he would take out his dinner of hard-boiled eggs from the top drawer of his bureau and go across the street to talk to Tom, who would be just pulling in his chairs for the evening. Perhaps a friend of theirs would pass; jokes would be exchanged. Loneliness would pass—time itself...and he would have survived the day to sell needles again tomorrow.

He began to reason with himself, like a man in a mist trying to discern his own headlight. Today was Tuesday; he had earned two dollars, which could carry him through Friday. But if for any reason he should not sell any needles between now and Friday, it would make it necessary for him to come out again on Saturday: the mere scarcities of the weekend would have dwindled to dangerous deprivations by Monday. And Saturdays were the worst days for selling: weekend kitchen-help blocking the threshold like cows, and the lady of the house busily engaged in work she had postponed during the week. With a great sigh, all the forces of reason united to persuade him that it would be best to try to sell at least one more packet of needles.

He picked his way with the utmost care down the gravelled path, because the one thing he hated—he made the philosophical point to himself in dialogue with the universal You—was getting those sharp stones in your shoes, under the arch of your sandals. Cut like the devil, then you had to sit by the side of the road, taking your shoes off. Made you feel ridiculous. One thing he had not yet become accustomed to in the nine years since he had left Michigan was this not having sidewalks in the suburbs. People down here just grew grass right down over the curb. True, the grass-covered area was public property, a full three feet off the curb, but it didn't *feel* public. Somebody else had planted the grass; somebody else had watered it and cut it and had kept the hot sun from burning it up, and had raked the leaves off of it: it was theirs, then. He had owned his own five acres of land, but that was before the Depression had brought tomatoes down to a quarter a bushel, and he had always believed in the right to nail a No Trespassing sign on your own tree: now it made him feel guilty to be walking on other people's grass.

And expensive grass too. He made a distinct effort this time to refrain from estimating, as he approached the corner lot, the cost of the gallons and gallons of water spiralling upward in snakelike revolutions and falling with a hiss on the green turf.

There was a girl on the front walk who reminded him a bit of his Susie at that age; she was wearing a yellow bathing suit and pushing a tricycle around with her small, white feet. To his shame he realized that she was watching him curiously. He noticed with surprise as he followed her stare that the buckle of his sandal had broken off and that a day's walking had grimed his toes with slightly comic circles of black. He wondered then, for the first time that day, if he had not sacrificed dignity for comfort in the upward roll of his cuffs which were now unravelling clownishly round his ankles.

"Mama's busy," the child intercepted him in a shrill, challenging voice before he could ring the bell. "My cousin from California's here, and we're havin' a party. They're all out back swimmin'. Nobody's in the house but Lola Mae."

The girl's protest made it clear that the rustic pine fence which he had thought separated the corner house from its neighbor encircled a swimming pool; he could hear the sounds of laughter, of splashing water, and the yap-yap of a small dog.

He started to approach the gate to the pool, but something in the spiteful tone of the child's voice discouraged him; he had been walking six hours, and had no more strength for the bravado of salesmanship: the quip and the rally and the elegant evasion. He turned instead toward the bench at the bus stop across the street, limping painfully where his bad knee had begun to gnaw like a toothache; he shoved the remaining five packets of needles into his pants pocket, mopping his brow at the same time with a great, knobby handkerchief.

Texas summers had become too much for him, but there was nothing for him to return to in Michigan. And it had been a smart idea of Big Bill's, after Susie's death, for him to stay on here a few more years, establishing residence for the TPD pension. The only thing Bill had not foreseen was the need in the past year for two kidney operations: even now his back ached, and from time to time he had fever.

He pulled the yellow bus schedule from his pocket. Crestview, Northwest Park, East End. He had a fifty-minute wait; it was bad luck, too, the bench being on the sunny side of the street. There was a flowering pecan right outside the fence around that swimming pool; but he was afraid they would think him some kind of half-cracked peeping Tom if he were to sprawl out under the tree. Besides, he vaguely resented the people in that house; it was as if they had done him an injury once long ago, which still rankled...The yapping of the dog he had heard—he saw now between the cracks of the fence—was that of a black poodle who had paused on the diving board while everybody—except those who were eating and drinking— was trying to coax it to jump. "Jump, baby, jump! Come awn darlin'—jump so's everybody can see you!" The dog must have jumped because he soon heard everybody laughing and applauding and the dog scampered around with a biscuit in his mouth.

All the drinking and laughing from the swimming pool made him feel guilty somehow, as if he hadn't managed things very well to be sixty-three years old and sitting all alone waiting for nothing except to be a little older. It made him feel like one of those welfare cases back in the Depression. He hadn't had much respect for those people back then: he and Emmy had always hoed their own row, the two of them pitching in and making fried pies for a while, using up all the fruit Emmy had stored from the farm and even some squash and pumpkin; and for a couple of years in the Thirties they had sold buttermilk in big five gallon cans to the Negroes of Detroit's Black Bottom, who had paid him in welfare tickets worth ten cents a piece. It seemed to him his tired body could still remember hosing those cans in the garage till long after midnight; and Emmy claiming, as her face grew flushed with fever that she *liked* to sit out there for company, trying to keep warm by the Franklin stove...One winter, when there had been nothing else, he had shoveled snow out in the Grosse Pointe area; but the high school kids had soon taken over the snow shoveling, they could do it so much faster...Those had been hard years between losing the farm and getting his first war job in the River Rouge plant, yet he thanked God he had never taken charity.

He had to admit that the hardest thing he had ever had to do was learn to work at that Ford plant: no sun, no land, no animals, nothing growing to your hand, no smell of dirt, no long silences suddenly shredded by the whoop of birds—nothing but the grit and tear of the sanding machine, the hellfire of the welder. He had already been too old to fight in the Second War, even if they had been willing to overlook his bad knee; but he was proud that he had been part of the arsenal for democracy, that in his fight for the Four Freedoms, he had once worked 101 consecutive days. Yes, he was still proud of that.

He shaded his eyes to peer into the wavery mirages down the street; the white heat waves in the glaze of afternoon sometimes looked like the bus coming over a hill. No bus—and he was "sure 'bout to burn up," as his friend María would say: the words now seemed to have a wholly literal ring. The water across the street, gizzling and hissing as it lashed its way across the grass, whipped him with thirst. He was tempted to cross the street now and kneel down as he would to a drinking fountain, and lap up some of that water; but pride held him fast...A good thing too, because there was the bus roaring in front of him...He must have fallen asleep.

Or could he have blacked out? he considered in panic. For suddenly it was extremely difficult for him to get the twenty-five cents out of his little leather purse while the bus turned, growling and curving toward Lamar Boulevard. And it seemed to him people were watching him, faintly disquieted by his appearance. He must be having a dizzy spell, else why were they staring? Had he or had he not yet put his quarter into the box? With a burst of decision that risked half the price of a hot lunch, he threw in two dimes and a nickel.

He felt tremulous but somehow triumphant as he sat down; evidently all was as it should be. Only falling asleep in the sun like that hadn't been good for him; he had sweated so hard he could feel the sog of perspiration through his clothes. At least people were no longer staring at him, that was good.

He was replacing his leather purse when he first noticed the small spreading spot. For seconds he sat in fascination till the darkness grew to medallion size, then to his horrified eyes seemed to grow wide as the dark side of the moon...and all the while, there had been no signal to his brain, reporting this treachery of the weakened flesh. Overwhelmed by a sense of public decency, hiding his body like a man naked in a crowd, he doubled over against the wall of the bus, jackknifing his legs together to conceal his shame. In a posture of rapt curiosity, he leaned out of the window staring at the ambulatory patients on the grounds of the State Mental Hospital on Lamar Boulevard.

In spite of the shame of his accident, the sight of these estranged figures shocked him into a relative calm; they laved his self-esteem with a consciousness of mental faculties still intact—yes, good for years to come, he assured himself. So long as a man could think his own thoughts, he reasoned, *real* thoughts—and yes, even live his own shame, he was still among the accountable. He watched the patients as they drifted unattended but aimless around the carpeted grass; the rosebush patches festooning the barbed wire every six feet merely added a note of wily-minded horror to the fact that behind that chainlink fence, fragmented minds, emptied of all desire but stillness, paced their pens like tranquilized steer. Doubtless he was not the physical man he had been, but he thanked God that he was still on this side of the dividing wire; he still knew the difference between right and wrong; he still knew what was the correct thing for a gentleman to do in public: and he had sense enough to know his shame was gratuitous—that though his kidney was weak, his mind was as strong as that chainlink fence.

Indeed Emmy would have been proud of him if she could have known how he had stood up under it all; she was never one to whine. He had even managed the funeral himself because Big Bill had been in a state of shock; and he helped his son-in-law pack and get off to the Air Force in Germany. He would never have believed, as he recalled Bill's skeletal face looking into the open grave, that within two short years Bill would be married again. It was too bad, he thought: he missed Bill's letters...He was thinking about those letters when he realized he had lost his needles. Frantically he emptied his pockets, even pulled open his shirt to grope inside. He looked stupidly down at his shoes, at his empty hands. Thrown out beside him on the seat lay his possessions: his purse, his handkerchief, a picture of his daughter before her death, the skeleton key to his room, and the yellow bus schedule. No needles. He jumped up.

"Stop the bus. I have to get off!"

"Take it easy. I can't stop in the middle of this traffic— y'think I'm crazy?"

He stood desperately peering over the driver's shoulder, gripping the bars like a man in prison.

"Where are we now? How far are we?"

"How far from where, Pop? Where y'going?"

"I'm not going that way. I want to go back. I want to get off."

"O.K. O.K. Mind your step. Don't fall, there."

A bluish-haired lady, immaculately clean, had run after him in the street, was handing him the treasures he had left on the seat of the bus; he noticed his shredding leather purse in her white glove.

"Thank you, ma'am." In horror he picked up his items one by one from her outstretched hand, trembling at what he had nearly lost...Fear washed over him, turning his flesh to water: was he growing forgetful, incompetent, senile? He stared around him. He had not realized they had gone so far; already they had circled the Capitol Building. Perhaps it was already too late to get back to that house with the swimming pool...And then, too, it would mean another fifty cents bus fare. For a moment it was his inability to make a decision which frightened him most of all.

He limped over to the grass of the State Capitol, just off Congress Avenue. He rested there a while, his elbows sunken dejectedly between his knees; when a policeman paused to look at him, he scrambled guiltily to his feet, he did not know why.

The ability to think oozed slowly back to his brain as he fingered the purse containing, thank God, a dollar and seventy-five cents. With a wrench of self-mastery he decided that what he must do was walk to McCrory's, just six blocks south. He would buy some more needles, and for twenty-three cents María at the lunch counter would fix him a hamburger that would carry him through the night. Then he would be able to return to his room to sleep, to a darkness warm and deep as life itself.

It was nearly closing time when he staggered into McCrory's. He was dry, exhausted, and the sight of María standing on a stool as she cleaned out the coffee urns made him feel like a man who had come home.

In the last four years he had become fond of her round, familiar face, just as he had grown to rely on the familiar face of his friend Tom in the antique shop, or as he had become dependent on the conventional nod of the postman who brought his checks with exquisite regularity: and he had learned, even, to care for people whose lives remained anonymous to him, but whose continued and invariable presence helped him to preserve his own identity.

María, he guessed, was no younger than he, but she looked a healthy fifty and could still get a job. Quickly she fixed his hamburger—he looked around him carelessly, not noting how she first glanced down the counter, then slapped two meat patties together; then he turned to watch her as she stepped back on the stool and reached her arm deep into the coffee urn, the floating flesh of her arms converging with the invisible boundaries of her bosom, so that her whole body seemed to swell into imagined eiderdowns of repose.

"You bring me the eggs, you want me to boil 'em," she reminded him. "I gotta cook for myself anyway, so bring 'em early. Then I don' use the gas anymore after supper—make it too hot."

Then "Bye-bye, Ben," she called out to him as he rose to

go, helping to identify him as a customer to the manager who stood at the main register, "I sure do thank you..."

He moved then to the other side of the store where he waited for service. The dime stores these days were partly self-service, and he was never sure whether he was supposed to get an article and take it down to the main register at the entrance, or to wait for one of those little Mexican girls. They were young girls, scarcely out of junior high, but it always seemed to him as if they had been working in dime stores all their lives. He noticed a bell on the counter with a card propped under it which said: If you wish to have customer service please ring bell. He smacked the bell with the palm of his hand, feeling a certain childish satisfaction from the sharp dissonance which rebounded from the empty aisles. Uneasily he looked around; not a soul issuing from the checkered layout of the empty store. The whole place was like some lavish make-believe, filled with squares and shelves and roundnesses of color, all for illusion...He stood listening and waiting, forcing his face into a picture of good nature in order to meet their impatience.

As he stood there, his eyes travelled impatiently up the corridor where he saw no one, and back again to the counter, the spectacle of whose array reminded him that he needed a few things, razor blades, one of those dime ball-points, some athlete's foot powder—but he steered his gaze resolutely away. He had learned too well the panic that followed impulsive indulgence before the first of the month. Over there at the end of the counter, half-hidden by the overflowing artificial flower display, were his kind of needles: sewing Susans—Seventy Gold Eye Needles, with Threader. He limped over wearily, as to a familiar face amid so many meretricious lures; he picked up and flipped through a stack of them, making a random count as they flew by, quick as a pack of cards beneath the dealer's expert thumb. More needles, all together, than he had sold since May—and five times cheaper than he had to charge...An inexplicable nausea fluttered at his stomach as the unanswerable question rose: why, then, should

anyone buy needles from *him?* He continued waiting, continued pushing the question down, deep into the consciousness of the Giersche who had never accepted charity; and
while he waited, there arose again that wave of nausea which
he recognized now as denial, and which rose again and again
involuntarily to his gorge while he stood there waiting, as it
seemed to him, for his strength to ebb away—waiting, always,
for his life to begin before it ended.

People paid him a dollar for needles they would never
use, that was the truth of it. They left, momentarily, their
swimming pools and flagstone patios, their cooled kitchens
and pine-panelled dens, their soundless carpeting, their
ambience of unemphatic command—and sticking their hand
out the door, gave him a dollar for Sewing Susans which they
tossed into a drawer never to be remembered. He saw now
that they did this out of pity and guilt, vaguely hoping that he
would survive. He envied them their margin of mercy, envied
them, too, because they would never go begging at the homes
of others, deceiving themselves that penury was pride. At the
same time the realization of his beggary, the mingled charity
and insult of their dollars rang like thunder in his brain.
Shame, swift as vertigo, scalded him; sweat and dark shadows
passed over his vision: it was such shame as a man might die of
if he accepted it; so in hot resistance he fastened his
resentment upon it, exacerbated it in quick self-defense to a
sense of outrage, cauterized it to sheer hate...

They had insulted and injured him, depriving him of all
that kept a man from death and exiled him to loneliness and
old age. And they were the same people who kept him here
now, waiting, in deprivation and exhaustion. They did not
need him; they could afford to ignore him forever, having
deprived him of everything, they had left him—these needles.
He began to pick up the needles in handfuls, his mouth
moving grotesquely at the absurd notion that these trifles had
been offered to him in return for all that he had lost; he shoved
them into his pockets, indifferent to their bulk as if they had
been cobwebs cleaned out from his past. As he stuffed his

pockets he stared idiotically at the old man in the mirror alongside him—at his dusty, dirty, hungry, hollow-eyed and terrifyingly risible face of a clown. He grimaced, squeezing the tears out at the corners—lifeless jellies.

His sense of insignificance was so abject that at first he failed to see how any action of his could have called for the authoritative haste of the salesgirl who, he now realized, was heading his way with a perturbed and angry expression. He thought at first of articulating an explanation for his folly—he must look like a madman with his pants billowing out; but then he began moving as fast as he could toward the exit as he realized that even his travesty of rebellion had become a crime...His walk became a jerky shamble as he projected his elbows to give himself balance and momentum, his head poking forward like a bird, and his burning face above all avoiding her baleful eye.

"Can I he'p you?" She was following along, briskly, not letting him out of her sight, her voice harsh, suspicious.

No, no, nothing...Never mind. He felt for the second time that day, the perspiration at his back, the sudden drench of fear and confusion...But she was no longer looking at him; she was waving her hand in a kind of salute to a whiskery, conch-headed fish of a man with frameless lenses on his nose, who stood staring at them from behind the reef of his cash register. He ran...looking, he hoped, like a simple, white-haired old man bravely making his way back to oblivion; but the girl was calling "Stop him!" and so he paced himself to a broken gallop, hurling himself upon the swinging door with a sharp, stinging crack of his knee.

"Stop him!"

The girl herself was after him now as he tried to merge with the five o'clock crowd, tried like a man bent on suicide to cast himself into a moving bus, clutching the doorhandle of the half-shut door.

"He took somethin'. Search him—I saw him—his pockets. Turn him over, you'll fin' it!"

Kicking furiously at their groping, depredating hands,

spitting in his rage at the faces so cruelly and stupidly bent over him, he rolled in the dust. They pulled the needles from his pockets; they pulled out his skeleton key, his little leather purse, his plasticized picture of Susie; then they tried to pull him around to his feet, to face the crowd; but he lay there stiff and immovable as death, his head covered with his hands, sobbing. He heard María saying:

"He lives near me, I know him three, four years..."

In America Begin
Responsibilities

Whenever Jacob spoke of the past, he would begin, always, with a description of his Bar Mitzvah, as if his life had not begun till then. For what he remembered most clearly from his youth was the little synagogue in Vilna where his widowed mother sat upstairs in the women's section watching him, with tears of joy in her eyes. From time to time wiping her cheeks with her handkerchief, roughly, as a woman does who has never known vanity. On her head she wore a grey wig, a *sheitel,* as all pious Jewish women did, her long hair having been cut when she became a bride; and over the wig, her Sabbath kerchief. He, Jacob, proudly kissed his *tallis,* the corner of which he had but a few seconds before touched to the Torah. It was his day of triumph, and before all the congregation he had recited aloud in Hebrew, his prepared commentary on the Law. He, the orphaned son of Velvel the glazier, had learned to read Hebrew—at what sacrifice only his mother who plucked chickens all day long for Shmuel, the ritual slaughterer, would ever know.

At times, when he had been as yet too young to remain home alone, or simply when he had hurt himself and had the vague longing to be near his mother, he would enter the ritual slaughterer's hut and, squatting by the door to escape the fetid air, he would watch his mother. The place was an inferno of dying fowl, of floating feathers flecked with red, of the scorched smell of pin feathers. From morning to night, every day except the Sabbath, his mother plucked, plucked, at the yellow flesh of birds, her own bloodstained fingers perpetually covered with white cotton-like feathers—her long white apron like a shroud dirked with blood.

Shmuel the ritual slaughterer would first slit the throat of the animal, then stuff it by its warty yellow black feet between the tight rim of the barrel, from out of whose depths Jacob could distinguish the rhythmic *cuk-cuk* of flying feathers, the drip of blood, and the spasmodic jerk of the expiring fowl as it thrashed itself more speedily to death.

At last, with a sigh his mother would hold the freshly dressed animal over the fires, and, while scaling the skin from its legs with one hand, she would say: "A nice Shabbos it'll be for them, *nu*—do you know how many geese they eat every year?" He and his mother had never eaten goose; in fact, they had considered themselves lucky when now and then some new bride, anxious to show how prosperous her husband was, would abandon, with a look of disgust, the peeled legs and slithering giblets. Then his mother would cook a fricassee for the Sabbath, more delicious than all the chicken he had eaten since in America. And they would have *challah* for the Sabbath too, as white as pollen, though they might have only black rye, if anything, during the week. In fact, during the War, they had come close to starvation. Had it not been for the herring or carp he would sometimes catch in the river near Vilna, they would perhaps, like the starving Gentiles, have eaten the dead horses, frozen in the snow. That is, Jacob would probably have eaten them; his mother would sooner have starved.

For weeks while the Germans had been advancing, they had lived on kasha and chicory coffee, so in spite of the cold he would often remain at the river the entire day in the hope of catching something. How clearly he remembered that bitter December day, nearly thirty years ago, when he had left his mother before dawn to go fishing. She lay in her bed weak and feverish, as he had thought, from hunger; so with stubborn determination he had remained at the river even longer than usual in the desperate hope of catching a carp, a tench...But when a wolf came lopping across the frozen river, he had finally run home in terror; it was only later that he had realized that it had probably not been a wolf at all but one of the savagely hungry dogs which roamed Russia during the war, abandoned and predatory as wolves.

From the moment he had approached the room which he and his mother occupied, he had smelled death. His mother lay on the wretched sofa whose sawdust entrails he could still remember, with their springs jutting out on either side of her. But she did not feel them. The filth and horror of cholera clung to her garments, to her rancid tongue; her stomach was swelled with black inexpurgable wind. He had not dared to touch her, but with a shriek of terror he had run to fetch the doctor. They had quarantined the whole building, and during the health inquiries, the government had wrenched him, Jacob, from out of the home of a neighbor, where he was hiding, and thrown him into the army.

In the army Jacob discovered that a uniformed Jew is a perversion of Nature; for the Jews are a people of the Book, and how had the Book, with its eternally unanswerable questions, prepared him to be a soldier? For a soldier is an animal with legs; he walks, he falls down, he shoots or gets shot at. For Jacob to be a soldier was an inversion of Universal Order: he could not think with his legs, which melted under him at the first cannon fire.

In his ignorance he believed the Czar's empire to be perpetual, and never dreamed that within a matter of months—soldiers, sailors, prisoners, peasants, Jews—all would be thrown into the precarious liberty of revolution. So rather than endure the life of a Jewish soldier, subjected to the cruelty of officers who treated him like a broken toy which could nevertheless be wound up and made to go at their caprice, he determined to starve...He lay in his barracks, reduced to the weight of an empty barrel, the mere staves of a man—till they dragged him out one night and poured sausage soup down his throat. He tried to set his jaw against them, but if he did not swallow, they said, they would fix the circumcised Jew once and for all.

A man may want to die; but there is something in him that recoils with violence at the thought of dying a sexless eunuch. So Jacob swallowed the soup and began sewing his roubles, one by one, into the lining of his clothes. Then at last one day he succeeded in establishing contact with a civilian named Drobninsky who had himself lived in New York City for a while and who now made his living by aiding Jews to escape: first from the army, then from Russia forever.

Drobninsky's method was simple but daring. Disguised as a civilian the desperate refugee would pitch himself toward the border—by droshky, by cart, by rail or by foot, until he reached the free port of Danzig. There Drobninsky would appear after a few days and would arrange for his departure for America by ship. Drobninsky warned him that the escape was dangerous; if the soldiers stopped him and discovered his desertion, they were liable to shoot him like a dog; but Jacob was adamant. His heart yearned for freedom. He said he would risk his life again and again if necessary to escape this hell. Besides, he was alone. He left no one to mourn for him.

"Alone? Alone?" repeated Drobninsky sadly. "Ah, how well I know what that means, to be in America alone. No, alone you should not be. You need somebody to take care of you. You want to study in a yeshiva house, then you still need a bowl of *lokshen* soup now and then, a place to sleep. What do you think, Jacob, to a wife? It's a good idea, you can't imagine. For a young boy in America there can be plenty of *tsoris* if he has nobody to keep him out of trouble. Let me write to my brother in New York, eh Jacob? I'll arrange everything—the passport—the bride. Only give me now a small down payment, and when you get to be a millionaire in America, you can give me a rouble now and then."

And true to his word, Drobninsky applied himself

conscientiously to the problems of immigration, including the marriage contract with the girl who was to be Jacob's bride: Bashe Gilmansky. So that there would be no misrepresentation —the applicants must be mutually assured of good health without deformities—photographs were to be exchanged. Drobninsky grunted with a paternal smile as he gazed down approvingly at Jacob's photograph: "With a face like that she'll have nothing what to complain."

Such talk, however, was a purely theoretical discussion of Paradise to Jacob until Drobninsky could effect his escape from the military. To this end, the cunning Drobninsky, with the organizational sense of a general, carefully selected a secondhand suit: "Too new it can't be," he explained. "They'd spot you in a minute in a new suit. No, it must be just a plain, nice suit." This suit, along with a pair of civilian shoes, Drobninsky carefully wrapped in a large bath towel such as the Russian soldiers were allotted at the turnstile when once monthly they were issued permits to attend the baths.

Thus, on that day when for the last time Jacob stripped himself of his uniform in the bathhouse, Drobninsky was standing beneath the bathhouse with a civilian outfit wrapped in a towel. At a prearranged signal Drobninsky thrust the towel through the bars—whereupon the anxiously waiting Jacob pushed his boots and uniform into one of the cupboards reserved for soldiers' gear, and with the celerity and precision of a borzoi dressed himself in the civilian clothes and left the baths.

Just outside the bathhouse, through Drobninsky's pre-arrangement, stood a droshky with a pair of deceptively idle mares, ready to tear away from Vilna forever. All afternoon and evening the mares' hoofs labored against the muddy spring roads, urging themselves onward to the crooning cry of the driver: "*Coom schon, coom, schon. Gehen sie, maidlach,*" till their soft black mouths foamed with the exhilaration and fatigue of the race. Then they were exchanged for a peasant's cart with a dray horse who plowed across the flat terrain with the stolidity of a mule. The peasant's cart was loaded high with over-innocent bales of hay, inviting surmise, and the peasant warned Jacob that as they drew nearer the border the soldiers often became more than militant: that they would not hesitate to stab through the hay with their bayonets—ostensibly in the search for deserters, but actually in the hope of laying their starving hands on a chicken or lamb enroute to market.

Jacob was willing to take the chance, however, and once when a soldier approached them, Jacob allowed the peasant to ransom them both with his remaining roubles and a loaf of rye. So although the last few miles were not so awful as he had feared, nevertheless even the sweetness of the country air was stifling to him. The smell of the new-mown hay under which he lay hidden, unable to move arm or leg, nauseated him; and as the morning dew seeped through the bales, mingling with the rank sweat of his fear, he could feel brewing on his body, a moisture of terror, yellow as tea.

But over the border all was joyous reunion; for at the free port Drobninsky awaited him with miraculous manna from America: a fifty-dollar dowry payment from Bashe's father, Morris Steiner, and a ticket for America by the fortnightly boat, which Drobninsky had procured for him with a false passport.

Drobninsky gave him also a photograph of his bride-to-be—which thirty years later his children were to find hidden away in Papa's low trunk with the metal corners: a round-faced girl with cheeks as plump as apples, wearing a white blouse which carefully exposed two round shadows, rich as jewels. Two wings of eyebrows flared up at him over a mouth not yet lined by rebellion or thought; and in the center of the face a soft mouth made for—certainly not for the heroic, but for warm kisses to swell the curve of the lip like a bee sting. The hair was bobbed in the latest style, a daring which struck Jacob with a feeling he could barely understand, it was like envy and awe combined. As his eager eye traveled forgivingly over the somewhat too-swelling hips, his gaze rested on the shining black shoes which adorned the daintily crossed feet;

and the sight of the rows of buttons upon the slim ankles, like sheltering peas in a pod, he heaved a great sigh. If it were possible to fall in love with a picture, Jacob fell in love on the spot with his bride-to-be and with their future. And as Drobninsky pointed out approvingly, though Bashe was several years older than Jacob, she was the only daughter of a manufacturer: poverty would never come to her. Drobninsky's praises of Bashe Steiner were in fact so unqualified that in a sudden rush of self-distrust Jacob asked himself why such a paragon should want *him*, a poor orphan who had barely begun his yeshiva studies. The uneasy thought occurred to him perhaps Bashe was considerably older than Drobninsky's report: or perhaps, even, she was no longer a virgin, a victim of a broken betrothal?...But when he recalled the lovely face of the photograph, he rejected this suspicion with guilty haste, as he would have rejected an impure thought during an hour of prayer.

"And *my* picture?" he queried somewhat hesitantly. "Was she—satisfied?" He would not have asked, but that he was in love and thus in his youthful vanity, he had for the first time become vulnerable. Certainly his mother had always said he was her pearl; a flawless jewel—small in size, but perfect: but then, was the vision of a mother likely to coincide with that of a girl, rich and accustomed to dandies who wore straw hats and shoes with spats? He began to mistrust his great good luck; but Drobninsky assured him that Bashe was enthralled; and showed him a note in her own hand—written in English!—this last alone would have melted a statue—in which she said: "Please send my warm regards to Jacob." There it was: *warm* regards! What could be more charming? He parted from Drobninsky with reluctant bliss, wishing to detain his benefactor so that they might pass the time till the ship arrived in talking about the wit, beauty and wealth of Jacob's fiancee.

Meanwhile Jacob wandered blissfully about the free port; his happiness seemed to him an almost supernatural blessing: springtime, a new life, prospects unimaginable for a handsome energetic bridegroom of sixteen; and freedom forever from the spectre of poverty and the tyranny of the Czar. As he wandered through the streets to the open market place, he contemplated his future happiness with leisurely gratitude: God had saved his life and God would help him in that great country where even a Jew could go to school and own property. According to the marriage contract drawn up by Drobninsky's brother, his future father-in-law was to provide lodging for the new couple for five years, during which time Jacob would continue his studies: Steiner's only son-in-law must be an educated man. But Jacob vowed that he would study not only *Torah*, but business, and American law, so that he could be Morris Steiner's administrator—ease him of the ever-increasing responsibility of one of the largest tanneries in the New York area—with a new firm opening in Gloversville which would soon supply all the ladies in New York City with long leather gloves.

Though Steiner himself was barely literate, Drobninsky assured Jacob that his future father-in-law would make him the keystone of a rising American family; Steiner was already advertising on the radio, and twenty years from now, Drobninsky said, there would not be an American anywhere who had not heard of Steiner's Gloves: for an enterprising young man in America, the sky was the limit.

As Jacob gazed up at the great blue-porcelain sky which spanned the piers of the harbor from which he would take his ship, he felt indeed that his world was limitless...The spring winds as he strolled toward the market place on his fourth afternoon in the city seemed fresh and piquant. As he passed a watchmaker's store he caught the reflection of himself between the hands of a great clock, as if the moment had stopped in awe at this blue-eyed, fair-haired, smooth-faced young man with just a wisp of a mustache, like pullen on his lip; and he grinned back in joy at the image and passed on to the market place—to gaze as naturally as the fox gazes upon the grape at the full-hipped Polish girls, who, he knew, kept warming braziers of coals beneath their layers of skirts to protect themselves against the March winds...It seemed to him he had never felt better.

There was a glow on his slim smooth body as he walked, and the brilliant colors of the marketplace had burned on his fevered vision with a never-to-be forgotten clarity: green onions and yellow squashes and giant turnips with purple streaks, like the eyes of an exhausted lover, and a halved pomegranate looking heavenward with myriad, ruby eyes. He saw a pair of mourning doves imprisoned side by side with some white turkeys; and he even remembered afterwards thinking what an odd creature God had created in the turkey, whose feathers were as luminous as angels and its face all red and purplish knots, like welts on unhealed flesh. And that had been his last clear thought before dizziness and nausea had knocked him with a blow like a Cossack's whip from his feet, and he lay suddenly in the marketplace, panting, his mouth open and something like fire issuing from his lungs. He heard someone say: "Don't touch him. Who knows what it is?" And his heart echoed in terror: "who knows what it is?"

In a rough litter made of pinned flour sacks they lifted him onto a peddlar's cart, and the nightmare of the ride began. They would not take him at the hospital nearest the market place because he was a foreigner, as good as on the high seas, and with a passport, they said, too circumspectly new. So the grueling ride in the cart continued, the driver cursing the fate which had brought him a customer so deathly sick that he might not live to pay his fare—and so strangely flushed with fever that he did not dare rifle through the sick man's pockets.

Finally his driver was told by a passerby (his hallucinatory memories, seared by fever seemed to make the figure of a nun...) that the Charity Hospital would take smallpox patients: they already had several cases in quarantine, she told the driver, and could expand their facilities in case of an epidemic...At the words "smallpox" and "epidemic" the driver crossed himself and no longer thought of his fare; his one concern was to dump this cargo of disease and disaster, and to pour a carbolic solution over himself and his wagon,

Jacob was never able to recall exactly how they carried him into the quarantine-room—a dank dark cellar of a room about thirty feet long, with twenty small beds, nearly half of them filled with patients like himself—some delirious, others exhausted from the sleepless struggle with itching scabs. Some few already in the shock of recuperation, lay motionless, staring at the ceiling, not yet certain whether they were alive. Over and over they had been cautioned not to scratch their sores; it spread the pus, they had been told, and caused terrible scars as big as bullet holes. Yet Jacob saw men who, in the maddening torment of their disease, tore at themselves with a spasm of curses, as if their flesh were mere rotting garments to be ripped in shreds. He himself, by an effort of will that later seemed more diabolical than human, had managed finally to restrict himself to an insane tapping with his fingernail upon the healing scabs: the faint vibrations at the rim of the scab seemed to temper the almost intolerable desire to claw himself to bits. And even so, when the nights were long and his fever was high, and the desire to scratch was like a wild effluvium on the brain, he could not remember the most rudimentary precautions; he would roll himself from side to side in the febrile blankets like a man on fire.

At last he sat, stunned, silent, in a twilight of recovery. Two ships had arrived in the harbor, en route to the Promised Land; and had departed. In all those weeks, he and the other patients had received no mail—had seen scarcely anyone: their food and slop pails were handed through the door. Only those nurses who had once contracted the dread disease ever entered; thus, they saw no one who looked different from themselves, with their faces like molten coals, red and shapeless, kept back from disintegration only by the tenuous scaffolding of bones beneath. They looked into no mirrors there, except what reflections they received from their tin soup spoons—shapeless and whorled with centrifugal scars, like their faces. So for a while Jacob was spared the ultimate, crucifying judgment of his eyes. In Jewish homes, when a death occurs, all mirrors are shrouded—and there seemed to him now a wise mercy in this covering of mirrors: he, the young handsome smiling Jacob that was, had died—let the dead not look upon their own sepulchered faces, devoured by mortality, lest their despairing souls never again know repose.

Yet, when his delirium had ended, it was another loss than that of his boyish face which plunged him into despair: and that was the loss of God. For ten years his dream had been to master God's Word; he had lived in childlike fear of His commandments and faith in His rewards. The Misnah, the Zohar, the Agadahs of the Torah—in these he had found man's purpose in life: piety and wisdom. And was this God's way with those who loved Him?

So that when Jacob was able at last to think again, he judged God harshly, condemning Him. For God, he swore, had failed him. Whatever may have been Jacob's sins in the past, he remained convinced that he had not merited a punishment so great. God was both arbitrary and inexorable: a tyrant. And so Jacob sat in the hospital courtyard rebuking God for His inhumanity. The April grasses sprang forth from the mud of winter; the ivy entwined the hospital walls; and the fragrance of the sap rising in the pine branches filled his senses till his whole body ached with the pain and the glory of it. All else held the power of renascence: storm, earthquake, and bomb could be drenched by rains, seeded by grass; the earth could melt and cohere again, bringing forth beauty. But man, God's most noble creation, could be shattered beyond recognition, his skull perforated fifty years before the worm would wind it. The emptiness inside him at the loss of God was worse than pain; he sat in silence, his heart wrestling again and again with the undeniable evidence: and he was bitter against God that He had not rendered his belief unassailable.

When the long quarantine was over, Jacob found the nurses had incinerated Drobninsky's new secondhand suit; but with admirable honesty or compassion, or both, they returned to him unchanged, in spite of its sharp chemical bath, the fifty dollar advance on Bashe Steiner's dowry. Also, an organization from a French-sounding town, Detroit, had sent another suit, lugubriously too vast for his present size, and new shoes with pointed toes, size 8 for his delicate foot, now more slim and delicate than ever.

The dimensions of the suit from Detroit oppressed him: were even the Jews so tall in America that their legs were as trees and their shoulders like strapping bears? His small size, slightly over five feet, had never troubled him before; if ghetto Jews were small, their women were even smaller, prematurely blighted by early childbirth and poverty. But now his size was a further ignominy, for the casual observer had no attractive point upon which the musing eye might rest. As he walked about the hospital yard, he hid himself from the women, for their gaze fell upon him like an axe—splitting his ego from the roots of his scarred scalp where the hair was just beginning to return in a stubby growth, to the tips of his pointed American shoes: Florsheims, a pale ochre whose fine leather finish had been marred by the spattering April rains leaving spots, like roseola. He noted how the female visitors regarded him—turning their amused glances upwards at first, from his slight figure in the ludicrously too large suit which dropped loonishly around his ankles till their gaze froze in horror at the doom of his face: a small blasted moon with craters wherever a healed scab had been torn away, scarring the face to inerasable woe as they peeled from the flesh leaving dessicated pits, hereafter to be guarded against dirt, against bearded manliness, against love—against the very sun; and above all against Bashe's black eyes.

All through the voyage he sat staring at Bashe's picture, at the limpid eye and succulent lip, and the skin like the breast of a dove; and he bit his lips and wept; for he knew in his heart that he had no gifts except the dazzling promises of boyish ardor with which to charm this avatar of the rich man's portion...And now he was nothing but a ruined husk, a blighted landscape.

What agonized him as he sat on board ship was the fact that he had been unable to write Steiner offering decently and discreetly to annul the marriage contract, return the dowry. As soon as the quarantine had been lifted, some officials came and drove him to the ship, stuffing him into steerage as rudely as over-baked bread. The space had been reserved and paid for, a batch of immigrants was leaving for America; so he was enveloped in a blanket and set on board deck with hundreds of other immigrants—some in good condition, others not so fortunate. And these latter trembled for fear they would be barred from the promised land at the very moment of arrival; for the officers at Ellis Island were reportedly uncompromising with any symptoms of illness. Jacob did indeed note one or two passengers who were lame, and several that seemed to spit too frequently into their broad spotted handkerchiefs. Yet there was not one with whom Jacob would not have exchanged his fate: a club foot, a weak lung, a sightless eye—with all these might a man yet stand with pride and be loved. But with a face like a sponge, what woman would ever caress him, saying as his mother had said: "*Wie shein du bist, meine zisse ponem.* How handsome you are, my sweet-faced one."

The voyage across was a disaster from beginning to end—with women and children sick on board deck, their faces the gangrenous green of dying soldiers. The men tormented him with questions concerning his illness—some out of pity, others slyly to determine whether he might still be contagious. One old woman, stunted with superstition, suddenly began clamoring that he was the Angel of Death and that his presence on board would bring down destruction upon the ship. And though they carried her away below deck and scoffed, afterwards, at her motions, they nevertheless continued to keep an apprehensive eye on Jacob as he walked back and forth in the wake of the ship, allowing the salt sea, with bitter indifference, to trickle in a mist upon his slowly-healing wounds, as with the smart of tears.

To climax it all, in the confusion of the ship's arrival, in the press of the crowds surging to the shoreward deck, he discovered that Bashe's dowry had been stolen, and while others were rushing to gaze with rapture upon the Statue of

Liberty, he was pushing through the crowds crying: "Bastards! Thieves! You've stolen my money. You're murdering me!" He sobbed and wrung his hands in despair at the realization that he was not to be allowed even this exempting grace: of pressing the dowry money into Bashe's hands and walking away. He had planned over and over again how at the first sharp intake of breath, the first tremor of fear, he would thrust the money into her icy palms and heroically disappear in the crowd...Afterwards, he was to think it bitterly symbolic that his first question in the promised land was: who has stolen my money? And these words were to ricochet from his mouth to his prospective father-in-law's and back again, striking the nerve at the root of his heart where feeling, pride, and shame had once flooded into radii of love.

"So—and you've stolen our money too," said Steiner with a sneer as he drew his trembling daughter toward the waiting taxi. "A tragedy we can all expect," he added loftily, making it hypocritically clear that, while he might be expected to adhere to a marriage contract with one of the riders of the apocalypse, he could never, no never, marry his daughter to a thief.

It had not even been a bitter triumph to Jacob in his humiliation that Bashe's face resembled her portrait only as a demon resembles an angel: for in her face had been no tenderness at all—only a furious aversion, a look of horror without pity: he was a toad who had failed to become a Prince, and he would never sleep on her pillow so long as she was Princess of the Tannery.

He saw her incline her head on her father's shoulder, saw the screwed curls at the neck bobbing, heard her sob in real or feigned hysteria, he was never to know which, "Papa, stop it. Please Papa stop it. I can't stand anything more today..." And then they drove away in the taxi, a green Oldsmobile, he remembered, one of the first American cars—as unlike the peddlar's cart on which he had been taken to the hospital as a dream is to life.

Doing It Like Velásquez

Your problem is relating to people. You enter the house, you smile endearingly at the Lady of the House, you "admire" her children. Five minutes later you are totally disgusted. The Lady of the House resembles a humanoid poodle, the children are all plaster reproductions of the original (but the original has been lost). Still, it's a job, isn't it: though you hadn't wanted to be a professional photographer, for years you were only a happy amateur, cherishing sunsets, picket fences, weathered houses—something to relax from after the intense concentration of your real work. Now it's your only future and how well you do it reenforces your own identity: Max Berman, Photographer. It requires merely that you continue to jolly up the procedures as you've done for months now: line up the kiddies, tickle their chins, poke a finger at their belly buttons, automatically obliging them to giggle. These sounds (you've learned) will stir the comatose Mommy to life, replace her buttered-crumbs smile with the glowing curve of a Madonna. Can it be done? Can you make plastic vibrate with Raphael? No, you cannot. You wish, like a proper cobbler, you'd stuck unto your last, never meddled in Pentagonal questions. What difference did it make what they did with your computations? The data was classified, you should have kept your mouth shut, but you wanted to object to what you felt was the "abuse of scientific method." O.K. Good, you objected, you don't have to worry about technology anymore, you can go on taking pictures for life.

At least, in the past few months, you've learned to resist the urge, like a call of nature, to pack up your gear, mumble excuses, and run home to your stereo. You've become competent, serene; you've learned to merely radiate your (understandably) inarticulate admiration for the genetic ciphers who've appeared before you in their pastel frocks or white collars; you've learned to ensnare their images so that (theoretically) fifty years from now, when they review their childhood nothings, they may luckily mistake it for Wordsworthian immortality. No, Berman, don't put it that way, there's nothing philosophical about it, it's a way to pay your rent, that's all. Medina Photos specializes in portraits (and now, so do you). Smother your esthetic reservations, summon up ruthlessness like a stage prop, and now, here's the house, 3002 Somerset Drive, one more gull to pay for Victorian frippery. ("Sell them the frames, sell them the frames," the route manager keeps reminding you, "the real money is in the frames.")

Your problem is, Berman, and you know it, you don't want to do portraits at all. You don't want to be responsible for what people have done to their faces. You feel too often like saying, "Look at this wreck of face (life), what can you expect me to *do* with it? How could you have done that to yourself? That dour scar at the mouth, for instance—you, Sir, Madam—started turning sour at twenty-four: thirty winters of discontent in that smile. Nothing Medina Photos can do anything about: just when you, Berman, are supposed to start selling extra prints, enlargements, frames, you begin to think you ought to sell them a whole new life (and buy one for yourself, Berman, while you're at it).

No wonder you're not doing so well, What you used to prefer (back when you still loved taking pictures) were natural

settings—sunsets, seascapes, driftwood. Settings aren't anybody's fault, you don't have to relate to them. If the birds are
clogged up and can't fly, that's ecology, not Character. You're
not Diane Arbus and you'd rather not see schizophrenics
splitting apart like some thready mitosis separating under
your microscopic eye.

Though it's true that from time to time, from sheer
madness or frustration, when you've had a particularly bad
day—today would do for an example—you've surrendered to
the temptation of truth-saying. You've said to yourself, O.K.
Berman, you blew the whole bit anyway, now let's do it like
Velásquez, show the whole rotten self complete with Philip
IV's mushy self-indulgent mouth, the Infanta's cherry lips and
empty eyes. But not very often. It costs money to do it like
Velásquez. Sometimes they get mad and won't even pay for
the proofs, much less lay out for more prints and frames. So
most of the time you've learned to suppress your itch for the
truth. You try to make every sitting the anointing of a King.
And that's prostitution, isn't it? By definition, I mean: doing
something for money that you used to do for love.

But who's to cast the first stone? Not at yourself,
Berman: let's get on with the job. You can see as you get your
gear out of the trunk that Mrs. Blander's been waiting for you
for some time: she's standing by the picture window, holding
the drapes open, and one of the kids has flown to the door,
yelling he's here, here he is! and is holding the door open for
you, literally jumping with impatience (you know from
experience, though, it's not you he's glad to see, but that when
you're through with him he can get out of his *poseur's*
clothes). Now you have this sinking feeling again, Berman,
you're not going to make it. It's been a rotten day, a day for
executions, not portrait-making, and you've just come off the
expressway, that whited sepulchre, sheeted over with smog.
You feel a little sick. Still, it appears to be a pleasant ample
brick house with ivied retaining walls, you hear the hum of air
conditioners, of a vacuum vacuuming, and there's a lot of
grass, always a comfort to look at: some trikes and bikes and a

compact parked in the driveway. Maybe the Lady of the House will turn out to be a winner and the kids all shipwrecked princelings in disguise. You growl at the glaucous air, you hunker closer to your equipment as you glide along the retaining wall toward the steps. You're like a carnie shellman, hoping your hand will be quicker than the eye, let's get it over with. But at the moment you're not at all sure you can even get through another sitting, no matter how gracious, genteel and ladylike the Lady of the House turns out to be: you just want to go home and forget the whole day which, right from the first sitting (9:00 a.m.) had begun leaking horrors like gas in a shaft.

Starting with the Echardts: a hell of a way to begin the day. You just weren't able to take that sort of exposure, Berman. There sat Amelia Echardt, nine years old and already struck down by some horrible wasting illness which (you gathered) would eventually melt down her bones like wax. You'd thought you'd freak out taking pictures of the two of them, the Stabat Mater and Amelia: you're not priest, doctor, magus. And there was the kid, smiling at you with the immaculate smile of the other world. The world you no longer believed in, the one you'd given up when you dropped all the masks of adolescence and said, there's no God. But if there's no God, Berman, what do you tell children on the way to the dark? You'd wanted to take an axe and smash up the whole place, with its whining ikons and Slavic mysticism. Barely able to see their damned faces for the blur in your eyes, you'd left without selling a single frame.

Followed by a sitting on the other side of the river. It'd taken you over an hour to find the tacky house which looked as if it'd been rolled down the cliffside to fall—slats loosened, nails jutting out—right beside the shitbrown river frothing with detergent: mill-stacks, our latter-day cathedrals, rose to the vaulted sky. On the kids' faces, Pompadour's beauty spots, lay tiny flecks of coal. At first you couldn't make any sense of it. Take pictures? Of this? Of them? The ugliness was a floating thing, a river full of jetsam. You wanted to argue with the woman: why throw away good money on individual poses? Listen, Mrs. Clogan, you wanted to say, I'm only an amateur myself and these seven portraits are going to cost you as much as an operation at your local surgeon. You even thought of explaining how she could do it herself: you get a pretty good camera, do this and that, it's simple and a great hobby too, etc. But you couldn't do it, Berman: you couldn't injure her sense of pride, she wanted to believe that the heavy sacrifice was worth it, that a mystery was about to take place: you, Berman, were some kind of damned expert and could turn water into wine.

So, like an utter fool, you'd sprung a gut trying to get the kids to look like something besides Cloned Clogans; in spite of your sweating efforts they'd come out looking alike, even to the thatches of hair like seven identical Cimabue aureoles, their seven mouths open with wonder at your wild gesticulating performance: they were a flock, not a portrait. But when you were leaving, Mrs. Clogan, a woman with a skin translucent as bone and a whisper of a voice (laryngectomy? you wondered, looking for scars) followed you to the door and thanked you several times, exactly as if she weren't going to have to pay for those thatched heads in solid gold, she said she thought they'd come out real good, and then suggested that you take a look (while you were in the neighborhood) at their local church, you could see the tower from her doorstep... Famous all over the world, she added, you'd probably heard of it. No, you apologized, you hadn't heard of it. But then, there was so much you hadn't...you left it for her to finish. She shook her head, mystified: an educated man, and you'd never heard of their cathedral, it was the pride of their community, built right after the Civil War.

You swallowed your shame and guilt, mumbled apologies and promised to bring the proofs by in a week or ten days.

And so it went: just before lunch, there'd been this elegant old lothario, Carpiello, who (he'd said) was being visited that afternoon by his granddaughter, and claimed that he wanted a really fine portrait of himself for a 'fine little widow' whom he was courting via the U.S. mails: 'the former wife of a Houston oil man,' he confided to you. Carpiello had ensconced himself in a brocade Windsor chair, an impressive-looking book on his rigid lap, his goatee and elflock whetted and brushed to a high aluminum gloss. "Be sure to include the ring," he'd abruptly directed at you, raising a monitory finger. (What about that granddaughter? you'd wanted to challenge him.) Maliciously you'd decided to give the oil man's widow a preprandial taste of the pleasures her mail-order lover might deliver her. You'd gloatingly included the wine-soaked nose stippled as trout, the sack of flesh slyly thrusting open Carpiello's fly, the prophetic flash of the white jewel on Carpiello's finger, like the mormal on the chin of Chaucer's cook. Then you'd fled to a park bench to gloat over your ill-gotten gains like some latter-day Puck gone mad with blight.

Then, after Carpiello had come Mrs. Perkins with her seven cats. Another client with disguised enthusiasms: the appointment was to have been with her niece (she said) but her niece had the flu and couldn't make it: but so that his (Berman's) trip wouldn't be wasted, would he mind taking some poses of Fluff, Scamper, Sambo, Puddinhead, Limerick, Pretty-boy Floyd and Ali?

But you weren't an animal photographer, you'd pro-tested. They were so sensitive (animals, you meant), and easily distracted. Didn't Mrs. Perkins feel she'd be better off calling Universal Dogs 'n Cats Snaps, they were terrific at that sort of thing? It seemed she'd tried them already, they'd had a falling out, they were not very *simpatico* with cats, preferring (rather obviously, she said) dogs. She purred at you persuasively, bribing you shamelessly by explaining that each one of the cats was to be done individually, a real kitty-portfolio, if you will, she mewed, and began immediately looking over your cata-logues for suitable frames ("the money's in the frames, Berman, never forget that"). So what could you do? You'd swallowed your already minimal professional pride. While you and Mrs. Perkins had wrestled claw to claw with seven individual sittings of Fluff, Scamper, Sambo, Puddinhead,

Limerick, Pretty-boy Floyd and Ali, you had plenty of time to muse over our human preoccupation with *seven*—our symbol of perfect order; our reconciliation of the square with the triangle; our seven basic notes of musical notation; our seven (original) planets, and our seven capital sins and virtues; and our seven lively arts and (even) our seven orifices of the male body; and now in the Age of Aquarius, even household populations—kids and cats—mysteriously fissioned into groups of seven.

And the mere thought of numbers, even their magic use (the "abuse of scientific method") made you nostalgic for your old job. What's a nice scientist like you, Berman, doing in a place like this—counting kids, cats, saints and lives, all going to St. Ives? You were meant for Better Things. You'd had good grades in college, you'd dressed neatly, were unilaterally polite to everyone. Not once had you épatéd les bourgeois, or had any urge to. You were going to use your brain to correct for natural error. Maybe later, you had thought, you'd get into space research. There'd been plenty of room in outer space for your talents, Berman. What happened? You used to have control. You believed in control. You thought the Scientists, like the war generals, had God on their side. Your job was a good one, with plenty of opportunity for advancement (company-subsidized improvement courses, all the trimmings). Then you'd started wondering what, exactly, your numbers were numbering. You preferred not to find out. You resisted information. But when Congress started cracking down, checking out even so-called classified data, you knew. And the Company lost no time in letting you know they knew you knew. You'd been restive for months anyway (the Company pointed out). Not really happy with your work. And now, Berman, (they said) your openly expressed views on the alleged "abuse of scientific method" sort of automatically cancelled your contract, didn't it? Like the joke about the Pregnant Nun, they'd smiled, you were a clear-cut case of heresy. The joke had made you aware, suddenly, that you weren't a WASP, something you'd not thought about before in relation to the Company.

They'd offered to promote you out of classified materials (they were Nice Guys, they'd observed affably, not Nuremburg defendants) into teaching newcomers the system, but you refused. You explained that teaching was not your thing, but to yourself you admitted that this was because you'd have to talk to newcomers, explain to them why this work was useful, valid, ethical, rewarding. And it wasn't, it was shit. It was a job. Like this one. Only, if you'd known how bad it was going to be (from seven kids to seven cats in one afternoon), maybe you'd have stifled your questions. Hell, they were going to have Big Brother some day anyway, what did you care how soon your phone was monitored, your activities chronicled, your love affairs transcribed, your business haunts listed, your cablegrams, letters and overseas calls recorded (you never sent cablegrams anyway, had never once received mail from China or the Soviet Union, you thought of Albania as a joke). It was all really irrelevant to you, since you believed in the whole schtick, you just wished you could make some private profits, own some private property, find a private woman and live the good life. But how? Not (God help you, Berman), by photographing these five little Blanders, the boys already aiming their forefingers at you (bang, bang, Berman, you're dead!) and the girls wrapped in rose-colored dresses smooth as shrouds. And although Lady Blander (convexly pregnant again) is rather sexy, you're now concerned with finding a spot stable enough to hang your lights from; but mainly you're trying to seethe with an importance you don't feel, engaging in this hyperactivity in order to cover your exasperation, you're already fed up with these not-yet-seven-but-almost-six little Blanders (especially the two who keep shooting you dead, *hey, kids, how dead do you want me? heh heh*) who are beginning to loot a mound of toys piled high as an igloo, toys which they'll soon be waving around in their portraits. You'd like to kick them in the shins, but you keep smiling and smiling, you villain, Berman. You'd also like to be allowed to ignore Lady B. altogether and get down to your job, it's after five, and you wish you were back at your apartment with your stereo...But it's impossible. She's explaining it all to you now, how the portraits are going to be for the kids' (maternal) grandfather and some pictures, of course, for herself which she's going to hang right above the fireplace. In oval frames, she adds, and she'd like the colors handtinted (*Oh good!* you try to gloat over all the money-you're-going-to-put-in-your-purse, Roderigo-Berman, but you're already furtively eyeing the Thomas clock on the wall). You're also sizing up everything with a professional eye: you have to guess what they're worth before you start pushing the junk. And you wish things were tacky, you would like (as it were) to be able to smile condescendingly at the barbarians in gold-plated boots, but the place is not bad—in fact, it's pretty damned nice, full of mauves and soft configurations, decorated like someone tuned into the history of art: things hung together. You hear again the humming of a vacuum going on in a room upstairs: while here below-decks all is crystal clean.

And the frames in oval, Mrs. Blander is saying. I mean, what do you think of ovals?—are they maybe too oldfashioned?

It isn't enough for her that you have to work here, she wants you committed to her esthetic, approving. O.K. Berman, on with the snow job. Here's where you earn your money by the sweat of your tongue.

No, no, no. Nothing's old-fashioned anymore. Nostalgia, you know. The older the newer. Not bad, Berman, a true bullshitter you're getting to be. You even manage to say something like, Nice place you got here, lady, which is evidently what she's waiting to hear, for she sighs with what looks to be an odd mixture of pleasure and guilt.

Thank you we've only just moved in. Adding: unable to resist citing a killing in the market, We got a really good buy on it.

Oh? You're cool, admiring: business acumen and all that. But, you wonder, why are you telling me this, lady?

I mean, they could have got at least four thousand more for it, they didn't have to honor our check. It was just that we were the first to make an offer—before the house had even been up for sale.

So, it's Absolution-time on Somerset Drive, is it, Lady B? O.K., if that's what you want, it's the least part of this gamesome game. 'Tis pity you're a whore, Berman, but absolution increases portrait-power, never forget the frames. So you nod sympathetically at Lady B. as if someone had just conned her out of a flat four thousand, instead of the reverse.

Yes. They were our neighbors, (pointing vaguely). Just down this hill around the corner. We had this tiny cottage, you should have seen us, it was like an army barracks with bunk beds and all.

You couldn't care less, Berman, if they'd slept in a bunghole, but you continue to nod, like one of these perpetual-motion gimmicks. You just wish she'd get the kids started, she hasn't said yet whether they're to be single sittings or *en famille* and you're got your sales pitch to get through yet ("the money's in the frames" etc.). And you're thirsty. You wish the Lady of the House would offer you a drink. Of water: even.

Then Captain Rawlins, that's the husband of the woman who lived here, I mean of the woman who owned the house, he got *very* sick. Like, no matter how much they've learned about it, it's pretty conclusive, you know, if it's 'inoperable.'

She's begun at least shuffling the kids around now, like arranging your poker hand, pair of jacks on one side, pair of queens on the other. But she doesn't stop explaining and confessing to you (why you, Berman? you only work here).

So we made Mrs. Rawlins an offer—through our real estate agent, of course, you have to be discreet about these things, people are naturally upset at such a time, they don't even want to think about what they'll need to do later...I mean, they always hope, don't they, that maybe they'll find a cure, or a miracle or something. She now bent over Littlest One, evidently he was going to be first.

He's going to be cranky soon, he missed his nap and it's time for Ulrica to give him supper...And I guess Mrs. Rawlins felt it best to have a sure buyer. Under the circumstances, I mean. So that's how we came to move here. To this house. It's more than twice as much house compared to where we were, you couldn't imagine how crowded we were, stacked up like... she deposits Littlest One on the sofa for his portrait, like cups in a china closet. She beams at you, Berman, so happy with her simile. Could you take the first ones of them all together, I don't know how long I can keep them all still, and they're sort of quiet now. Could you?

You could, you would, you do, but your blood is still curdling from her necrophiliac confession (*mordre will out*) so that, confused, you trip over your own cord, the lights fall to the floor, for a few seconds you are plunged into darkness. O.K. kids, you cheer bitterly: abandon all hope ye who enter here. Then the lights flash on again, all except one. Angrily you change a bulb. Pretty damned dark in here, you growl, making some sort of sweeping moral summary. Then, mollifying, (remember the frames!) I mean, for such a big house with picture windows and all.

That's the disadvantage, she agrees quickly. It's a northern exposure. We noticed that when we finally came to make the deposit. I mean, we did have to identify who it was our realtor was representing, finally, so when we came to give her a check, the check being a kind of contract, you know, we had some second thoughts: did we really want a northern exposure? But Dick said jokingly, what difference does it make, you can always send the kids to play in your neighbor's yard (she, pointing). So we made the deposit and about a week later Captain Rawlins passed away and she, Mrs. Rawlins, could have put the house up for sale and gotten whatever she asked for it, the price of real estate has nearly doubled in this neighborhood in the past few years, you know, but she said a bargain was a bargain. I mean, she could simply have torn up our check...And then Mrs. Rawlins just sold out everything (again pointing) furniture and all, and went to live with her daughter in California. Just like that, she sold everything. So it is dark, I know. But you can't have everything.

Lady B. smiles at you philosophically and you, Berman,

grin back at her toothsomely, while signalling up to God, Whom of course you don't believe in, that here's a proper case for Him, that you hope to hell He's listening to all this and has a nice chunk of retribution ready for Mrs. B. on her way to Jesus.

But suddenly your toothsome, gamesome role becomes real, a demon has invaded you, you're going to do it your way, you're going to photograph the Blanders, red in tooth and claw. It may cost you your job, but it's worth it: how many times a week do you meet the local Gorgon face to face?

Now, heh, heh, Berman, you begin to line them up, catching their names in mid-air like a juggler, you concentrate on their gloss, their veneer, their round heads set in sturdy necks, the soft, cared-for skins, all gazing out at Milady like images in a pond. So many round heads, so many square shoulders, they become a geometric pattern, an object, not persons: your curse on this image shall be, Berman, the viewer's conviction that no persons shall rise from these ashes. You do your comic act (chins, bellies), not the time to stimulate smiles but to agitate the clutching fingers, anticipating the webbed feet of snakebirds and cormorants, ready to dive under, ready to survive on anything, the foddered food of picknickers, or small fish below. But Blander herself is smiling and her smile is very pretty. Hang it all, the Infanta didn't smile, that was Velásquez's secret, it's hard to limn the lamentations on lust, gluttony and pure churlishness when they insist on smiling. So you decide to look glum yourself, you stop photographing, you start *tssk, tssking* in false dismay, you look solemn, you pretend something's gone wrong, that you've lost all the wonderful poses after all. Instantly Lady B.'s smile dries on her lips, a look of annoyance not-yet-ready-to-explode-into-impatience, draws Lady B.'s brow into two fine, whittled lines, the curve of the Madonna lip droops into discontent (she doesn't want to have to keep the lid on the kids for another sitting, she'd rather get rid of you right now, Berman). But now swiftly turning your camera, you take Lady B. stripped of all her blandishments: she has just seen a galaxy

of little Blanders disappear into the coiled film, which you're
still pretending to regret having lost somehow, heh, heh. Now
you affect to rescue all, you appear to court her good nature:
but the transition is too much for her, her smile has smeared
like grease paint, and you put that in too. The boys meanwhile
have begun grabbing from the plates which Ulrica has set for
dinner. They ravenously shove tomato slices into their
mouths, oozing seeds on their new suits. Lady B. nearly
stomps at them to stop it, stop it this minute, and you add her
rage to the Directory of Blander Talents, catching another
shot. (If she knows it's Herself Surprised being shot, she
doesn't let on.) At last, the kids are shoved back onto the sofa.
Frustrated now: they've seen a jello ring with bits of fruit on
the table and they long to poke into it as into a piñata: what
will come out? Quietly sucking in your Mephistophelian
chuckle, you entrap them now, their lips bleeding ripe-red
tomato seeds, their eyes mesmerized by the wizardous green
eye of the jello ring. The girls, you note, are subdued by all this;
one begins to suck her thumb, you catch the pose just as Lady
B. flushes the hand out like a bird; the other daughter,
frightened by something happening which she does not
understand, shrinks into a corner of the sofa, trying to smile,
her legs crossed at the ankles, arms hugging her chest, only the
nerve ticking under the eyelid revealing her unnameable fear
at something rampant in the house, a license to cruelty which
hovers (like *you*, Mephistopheles-Berman) in mid-air. At last:
you've taken dozens of pictures, not for Lady B. but for
yourself (O.K., Hogarth-Daumier-Berman, there they go, into
the Museum of Modern Art!) So you're vague, non-committal,
when Lady B. asks you when they'll be ready, she'd like them
for gifts, etc., explaining again about the fireplace and the
ovals. You promise, with your malevolent wolf's grin, to
return with proofs in about a week. Privately you're convinced
she won't pay up, not even for your terrific two-hours' work
(damn, it *is* late, and the kids are jumping with tension,
wanting supper to come and this Stranger to go). Lady B. now
asks you very politely, very coldly, to come back when her

husband's home so that they can make choices together from the proofs, she never makes decisions of that sort without Mr. Blander, so would you mind—as they're leaving the following weekend for their vacation—would you mind coming Saturday morning?

Saturday morning, bright-eyed and bushy-tailed, you look over the proofs you're about to bring to the Blanders, and you whoop with demonic joy: they're surely going to be part of that one-man show in the Museum of Modern Art, circa 1984, to be entitled "Velásquez Redux" or "Daumier in the Age of Aquarius," or perhaps, simply, "Survival!" leaving it nicely ambiguous as to who or how anyone survives in our intergalactic age. So when you park in front of the Blander house, it's for your own dyspeptic kicks, Berman. You don't expect anything to come of it, the minute Lady B. sees them, she's going to howl with outrage.

The house, you note this Saturday a.m., seems vaguely different. Everybody's got to have some kind of shelter, you allow generously, so why not the Blanders? All bikes, trikes and compacts have been removed from the driveway, so it looks just like another one of those rambling brick houses with ivied walls, a house just trying to survive like the rest of us (but perhaps more highly endowed with some mysterious *élan vital*, Berman, and so does a lot better than you). But anyway, you're in a gracious (as distinct from a vicious) mood, and you're willing to let the Blanders keep their jello rings, you've got what you want.

So it's to your genuine astonishment that Lady B. begins *oohing* and *aahing* at the proofs. You're utterly baffled by this, you feel you flayed them alive, showed then craw, maw and sinew, with real flames issuing from the mouth of Dragonlady. But her husband, too, stands beside us whilst, one by one, Lady B. hands him pose after pose, *isn't that just darling, isn't that just perfect?* till you wonder if it's merely you, Mephistopheles-Berman, who've been glaring, red-eyed and devilish, at the innocent world. And then you realize: she doesn't see it, he doesn't see it. Only you see it, Berman, and those nice people who are going to be strolling through the Museum of Modern Art in 1984, they'll see it. And isn't that wonderful? You can now go round like the Red Cross Knight having adventures, taking pictures, and every Dragon will think she's Una: such is the power of allegory. And thus is the poet rebutted once and for all: God did not give us the giftie to see ourselves as others see us, but the giftie not to, never. And you, Berman, can profit from His neat little arrangement: you can go on photographing Gorgons and Dragons who will go on seeing themselves only as King Philip IV and the Infanta. You can go on doing it like Velásquez.